D0373691

"I saw Kit."

Cori's voice lowered. "I saw my husband's eyes. Clearly. Now take your hands off me this instant or I'll have your badge and your career."

Joey let her hands go. Cori was not going to listen to what he said. He'd thought if he could hold her long enough to finish, the weight of the truth would finally make her believe that her husband was dead.

Cori stood. "I'm out of your program, Mr. Tio. I'm not a witness for anything. My husband is alive, and I'm going to find him. I don't need you or anyone else."

"Cori, please..."

As she turned away and stormed across the restaurant, Joey wondered at his own motivations—was he reacting to Cori this way because he was her Witness Protection Program handler...or because she was such a sexy woman?

Dear Reader,

A Christmas Kiss is the first in a three-book series that takes a look at what might happen to citizens who get caught up in the witness protection program. When my editor, Julianne Moore, approached me about the idea of doing a series based on three female witnesses who all see the same crime committed, it sounded, well, intriguing. My imagination started spinning. As a former journalist, I've always been fascinated by the fact that several people can "witness" an accident or event, but none of them sees exactly the same thing.

Then a friend of mine who works with the Mobile Society for Prevention of Cruelty to Animals told me the story of how she came to own the world's most lovable Doberman. She got a call that the dog and nine puppies had been abandoned. When she went to check it out, she discovered that the former owners had simply vanished. The food was still on plates on the kitchen table. Books and records were on the shelves. It was as if they'd gotten up to answer the phone and never returned to their lives.

It's a leap of imagination, but what if these people were part of the witness protection program and had to be moved—instantly.

The idea of writing a book with this kind of built-in drama was irresistible. And when I discovered that Cassie Miles and Dawn Stewardson were going to write the second and third books in the series, I was hooked.

I hope our "witness protection" series hooks you, too.

Best,

Caroline Burnes

A Christmas Kiss
Caroline Burnes

Harlequin Books

TORONTO • NEW YORK • LONDON
AMSTERDAM • PARIS • SYDNEY • HAMBURG
STOCKHOLM • ATHENS • TOKYO • MILAN
MADRID • WARSAW • BUDAPEST • AUCKLAND

To Ouzo and Garp

ISBN 0-373-22399-4

A CHRISTMAS KISS

Copyright © 1996 by Carolyn Haines

Printed in U.S.A.

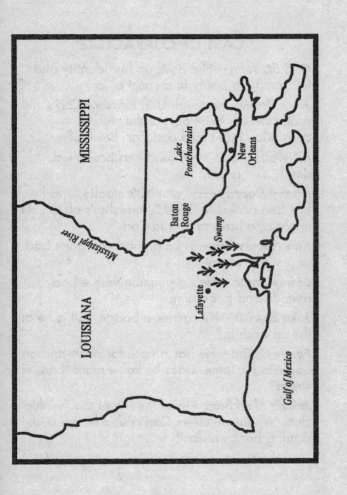

CAST OF CHARACTERS

Cori St. John—She gave up her identity and her family to testify in a court of law.

Joey Tio—Is the tough U.S. marshal Cori's protector...or is he part of the web of corruption that could cost Cori her life?

Kit Wells—Cori's husband was presumed dead...but is he?

Danny Dupray—He was Kit's stoolie, and he has free access to the U.S. marshal's office. He might also have access to Cori.

Ken Applewhite—Is he a good cop gone bad or just a grouch?

Bailey Smith—He's a gunman with a bad attitude and good aim.

Jake Lewish—He carries a badge, but is he on the up-and-up?

Farris Quinn—He has a nose for news and an appetite for fame. Does he know more than he writes?

Jolene Markham—lived the life of the Twinkle club. When she offers Cori a safe haven is she signing her own death warrant?

Prologue

December 15, 1993

The cold draft blew through Augustine's bar and settled tightly around Brently Gleason's trim ankles. She checked her watch and felt a flutter of anxiety emanate right from her heart. Kit was late. And he had assured her he was never late.

Brently crossed her feet and thought of her older sister, Lane, who was always teasing her about her tiny ankles—saying she should have a message taped to one of them, like a carrier pigeon. It was a backhanded compliment, which was Lane's way, but it didn't help a shy young woman with a zero level of confidence in her social skills.

But Kit did. Kit Wells. Brently said the name silently to herself and pressed her feet together tighter, glad that she was wearing her new, festive Christmas socks and the red sweater that made her mahogany hair sparkle. How had she been so lucky to attract the attention of the handsome police detective? Even as she checked her watch, she smiled at the memory of their first meeting. She had called the New Orleans Police Department, better known to all city residents as the NOPD, to complain about the noise and the "bad element" from the bar next to her studio. The lowlife who ran the club was out in the street threatening to pistol-whip one of his dancers. She had finally had enough and insisted that a unit be sent, stating she would press charges.

Kit had come to take her complaint, a professional worn-out with the endless bickering of the mishmash of tenants in the crowded French Quarter of New Orleans. Watching from her studio window, she had seen him drive up to answer her call. He had parked halfway in the street, as if he were in a movie, with the blue light in his windshield flashing away. No siren, though. Just the light. Getting out of the car, he had been big and smooth, and he had walked up to the bar owner and pushed him back from the girl. A gesture that spoke of his power and his contempt for men who made their living off women. Kit had all the makings of the man of her dreams.

As she relived their first meeting, she sipped the wine she'd ordered and checked the big front door of the restaurant-bar, hoping for a glimpse of a sandy head and strong shoulders. Augustine's wasn't big, and it was always packed. It virtually reeked of the history of the city, which claimed kinship to French, Spanish and Indian heritage.

"Are you ready to order, ma'am?" the waitress asked for the third time.

Brently looked into the face of a pretty woman with jeans and a sweater just a little too tight and an attitude a little too tough. "I'm, uh, waiting...I haven't made up my mind." She'd feel like a fool if she said she was waiting for someone and Kit didn't show. After all, she didn't know him *that* well, and he was working today. What if he'd been called out on a homicide or some other crime spree? Would he at least telephone the restaurant and let her know? Perhaps he'd left a message at her studio. She thought about going over to the pay phone and calling her answering machine.

"How about another glass of water?" the waitress asked sarcastically.

Brently heard the irritation in the woman's voice and knew that she'd occupied the table too long without ordering food. She'd occupied space where a tipping customer might have sat.

"I'll have another wine." Brently glanced at her watch. It was twenty after twelve.

A blast of air much colder than the normal December temperature drew her attention to the door, and a tall, broad-shouldered man with his face red from the sting of the wind stepped inside. In five long strides he was at her table. Ignoring the waitress, he bent to kiss Brently's cheek. "Sorry, we had a body down in the river, and I had to wait for the pathologists."

"It's okay." Brently felt positively light-headed with relief. He'd come. Until then, she hadn't acknowledged how much this lunch meant to her.

Kit took a chair opposite her and signaled the waitress for an iced tea. "I'm on duty," he said. "Not like you artistic types. I hear you paint better when you're relaxed."

"I may paint better, but I'm not so sure I can hang pictures straight, and that's what I have to do this afternoon. Remember?" She tried to sound casual. "We're having the opening for Selma Gray's show tomorrow night. Our big Christmas gala."

"The artist from Alabama?" Kit nodded. "This is the event I have to wear a monkey suit to." He grinned to take the sting out of his words.

"That's the one." Brently beamed. He was coming.

"Wouldn't miss it for the world." He motioned the waitress back to take their orders. "Although, I don't have a clue what those modern painters are doing with their splotches of color here and there all over the canvas."

Brently laughed out loud. "Selma is a primitive. Bright colors, simple figures. Her paintings tell a story. You'll love her work, and her, too."

"If you say so." He pointed to the menu. "Want to split a *muffaleta?*"

"Wonderful." The big sandwich with salami, Greek olives and bread fresh from the stone ovens was more than enough for two hungry people.

As another blast of cold wind swooped over the stone floor, Brently and Kit looked up at the man who swept in with the chill and the faint tinkle of Christmas bells from one of the street vendors outside.

"Isn't that Ben DeCarlo?" Kit asked.

Brently studied the handsome man who stood in the doorway, his overcoat impeccably tailored, his eyes hooded. The sun-streaked hair was honey-brown, but there was a faint hint of darker stubble on his lean jaw. The trademark cleft in his chin was a dead giveaway. "That's him. I heard he was going to run for the senate seat that Crosby is vacating." It was a rumor ripe in the French Quarter—and probably all over the state. The DeCarlo family was big, powerful and, some said, hardly ever on the right side of the law.

"Why shouldn't he join the rest of the crooks in Washington? He'll fit right in." Kit shrugged his shoulders. "It's all I can do to keep up with city politics. I hope DeCarlo runs and wins. It'll be one less crime boss for me to worry about."

Brently shifted her wine so the waitress could put down her plate. When she looked up again, Ben DeCarlo was still standing in the doorway. His gaze was fixed at the back of the room.

"Listen, before I pick up this sandwich, I want to wash my hands." Kit stood. "Police work isn't the cleanest business in the world." He was gone just as the waitress brought catsup and mustard and whirled around to another table.

Reaching for the pepper, Brently caught sight of Ben DeCarlo moving through the restaurant. Something about his stride made her pause in mid-reach. He passed her table and kept going, his gaze never shifting. The dark brown overcoat flapped at the back of his calves, just a shade lighter than the expensive Italian shoes he wore. He didn't stop until he reached a table in the back.

"Ben?" An older gentleman at the table started to stand. "Come and have lunch with us, son."

"Sit and eat with us...." the woman said, her words trailing off as she motioned to a chair beside her.

Brently had a clear view of the table. She watched as DeCarlo reached into his coat. The gun he withdrew was dark, deadly-looking.

"I won't run for senate. I'm sick of you interfering in my life. You may run this town, but you don't run me!"

The two shots that rang out seemed to freeze everyone. Brently felt the pepper shaker slip from her fingers but she was unable to move her arm. She watched in horror as blood blossomed on the chest of the man as he fell back in his chair. The woman, who was still sitting at the table, slumped to the side, blood gushing from her throat.

Ben DeCarlo turned directly to face Brently. His handsome face was twisted into a mask of rage and hatred. The gun was still in his hand, and he aimed it straight at her for a split second. Then he turned and began to run.

Chapter One

December 14, 1996

The Café du Monde was bustling with activity as the woman now known as Cori St. John took a seat toward the rear of the open restaurant. Grateful for the warmth, she wrapped her hands around her cup of steaming café au lait and smiled at the young Vietnamese waiter who served her and quickly withdrew. He had no time to waste. The wrought-iron tables of the café were filled with Christmas tourists, all eager for the delicious mixture of steamed milk, sugar and the rich coffee famous in New Orleans. The café also boasted the best sugar-coated doughnuts, called *beignets,* served piping hot and messy. After a burst of warmth and sweetness, the eager shoppers would be ready to continue their holiday shopping sprees. There were only ten shopping days left until Christmas.

Instead of looking around at the splendor of Christmas that bedecked every shop along the two-mile strip of the Riverwalk shopping zone, Cori stared into her coffee as if she could read the grounds like some of the old voodoo women she'd once known. But she didn't have to read coffee grounds to see her future. The surface of her coffee was as smooth and blank as her life. How could you have a future when you had no past?

A lone trumpet player strolled up to the side of the café. A grizzled African-American, he looked homeless and hopeless. When he lifted the horn to his lips, a rocking, jazzy version of "I'll be Home for Christmas" had the breakfasters clapping their hands and tossing money into the open trumpet case.

Cori glanced away. Once she had loved New Orleans. She had loved every smell, every sound, the way the rain fell and glistened in slick pastels on the cobblestone streets. The city had been uniquely alive—and so had she.

And Christmas. It had been *her* holiday. Her favorite time of year. The one time when she had believed that every wish could possibly come true.

Especially the wish of love.

She felt her throat begin to close, and she swallowed the hot coffee to block the emotion. She shouldn't have come back here. In doing so, she had violated the terms of her contract with the federal government. Her handler in the witness protection program would be the first to say, given the pending retrial of Ben DeCarlo, that she had foolishly endangered her life. The efficient Joey Tio, from the U.S. Marshal's Service, had been mad as the proverbial wet hen when she had informed him that she was coming to New Orleans to discuss Kit's disappearance with the authorities and demand to see the investigation they had so unsuccessfully launched.

She had never met her handler in person, but she had a pretty clear mental picture of him, based on his accent. He had the soft, rising pronunciation of the southern part of Louisiana known as Acadiana. If he was a son of the region, he would be dark-haired and dark-eyed—and fiery. She had heard the fire as well as the accent in his angry voice when he'd told her to "stay the hell out of New Orleans if you know what's good for you."

Well, that was just tough. Joey Tio and the rest of the marshals went home every night to their wives or children or girlfriends or mothers. They had a life, complete with a past, present and future. And she had nothing. Not even the satisfaction that someone was still looking for Kit. They'd abandoned the search for her husband more than a year ago. Just up and quit. More pressing cases, Captain Blake, formerly Kit's boss—and supposed friend—had said. There were others with more desperate needs, he had reminded her.

No one had taken into consideration how desperate her need truly was. There had to be some resolution to her marriage to Kit, even though there was some question whether it was even a valid marriage. In her mind, she had made a vow. A lifetime commitment. That type of commitment didn't come cheaply for Cori.

As a member of the witness protection program, she'd given up her right to be in New Orleans. For two years, ever since DeCarlo's first trial, she'd given up any contact with her family. She'd given up the name Brently Gleason and assumed a new identity. Cori St. John of Houston, Texas.

What she wouldn't give up was the belief that her husband was alive.

She felt the prickle of gooseflesh along the nape of her neck and knew it wasn't the December weather or the song the trumpeter was now blowing on the horn.

Reaching into her purse, she fished out the tiny foil-wrapped chocolate. As a child, she'd called the candy a silver bell. Later on, she'd called it a kiss. A chocolate kiss. Her favorite treat, especially at Christmas. The little drops of sweet chocolate had been a coded communication between her and Kit during the year of their engagement. She felt the tears building in a wave she no longer wanted to withstand. Kit had even tucked the box holding her engagement ring into a bag of chocolate kisses, knowing it wouldn't take her long to find it in such a tempting place.

Her hand trembled as she put the candy back in her purse. The diamond solitaire she wore beside her wedding band caught a flash of morning light. Cori fought to control her emotions—and her imagination. She had found three kisses on her desk in the small studio she ran in Houston. At first she had tried to pretend that some child had simply left his or her stash of candy. It made a lot more sense than to jump to the conclusion that her dead husband was "haunting" her. Or so she had convinced herself.

Until two days later when she'd found three more kisses on the dash of her locked car.

Either Kit Wells was alive, or she was losing her mind. And it was the latter that scared her a lot worse than the former. No one had a key to her car or her studio. There had been no sign of forced entry into either place. Was it possible that she had put the candy in both places and had no memory of doing it? The possibility made her chest ache with terror.

The sensation that someone was staring at her made her turn around suddenly. She found the startled gaze of a man who was looking over the top of his newspaper directly into her eyes. He gave a smile and a nod and looked back at his paper.

Cori felt the flush touch her cheeks with color. The man had been staring at her, true enough, but only with mild interest. She had wheeled on him like a caged tiger. Out of the corner of her eye she saw him toss money on the table, stand and leave. So much for his breakfast. Her wild-eyed stare had motivated him to get up and get away.

It had been more than a year since she'd looked at a New Orleans paper, and Cori reached across to the now-vacant table and picked up the man's discarded *Times-Picayune*. As she had anticipated, the possible retrial of Ben DeCarlo was front page news. There was a picture of him standing outside his Angola State Penitentiary cell block talking into a microphone, always proclaiming his innocence.

How could a man who had walked into a restaurant and cold-bloodedly killed his mother and father at point-blank range even pretend to be innocent? Cori felt the old anger boil. One reason she was such an astute art dealer was because of her ability to remember detail. She could recognize talent and remember the unique style and brush stroke of an artist, the exact shades that marked a painter as original, the curve on a line of sculpture that told of the creator's talent. Time and time again she'd been able to pick up a budding artist for a song and sell him for big money when he developed a reputation.

Before she'd left New Orleans, she was gaining an impressive clientele of serious collectors, as well as an audience for her own work. Kit had often teased her that her memory was nearly photographic. It was that talent that had made her such an important witness at Ben DeCarlo's trial.

All of that was gone, along with Kit, and her sister, Lane. Her parents. Her nieces. All gone. Because she had witnessed a brutal murder and had then fulfilled her duties as a citizen. She was paying the price for doing her civic duty.

She flipped the paper, hoping for something to take her mind off her personal troubles. At the photo of a man in a black dinner jacket and big smile, she stopped. He was familiar. She scanned the story quickly, gleaning the facts that Emmet Wyatt had been shot, execution-style, and stuffed in the trunk of a rental car and left at the docks.

The reporter who wrote the story, Farris Quinn, had drawn the link between Wyatt and the DeCarlo retrial. Even as she read, Cori heard the blood thrumming in her ears. Emmet Wyatt, the man who was dead, had been one of the five eyewitnesses at Ben DeCarlo's trial. His name had been Kyle Johnson, and he also had been placed in the witness protection program.

And now he was dead. Murdered the day before, not all that far from where she sat this moment.

She scanned the story again, hoping for the details that would give her enough information to form the rest of the picture. Why was Emmet back in town? Why had he returned to New Orleans? Had something happened in his new life that had triggered a part of the past he could no longer ignore? Or had he been lured back to the "Crescent City"—possibly just as she had been?

Farris Quinn's story dangled a few suppositions, but there was no hard proof either way. The New Orleans Police Department was predictably silent. Just as they had been when Kit disappeared—right after she had testified against De-Carlo.

And now Ben DeCarlo had won a new trial. "New evidence" had been discovered by his defense team, and the trial date had been set in January. Cori had been informed by her handler that she might be expected to testify again. Of course, if that was necessary, she would be supplied with a *new* identity. Another new life. Another empty pretense.

Until that time she was "to remain in Houston and do nothing that might blow your cover." Joey Tio's exact words. The words she had deliberately disobeyed.

She folded the newspaper and left it on the table along with a five-dollar tip. After all, it was Christmas, and somebody should find some pleasure in the holiday.

Exiting the café, she walked across Decatur to the alley where many of the talented street artists plied their work. She had an appointment with Captain Blake in the police station, but she'd allowed herself some time to travel to familiar landmarks. She wanted to confront the past. She *had* to.

The morning was young, but the sidewalk artists were already working. Some took the easy tourist dollar with caricatures. Others hung their oils and watercolors on the wrought-iron fence that surrounded Jackson Square. A cluster of tarot readers worked a steady trade while two young African-American boys did a lanky-limbed tap dance with bottle caps pressed into the soles of their tennis shoes. Clapping for the tap dancers, she left two dollars in their hat and scanned the work of the artists. Some were very good, others not worth a glance. Even as she studied a haunting watercolor of the cathedral on the square, she found herself looking past the wrought-iron enclosure into the center of the park.

Soaring into the morning sky, a magnificent fir tree glittered and shone with tinsel and ornaments. It would be beautifully lit at night. Just as it had been on the eve of her wedding. Two years ago, she and Kit had married in the park, a Christmas Eve ceremony lit with candles and the brilliant future they had planned together. A future that had lasted hardly more than two hours.

Cori started toward the cathedral. Her old showroom was only a few blocks away. She'd heard it had been sold to a young couple who were doing well, but she wanted to see what artists they were hanging—just a glance in the window. And then it would be time for her appointment with Kit's old captain.

She caught a movement out of the corner of her eye. A man was standing beside a large magnolia at the corner of the square. His wide shoulders made her halt in her tracks. When a light breeze ruffled the magnolia leaves, a shaft of sunlight filtered down onto his sandy blond hair, longer and curlier than she remembered it.

"Kit?" She spoke out loud, a whisper of a question that took all the breath in her lungs. "Kit!" She knew it was him. Before she could think, she started running toward him.

A crowd of giggling young girls, their arms filled with shopping bags, stepped in her way. Unable to stop, Cori plowed into one teenager, sending her sprawling to the flagstones. Cori didn't stop. She jumped over the girl, nearly losing her balance in her high-heeled boots. Her forward momentum carried her on past the girls, who were yelling angrily.

The man was gone. The shadows beneath the tree were empty.

Cori saw a blur of movement across the busy street. The man had crossed among the parked carriages and had managed to navigate Decatur Street. He was headed for the French Market. Purse banging against her side, she started to run again.

She heard the blare of a car horn, the squeal of brakes and the horrified cry of the people sitting in the Café du Monde. By the time she turned to look, it was too late. The car was careering toward her, brakes locked as the driver attempted to stop before he struck her. There was no place for her to go. Traffic coming from the other direction couldn't stop in time.

Through the gnarl of traffic, a dark-clad man seemed to fly over the hood of the car. He struck her with such impact they both tumbled into the gutter of the street, startling one of the carriage mules into a near stampede.

For Cori, the world rocked in a carnival ride of blurred sights and pain. Before she knew what was happening, she was hauled to her feet and confronted with the snapping black eyes of a man who looked ready to strangle her.

"What the hell do you think you're doing?" he demanded, his strong hands gripping her shoulders and shaking her for good measure. "You want to commit suicide? You want a stay in a hospital bed?"

At last her focus began to clear, and she took in the mouth drawn tight by fury, the olive complexion slightly paled by fear. The wind ruffled his dark brown hair. Cori looked past him to the place where she'd last seen Kit. Why had he run away from her? She had no interest in anything, not even her burning knee and bleeding elbow, except finding Kit Wells.

"Come on." The man said, roughly pushing her up on the sidewalk and toward Jackson Square.

His anger drove her forward without protest. When they came to an empty bench, he pushed her down onto it and stood over her, huffing with exertion and the residue of adrenaline that had precipitated his bold rescue.

"I ought to thank you," she stammered. She was still disorientated, but she wasn't certain if it was from the hard knock she'd taken onto the pavement or because she'd seen Kit. She rubbed her knee, which had begun to throb. Blood soaked through her dark pants, a sticky wetness that wasn't visible at first. She pulled her hand away and looked at the stain on her palm and fingers.

"Are you hurt?" The man bent down, his fingers now gentle as he probed at her leg.

"It's just a scrape." She wanted to push him away, but it would require too much energy. "Really, it's just a brush with the pavement. If you hadn't..." She thought of the car, the terror of the man's face behind the wheel when he knew he couldn't stop. "You saved my life."

"And you're going straight back to Houston, Texas." He looked directly into her eyes from his kneeling position. "Right this minute."

Cori's eyes widened. How did he know where she was from? "I . . ." Words wouldn't form.

"I'm Joey Tio." He lifted one brow in a gesture that made him look more dangerous than amused. "I told you not to come here." He looked around. "One of the five witnesses was murdered down at the docks yesterday. The retrial is set for January. Your life is in extreme danger, Ms. St. John. I can't believe you were stupid enough to ignore my orders."

The facts were not slipping into place easily, but Cori was finding some sense. "You've been following me?" How else could he have been right on the spot to rescue her?

"My job is to make sure you're safe and protected. You're a very valuable witness." Anger now accented his words. "Although you're making it very difficult, I have no intention of allowing you to die before DeCarlo's retrial. I'll do whatever is necessary."

"Even risk your own life?" She hadn't meant the words to sound so sharp.

"Most witnesses don't expect such heroics, but then we do have the occasional one who is so self-involved that she endangers all of us." He stood up. His fingers wrapped around her upper arm. "And *those* we treat with necessary force. You're going home right this minute, if I have to sit on you the entire way."

Chapter Two

Cori had been propelled halfway down Decatur and nearly to the parking lot where she'd left her car before she gathered herself enough to jerk free of Joey Tio's bruising grip. Her knee throbbed with each step, and his fingers were only making matters worse. Besides, she'd come to New Orleans for an appointment. Just as she twisted free of him, she turned to face him. She was average height, but her gaze was squarely at his sternum. She had to tilt her head to look him in the face.

"Back off," she said succinctly. She was not a woman who often took a forceful stand, but years of running an art studio had taught her a little something about pushy people. Artists were notorious for temper fits and prima donna behavior. She'd learned the hard way that if you gave an inch, they'd take a mile. Joey Tio seemed to be the same personality type. He was going to bully her back to Texas if she didn't put her foot down—pronto! And she had no intention of leaving Louisiana until she'd tracked down the man she'd seen beneath the magnolia tree.

Her heart told her it was Kit, but even if it wasn't, the man was watching her. She was sure of that. He wanted something. There was a reason for his interest, and her gut told her it had something to do with Kit. All Cori knew was that if she put herself in public places, the man would watch her again. The next time she would speak with him.

Joey stopped, caught more by the fire in her green eyes than by her words. From the first moment he'd picked up Cori St. John's trail in the Riverwalk parking lot, she'd seemed more hunted doe than stalking panther. Now the cat imagery was definitely more applicable. Strangely enough, he felt a small wave of relief. When he'd watched her run into the middle of the street, he'd thought she was committing a form of suicide. Now, though, he could see the fire in her spirit. She hadn't completely given up on life—yet. And that was a good sign.

The U.S. Marshal's obedience to her order to back off was so unexpected, Cori could think of nothing else to say. "Quit gawking at me," she finally snapped. "I'm not some kind of specimen or something."

Joey was not a man who blushed easily, or often, but a hint of embarrassment tinged his natural olive complexion with a dusky rose. He had been staring. His thoughts had gone from protecting Cori St. John straight to registering the unusual features of her face—her catlike eyes, pale skin and dark hair—right on to speculating a few, more personal things about her, such as what man in his right mind would walk off just after the wedding ceremony and before the honeymoon?

"I have an appointment with Captain Blake." Cori had decided that she was not going to give any further details of her plans to her "keeper." It was his job to get her out of New Orleans. Out of Louisiana, for that matter. He had no interest in finding her husband. His job was to keep her safe and ready to put on the witness stand when Ben DeCarlo came to trial again. Joey Tio would only laugh at her stories about spontaneously appearing chocolates.

"Ms. St. John, the investigation into your husband's disappearance is closed." Joey tried not to sound condescending, but he'd gone over her file and knew of her repeated attempts to reopen the case of her husband's disappearance. Kit Wells had been one of the NOPD's brightest police detectives. And he had left his job and his wife without explanation. His body had never been recovered, but the basic belief of all the local law enforcement officials was that Kit had taken a bullet intended for Cori. Although there was no solid proof, the law officers Joey knew felt that Kit had been abducted and murdered in retaliation for Cori's testimony at the DeCarlo trial. Cori wanted to reopen that mess. To probe further into the matter would only bring anguish for her. Anguish and guilt. Why couldn't she see that and let it alone?

"I have new evidence." Cori had meant to keep her mouth shut, but she couldn't.

"What kind of evidence?" Joey kept his tone flat.

Cori shifted her weight. Her knee was throbbing, and she could feel the blood trickling down her leg. All she wanted was to make her appointment with the captain and then slip down into the free-for-all atmosphere of the French Market and hunt the man who looked so shockingly like her "dead" husband. She certainly didn't want a marshal hanging around. Kit could spot another law enforcement official a mile off. Whatever his reasons, he was hiding from the law, too.

"Are you okay?" Joey saw the fevered look that came into her green eyes. It was almost haunted, a hopeful look laced with pain. And her breathing had grown unsteady. He put his hand on her arm, this time gently. Without thinking, his fingers brushed her cheek, feeling for her body temperature to see if she was too cold or too hot. Her eyes looked slightly like a shock victim's, and her behavior had been bizarre.

At the touch of his fingers, Cori gasped. The gentleness was so unexpected, so much a part of the life she had put behind her, that she felt that light brush across her cheek all the way down to the tips of her toes. Even her throbbing knee gave a moment's respite.

Joey thought she was going to faint. One arm moved deftly around her shoulders while his other arm caught her behind the knees. In one smooth movement, she was in his arms. "I think we should stop by an emergency room and have you checked out," he said. He found that he did not dare look down into her eyes. He stared ahead and started walking. The hundreds of tourists all seemed to turn and stare, and Joey felt a growing apprehension about the attention he and Cori were drawing.

"Put me down." Cori at last found the words to protest. Finding herself scooped into Joey Tio's arms was the last thing she'd expected, and the very first thing her body had reacted to. He was a handsome man. A strong man. And her body had suddenly decided to kick in and remind her that she was a woman. Cori felt a tide of betrayal by her own foolish flesh and a wave of anger at the man who had initiated this confusing mix of rocketing hormones.

Seeing a small alleyway that was walled on either side by tall brick buildings, Joey took the opportunity and stepped down it. Hidden from view, he eased her to her feet in the narrow confines that put them chest to chest.

"How dare you do that," Cori said. She could hardly breathe, he was so close to her.

Joey felt her physical closeness, too, and the sudden, totally unprofessional images that leapt into his mind made him step to the side so they could have some distance apart. "I thought you were going to faint," he said. He noted the lively color on her face, the fire that danced in her eyes and made her seem older *and* younger than her twenty-nine years. Obviously he had misread the signals. Cori St. John was a lot more likely to explode than faint.

"I'm not about to faint, and I'm not about to go back to Texas." She put her hands on her hips, taking up the narrow alleyway. "I saw my husband today. I saw him! That's who I was chasing when I . . . you . . . when you got me out of the street." She saw the look of disbelief he didn't bother to hide.

"Go ahead and sneer, just like all the rest of the policemen who claimed to be Kit's friends. All of those men he worked with day to day who gave up looking for him two months after he disappeared. Well, I'm his wife, and I know he isn't dead."

"If he isn't dead, why did he run off and abandon his bride?" Joey asked the question quietly, and he saw that it did its work as neatly as the sharpest stiletto. Cori St. John actually sagged. But this time he knew better than to touch her. Not even if she dropped to her knees in the dirty alley.

Cori found her mouth suddenly too dry to speak. She stared down at the tips of her boots and tried to manage enough moisture to answer the question she'd asked herself a million times. Why hadn't Kit taken her with him? If he had to run to protect himself, why hadn't he taken her? She had already given up her life, her family, everything she loved—except him—when she'd testified against Ben De-Carlo.

"I'm sorry," Joey said, and indeed he was. He'd never damaged another person so badly with words. "That was out of line, but you are in a very dangerous position, Ms. St. John." He wanted to help her, to simply offer the protection of his arms. Once again, Cori St. John had transformed, this time from a cat back into a doe. And the deer didn't seem to have enough heart left to elude the hunters.

When she didn't respond, or even look up at him, he continued. "By coming to New Orleans, you've violated the conditions of your protection."

She still didn't look up.

"Legally, we can withdraw all of our help and support. You'll be left alone, without any official protection." Joey couldn't help the feeling that he was sinking lower than the belly of a snail. Everything he said was true, but... "If you'll just go back to Texas and stay out of this city until the retrial, I'll do whatever I can to make sure this doesn't get reported." As soon as the words were out of his mouth he wondered where in the hell they'd come from. He had just agreed to violate the rules of his job. And the woman standing in front of him had not asked for any of it.

"I can't go back now." Cori finally looked up at him. It was his last bit of kindness that gave her the courage to stay and hunt for Kit. Maybe Joey Tio didn't like what she was doing, but he understood. She heard it in his voice. "Kit Wells is in this city. I don't have a life, Mr. Tio. I have an existence. I buy and sell art. I paint a little. I eat, and sometimes I sleep, but not very well. I look for Kit every time I glance out a restaurant window. Every time I walk into a park. I look for him in my dreams. I simply can't go forward until I find him, or find the proof that he is actually dead."

"After the retrial, once Ben DeCarlo is permanently behind bars..."

"No!" Cori shook her head. "No. Two years of my life are gone. The first time I testified, Ben DeCarlo was supposed to get the death penalty. He got life. Now he's getting a new trial. This could go on for the rest of his life, or mine. No. I have a right to live. And I can't begin until I find

Kit. Dead or alive.'' She turned and started out of the alley. Her knee was completely stiff now, and she limped, but she didn't care. She was going to the NOPD and she was going to see the file. Come hell or high water.

Joey Tio reached for her, but thought better about touching her again. There was something that happened between them whenever flesh met flesh that was better left unexplored. What he had to do was bring this witness into line.

"You walk out of this alley and turn to the left, toward the French Quarter, and you're out of the witness protection program. There's nothing I can do for you. On the other hand, if you turn right and go with me..."

She hesitated but kept going.

"Cori, you're signing your death certificate. One witness is dead. Did you ever stop to think that the man you thought you saw was a plant, a setup to draw you out?"

Cori faltered. Her hand went out to the alley wall to brace herself. Joey Tio had struck a nerve.

"Think about it, Cori." Joey saw he'd gained an inch of ground. He pressed forward. "This man you saw. He was in shadow. He wore a coat something like one you'd recognize. A coat that disguised his physique."

"His hair..."

"How hard do you think it would be to do a perfect dye job? There were photos of Kit easily accessible by De-Carlo's ranks." He saw he was shaking her.

Cori clutched at the memory of the chocolate kisses. "It wasn't just seeing him. Someone left something in my studio. In my car. Something that had to come from Kit. Something only he would know the meaning behind."

Joey felt a tingle down his spine that signaled real trouble. His gut was telling him that there was more to Cori St. John's desperate trip to New Orleans than determination to see the NOPD captain who had headed Kit's investigation. Something—or someone—had pushed her into this trip. All of his senses snapped into full attention as he scanned the opening of the alley. This woman was in danger. If not from DeCarlo, then from herself.

"What happened?" he asked her.

Telling Joey Tio she'd endangered her life because she'd found candies would be foolish, so Cori merely shook her head.

"If someone has threatened you, or made contact with you..." He thought again of Emmet Wyatt. Wyatt had picked up a new life in Atlanta, Georgia, with barely a hitch. Not the kind of man to develop lasting relationships, he'd left New Orleans with the nest egg provided by the sale of his restaurant and the money supplied by the WP program and developed a plush life-style in Atlanta. Why had he come back to New Orleans? Why had he chosen to dance with death by returning to a past that he knew could kill him?

Cori started walking away from him.

This time when he reached for her, he caught her shoulder. Ignoring the feel of her bones and muscles clearly defined beneath her sweater, he restrained her. "One witness is dead. As you pointed out, that's a certain amount of failure on my part. Emmet Wyatt was my responsibility. He made it back to New Orleans, and I had no idea he was coming. Now, if someone is luring back the DeCarlo murder witnesses so they can knock them off one by one, I *have* to know."

For the first time, Cori looked past her own predicament and saw that her actions gravely affected others, including the man who stood before her. Assisting her was his job— not following her around to keep her from killing herself in traffic accidents. He had not asked for the responsibility of protecting her any more than she had asked to be a witness to a heartless double murder.

He saw the softening of her anger. Joey released his grip on her, his hand still warm from the contact. "Look, we've gotten off to a bad start here. I don't think tackling you in the street was exactly the best introduction I've ever made." One eyebrow lifted, and this time it was self-mocking.

Cori felt the tears, always so near the surface, begin to well in her eyes. The last thing she needed was a show of kindness.

"Since you're already here, let me take you to a place, a safe place, where we can have some lunch. We can talk. You can tell me what's happening, and I promise that I'll look into it."

"Do you know how many times cops have promised to look into Kit's disappearance? Except they never look far enough to find his body." There was no fire in her words, and Cori knew she was near defeat. Had she really seen the man under the magnolia tree? Or had she dreamed him up because she wanted to find Kit so badly? Even a glimpse of Kit would feed her desperate fantasies for another few months. Until the retrial. Until she was moved and had to start all over again. And then? Would Kit suddenly come to visit her in another city with other tidbits from the past?

Joey took her elbow and ushered her out of the narrow alley ahead of him. At the sidewalk he eased her to the right, toward the parking lot where she had not wanted to go. Now, though, Cori did not resist. Her hard-edged facade had crumbled.

Instead of going to her Saturn, Joey steered her toward a racy black sports car and opened the passenger door. She got in without a word. For the moment, she didn't care where she went as long as she didn't have to make a choice. She felt herself slipping back into the lethargy that had marked the past two years of her life, since she'd joined the witness protection program. The only decisions she'd made had been professional—which artists to buy and show, what presentations, what dates and times. That work had been her lifeline from one day to the next.

Once behind the wheel, Joey cast a look at her, his eyebrows furrowed with worry. She seemed almost catatonic, as if by giving up on going down to NOPD headquarters she had given up on everything. He drove out of the Quarter and headed toward Lake Pontchartrain. In the heavy Christmas traffic, he had to pay strict attention to the road, but he had several moments where he glanced at Cori only to find her gaze distracted, her attention focused in a place so internal he worried that she had left reality behind.

"I'm okay," she finally said without even looking at him. "I just don't know what to do anymore."

They were in a neat neighborhood of white frame houses on a street lined with old oaks that canopied the road. Joey pulled into a driveway, relieved to see the red Mazda parked there. When Cori didn't move, he got out and walked around the car to open her door.

She looked at the house, then up at him, confusion apparent.

"We can talk here," he said, helping her from the car.

She followed him like a puppy, and Joey felt another spurt of worry. Would this woman be able to testify again? He'd heard her take the stand at the first DeCarlo double murder trial, and Cori St. John, then known as Brently Gleason, had been one of the strongest eyewitnesses he had ever heard. She had remembered acute detail, convincing detail, and he had been told she had a type of photographic memory that nailed down scraps of information with perfect recall. But looking at her, it seemed as if she might have trouble remembering how to dress.

When she stumbled on the brick steps because of her injured knee, he steadied her. Before he could say a word, the screen door flew open and a tall, slender woman with black curls that hung to her waist rocketed out onto the porch.

"Joey! What have you done? Look." She pointed at Cori's blood-soaked leg. "Why is she even walking? You're plenty strong enough to carry this woman. Why is she limping along, you big galoot?" Dark eyes that exactly matched Joey's snapped onto him. "How did she get hurt in the first place, Joey?"

Instead of trying to answer the flood of questions, Joey put his hand on Cori's shoulder and gave her a little support. When the dark-haired woman paused to draw a breath, Joey finally spoke. "Cori St. John, this is my sister, Laurette. Laurette, Cori is…she was in an accident over in the Quarter. She wasn't feeling well so I thought we could come here for a cup of coffee *and some privacy.*"

Laurette's dark eyes rolled. "The woman is bleeding, and you want privacy? The saints should walk beside you, Joey Tio. Your skull is as thick as dried swamp mud." She shook her head. "Sometimes I think you have moss for brains. If Mama could see this…"

"Laurette…" Joey's voice had a warning tone. He was already beginning to regret bringing Cori here, but it was the only truly safe place he knew. Safe from the prying eyes of anyone who might be watching Cori, and also safe from the intricate web of personnel and contacts that made up the witness protection program. Cori had indeed blown her cover. Legally, the U.S. Marshals could wash their hands of her and assume no further responsibility. But if he could get her out of town, maybe he could patch up her cover until the trial. And maybe she could be kept safely out of harm's way, if she cooperated. Then she could have a new identity and start again.

"Come inside." Laurette had her arm around Cori's shoulders and was half dragging, half carrying her inside. "My brother Joey was raised better than to leave a woman bleeding on the front porch. He was taught proper behavior. But he is a big man with his badge and his important business, and he has forgotten the courtesies and manners our mother taught him." She cast a dangerous look over her shoulder and muttered something in French.

"Laurette!" Joey warned.

"Don't speak to your older sister in that tone, Joey." Laurette never stopped as she assisted Cori past a massive fir tree that touched the ceiling and was decorated with multicolored lights, white crocheted snowflakes, angels and red glass ornaments. Beneath the tree the floor was covered with presents. The cool, spicy scent of the tree gave way to the warmth of a kitchen bubbling with the smell of gumbo and corn bread. "And just in time for something hot." She eased Cori into a chair at the red-checked tablecloth, and in less than twenty seconds she had placed a steaming bowl of gumbo and a hot piece of corn bread in front of her.

"Sit," she commanded her brother as she motioned to another chair. "Cliff isn't coming home for lunch, and Angela is Christmas shopping with the neighbors. As soon as this injured one eats, we'll look at her knee."

"I'm fine." Cori was surprised that she could manage to get a word in edgewise between the brother and sister. They were so alike, and yet so different. Where Joey's voice carried only a hint of the Cajun dialect, Laurette's was the voice of that unique region of Louisiana. Cori looked from one dark, worried pair of eyes to another. If they were not close in spirit, they were almost identical in looks. The arch of their eyebrows was perfectly matched, as was the widow's peak that marked their smooth, olive foreheads. Even the full cupid's bow of their upper lips, over a lush bottom lip, were exactly the same.

"Joey is my younger brother," Laurette said as if she read Cori's mind. "People sometimes think we're twins, but I'm older, and therefore he has to *listen* to me." She got up and quickly placed gumbo in two more bowls. Before she took her seat they all had corn bread and butter, gumbo and big glasses of sweetened iced tea.

Cori had not intended to eat, but the spicy food tantalized her, making her mouth water. Joey and Laurette had no such reservations. Laurette mumbled a prayer and they began to eat. Cori lifted her spoon and let the delicate blend of spices and seafood invade her mouth. One spoonful followed the next until her bowl was empty, and she looked up to find duplicate expressions of satisfaction on the two faces across from her.

Patting Joey's arm, Laurette turned to Cori. "So, when is the wedding?"

The words stunned Cori. She looked up to find that Joey looked as shocked as she was.

Laurette saw the amazement and focused on her brother. "Surely this is a wedding. For ten years you live in New Orleans and never once do you bring a single girl anywhere near the doorstep of my house. Now you drag in this half-starved child with her leg bleeding. I was certain you'd asked her...." At her brother's glower, Laurette finally fell silent. Her gaze fell on Cori's left hand where the wedding band and engagement ring sparkled. "Oh, my," she whispered. "I've made a terrible mistake."

Cori recovered first. "It's okay." Laurette was a warm-hearted woman, and her love for her brother was more than clear. "I, uh, sort of work with Joey. He saved me from getting run over, and I was a little...out of it. So he brought me here to talk." She looked up and saw gratitude in Joey's eyes. For the first time in a long time it felt good to be able to do something helpful for someone else.

"Here I make an issue of Joey's manners, and I had assumed..." Laurette couldn't look at her brother. When she did, the fire was back in her eyes. "But it's a natural thing to assume. He's thirty-four. An old man by my family's standards. And no girl on the horizon. No one to hold in his arms and dance when the fiddle plays fast and sweet." She leaned forward. "No one to hold and start a family."

"Laurette!" Joey's face was darkened with what could either be embarrassment or anger. "This is not the time or place. This is business."

Laurette was totally unimpressed. She held up her hands and turned to Cori. "Business! Business! That's all I hear from my little brother. Everything in his life is business, and all the while he grows old and shriveled and his juices will dry before he produces a single son to carry on the Tio name!" She stood up. "Well, tend to your *business*, Joey. I'm going to decorate the front porch." She walked out of the room and let the swinging door to the kitchen flutter to and fro in her wake.

Joey looked down at his hands for a long moment before he stood and cleared the dishes from the table. At the sink he ran hot water and squeezed detergent over their bowls.

Cori had nothing to watch except him, even though the movement of his muscles beneath his cotton shirt made her slightly uncomfortable. When it was clear he could think of no way to get around the embarrassment his sister had caused, Cori spoke. "You're lucky to have a sister who loves you so much."

He turned the water off and turned around. "I know." His smile was sheepish and proud. "We're the only two children. My mother was sick for a long time and died when

I was twelve. Laurette felt she had to step in and take over, even though by then I was mostly grown."

"I have a sister." Cori thought of Lane, the cool professional writer who lived in New York and worked as a producer on a network news show. Lane knew Cori was alive, and knew that in order for Cori to stay alive they could never be sisters again. That was how the WP program worked. Now, though, Cori felt as if it might be worth her life for one conversation with someone who loved her.

Joey nodded. He knew all about Cori's family. Her sister, married with two daughters. Cori's parents were dead. Her father was killed in a traffic accident and her mother had died of a heart attack shortly after the DeCarlo murders. It was one of the reasons Cori had agreed to go into WP. That and the fact that her fiancé, Kit Wells, had agreed to go into the program with her. She had not thought she would be so very much alone.

"I've had enough of this," Cori said. Her decision was made.

Without asking, Joey knew what she meant. He'd seen witnesses fall out of the program many times before. The loneliness, the isolation from family, sometimes it was just more than a person could bear. And a lot of times those people ended up dead.

"Cori, stick it out until Ben DeCarlo is retried."

She felt a flush of anger. She had nothing left of her life, while Joey Tio had a sister who worried about him, a niece, probably a hundred aunts and uncles and cousins. And all he was really worried about was having his witness available for the retrial.

"I can't," she said, starting to rise. "Please take me back to my car." She checked her watch. She'd missed her appointment with Captain Blake, but she could still demand to see the investigation file on Kit.

"Cori, you're not thinking about the danger."

Her smile was sad. "No, I suppose I'm not. I'm thinking about the fact that I don't care about the danger. Don't you see, Mr. Tio, I just can't do it another single day. Kit is alive." She reached into her handbag and withdrew the chocolate kisses. She lined them up on the table in a neat row. "He left these for me. Three in my locked studio. Three in my locked car."

"Chocolate candy?" Joey picked them up and knew they could have been bought in any gas station or convenience store in the world.

"It was a signal between Kit and me. He would leave three kisses for me whenever he came by the shop and I wasn't in, or sometimes on the pillow in the morning...." Her voice broke and she turned away from him, her hands on her face to hold back the emotion that almost overwhelmed her.

Joey was beside her, his hands on her shoulders, bracing her, trying not to interfere with her grief but also trying to stop her from falling apart at the seams.

"Don't you see? Kit is out there. He's trying to tell me something. He wants to come back," she said, knowing she sounded desperate, stupid and horribly lonely.

"Ms. St. John..." Joey's voice was calm, soothing. "Anyone could have left that candy. You can't assume it was your husband."

Cori had no fight left. She stepped out of his hands and finally turned to face him, not even bothering to wipe the tears from her cheeks. "That's where you're wrong, Mr. Tio. I can assume anything I want. If it isn't Kit, then I am losing my mind. Either way, I can play by any rules I decide on."

Chapter Three

Cori opened the car door and put her foot on the gravel pavement of the Riverwalk parking lot. Around her was the constant motion of shoppers loading trunks, hunting for parking spaces, laughing in the cold December air that seemed to hum with the excitement of Christmas. Her knee had given up the terrible throb and settled for a dull whine of an ache. "Thanks for trying, Joey." She couldn't dispel the look of failure on his face, but he had tried to help her.

"Leaving the program isn't the solution, Cori."

"It is for me." She shrugged. Somehow the visit to Joey's sister's house had calmed her, had forced her to see clearly all that was missing from her world. "I don't have a life."

"Hunting for a man who disappeared from your life, deliberately or otherwise, isn't a great new beginning."

"I know." They'd argued about this for at least an hour at Laurette's kitchen table. What or how much Laurette heard, Cori had no idea. She had been busy stapling colored lights around the front porch pillars when Cori and Joey had finally exited. The look she'd given both of them had been sympathetic, but she had offered no advice.

"Cori, I'll have to report this." Joey found his reluctance to do so very unsettling. He'd been in the program long enough to know that WP worked only as long as the participants played by the rules. Cori was taping a target to her back, especially with a new DeCarlo trial just around the corner of the New Year.

"Do your job, Joey. Write it up." She got out and leaned down to look in the car windows. "No matter what happens, you tried. I thank you for that. I don't feel that the officers who claimed to be Kit's friends have really tried. If I felt that all efforts had been exhausted, maybe I could give up. But the candy confirms my belief Kit is alive, and he's trying to communicate with me."

They were back to the candy. The tiny little silver bells that had glittered on his sister's table like the proverbial thirty pieces of silver. Unless Cori, in some state of mind where she wasn't aware of her actions, had actually left them for herself. He looked into her dark eyes and saw the demons dancing there. She was a tormented woman. Her subconscious could have gotten the upper hand. Even as he thought it, though, he didn't want to believe it. He *wanted* Cori St. John to be a healthy woman with a chance at happiness. If she lived long enough.

"Thank you." Cori stood up and closed the car door. She walked over to her car and got inside, but she didn't crank the engine. Joey knew she was not leaving. She was only waiting for him to give up and go back to the office to report the fact that she was out of the program.

And on her own more than she had ever been before.

Cori sat in her car and waited until Joey drove away. Watching the black Supra disappear, she felt a sense of loss that was far too acute for a man she'd met only hours before. It was just a sign of how desperate she was. Officially, Joey Tio was out of her life.

She left her car and walked to one of the shops that paralleled the Mississippi River and found peroxide and Band-Aids, then moved to a bench on the levee where the sun

shone brightly. While paddleboats that offered scenic tours,
dinner and dancing drifted along on the deceptive-looking
current of the yellowish river, she repaired her knee. Joey
had repeatedly offered to clean her leg, but she had not allowed him to do so. The idea of his hands...well, it wasn't
a good idea. She poured the peroxide and gritted her teeth
against the sting. The injury was certainly not life threatening, but it was painful and a nuisance. Just the sort of
thing to plague her when she needed to cover a lot of ground
on foot.

When she'd patched herself up as well as possible, she
gathered her things and set off for the French Market. It had
once been one of her favorite places. She and Kit had developed a weekend routine of coffee and *beignets* at the Café
du Monde, and then a stroll through the vegetable vendors
for a string of elephant garlic or the delicious peppers that
grew only a short distance away in St. Tammany Parish. The
Big Boy tomatoes were always ripe and firm, smelling as
only homegrown produce can. Cantaloupes, melons, sugar
cane during Christmas, all of the wonderful smells of a state
and culture rich in history, tradition and soil.

And Kit. Always Kit with his laugh and his antics.

She passed through the south end of the market, letting
her eyes wander over the fruit and produce but not stopping to buy any of it. She didn't cook anymore. There was
no point, or pleasure, in cooking for one. She moved on
with the general drift of the loud milling throng of shoppers. Next came the jewelry and crafts, the tables of sun-
glasses and unique earrings crafted by local artists. The
boxes of secondhand books where a signed first edition
might rest against a crate of pulp fiction.

T-shirts and sweatshirts, all bearing slogans and logos that
had become symbolic of the many faces of Louisiana, were

crammed table to table, as vendors cut prices in loud, bantering voices, vying for the tourist Christmas dollar.

"Hey, hey, little fox, this green is the exact color of your eyes." A smiling vendor held out a sweatshirt that was a deep shady green. "For you, six dollars."

Cori shook her head. She had come to look for something other than sweatshirts. If—when—she saw Kit, she didn't want to be hampered by shopping bags. She would have to move fast to catch him. Then he would have to answer some questions. Why? Why had he married her and left? Why hadn't he let her know he was alive? Why? Why? Why? And most especially, why on the night of their wedding?

Joey had raised that question. And others just as painful. She had not responded because she didn't have an answer. Maybe when she did have one—an answer that wasn't something she'd imagined or made up—maybe then she could put the past behind her and go forward.

What wasn't fair was that she was in more of a prison than Ben DeCarlo was. She still watched the news out of Baton Rouge. She'd seen DeCarlo, his handsomeness only heightened by the leanness of his jaw, the hungry look that had come into his pampered face since his incarceration at Angola, the maximum security prison farm in Louisiana. Somehow, prison had made him even more handsome than before.

If she closed her eyes, she could still see him coming in through the big door of Augustine's. She could smell the fresh garlic bread baking at the nearby Le Croissant du Jour as he swept through the door, his dark brown overcoat flapping in the breeze. She could see the honey-blond streaks in his hair. They looked professionally done, but after she'd seen him on television at the prison, she knew they were from the sun, not a bottle. She also saw the anger in his blue eyes, flickering deep, almost hidden but not quite. He was a dangerous man who intended to have his way. The wine merchant-cum-politician who would have inherited the most powerful crime family structure in the city—if he'd only waited for his father to die a natural death.

What was it Shakespeare had said about children? Sharper than a serpent's tooth. It had long been alleged, by Kit and all of his cop buddies, that Antonio DeCarlo had been responsible for a lot of people taking a swim in the murkey depths of the Mississippi River. Dixie Mafia. And Antonio DeCarlo had been the reputed head of the Louisiana branch of "the family." Of course, officially there was "no proof of any mobsters operating in the state." No *solid* proof. But the law enforcement racketeering specialists called RICO were all over the DeCarlo family at the time Ben killed his parents.

Kit's disappearance was tied to the double murder—and her testimony. She had concluded her testimony on December 22, the last and most powerful of the eyewitnesses to the murder. Kit had disappeared December 24 about nine o'clock in the evening, while Cori, still in her bridal gown, had been dancing at the elegant reception her sister had organized at the exclusive Riches'. Kit never made it to the reception. He had gone to check on more champagne, a trip only a few blocks out of the way, but it had been a special champagne. The perfect ending to a perfect day, he'd said. And he had never returned.

She forced herself to remember the times Kit had talked about the murder case, searching his past casual conversations for some clue that she had overlooked. Kit had it figured that Antonio was getting ready to put Ben out of the family, and that's why he was hit. The bold daylight hit was Ben's last attempt to grasp control of the family crime unit, even if he had to call the shots from behind Angola's miles of concertina wire. It had been an interesting theory, and one Kit enjoyed talking about.

Personally, Cori would have been only too glad to bury the images of that day forever in the far reaches of her mind. Only Kit's gentle persuasion, his total belief in the duty of each citizen to participate in justice, had convinced her that she had to testify. That and the promise that he would go into the WP program with her; they would build a new life together.

The sound of a loud whistle drew Cori out of her reverie, and she found that she was at the end of the market. Her favorite pizza place was only a block away, and she considered stopping for one of the small, thin-crusted pies topped with sweet peppers, cheese and thick slices of Italian sausage. She had forgotten all the delicious temptations of New Orleans.

She took a seat on an empty bench and scanned the crowd instead. She could only use her body as bait, hoping that the man she'd seen earlier would find her. In a city of more than half a million, she had no way to track him.

The wind off the river was cool, and she drew her sweater closer around her. She could wait. In the past two years, she'd gotten very good at waiting.

JOEY PUSHED THE CAR to the limit of safety as he sped to the Marshals office. His intention was to report that Cori St. John had broken her cover and was in New Orleans, and was in grave danger. If he alerted the entire office, perhaps they could pull together some kind of tailing unit that might be able to keep her alive until the trial. But he knew that was next to impossible. They didn't have the manpower for that kind of operation, even for a day or two, much less several weeks. No, but court action could be taken to place Cori under protective custody. She'd be madder than a panther with a knot tied in her tail, but she would also be alive—and able to testify.

That was the goal he had to keep in mind. Cori was a key witness in keeping Ben DeCarlo behind bars and off the streets of his city. Ben's absence hadn't cut down on the gangland style deaths; if anything, since his incarceration, the bodies found in trunks, the execution-style slayings, were becoming more and more a part of the scenario of New Orleans. But Joey could only guess that if Ben were out, the body count would climb even higher.

As he forced his train of thought along these lines, he could still see Cori's green eyes, shadowed with self-doubt and so much pain that she obviously didn't believe she could be hurt worse. Well, she was wrong about that. If Ben's men had any idea she was in town—a target so simple to take down that it made deer-hunting seem like brain surgery—she wouldn't last through the night.

Ben DeCarlo wanted out of prison. And Cori St. John was one of four people left who could see that he didn't get out.

Joey's long stride carried him from the parking lot and into his office and directly to the file cabinet, where he pulled Cori's file. He'd read it several times, but after his encounter with her, he wanted to refresh his memory. Especially about Kit Wells and his peculiar disappearance.

He flipped through the pages of the file, noticing that for a time after moving to Houston Cori had dyed her hair a dark shade of brown that rivaled Laurette's tresses. But she had gone back to her natural mahogany that so perfectly set off her eyes. She was thinner than she'd been when she married Kit. And so much sadder that he sat and stared at the photo of the bride in her candle-lit gown. The wedding had been in Jackson Square, at night. A candlelight ceremony that used the Christmas beauty of the park perfectly.

An artistic wedding that showed Cori's talents to their fullest.

But the true artwork was the glow on her face, the way her eyes held on to the figure of Kit Wells, handsome in his tuxedo...and with just a hint of something in his expression. Joey lifted the picture closer. Why hadn't he noticed before? There was a trapped look in Kit's face. Maybe it was just the huge commitment of marriage. Or maybe it was the fact that he *knew* he wouldn't stick around to see the wedding through.

Joey lowered himself into his chair, the photo still in his hand.

Maybe Cori St. John wasn't as crazy as the members of the NOPD thought she was. Maybe Kit Wells had found himself in a place so tight he'd had no choice but to cut and run.

Joey tapped the photo against his desk and leaned back in his chair, closing his eyes for a moment. He visualized the scene from earlier in the morning. He'd been in the shadows cast by the awnings at the Café du Monde. Cori had been across the street, staring at the artwork and watching two kids who were hustling coins from the tourists with a tap dance act. He'd surveyed the scene carefully, waiting for a time to approach Cori and to try to drag her back into the net of the WP program. Captain Blake had alerted the U.S. Marshals that Cori was headed to New Orleans. As her handler, he'd been prepared to intercede, intercept and protect.

And then she had frozen, staring into a corner of the park. Before he had a chance to figure out what she was looking at, she'd run headlong into the traffic. By the time he'd launched himself across the street and knocked her out of harm's way, whatever, or whoever, she'd been watching was gone. If there had been anyone there to begin with.

He picked up her file and reread the familiar notations. The first year into the program she'd been a model witness. She'd made the move to Houston, established a new studio, started a new life. She'd buried herself in the day-to-day of a big city where even successful art studios didn't call much attention to themselves.

She'd called the NOPD regularly to check and see if any progress had been made in the investigation into the disappearance of Kit Wells. Weekly calls. As regular as a paycheck. Always asking the same questions. To the point where Blake had begun to view her as a nuisance.

Six months ago, when Blake had told her firmly the case was closed, that Wells was considered dead and that as his beneficiary, she would receive all his benefits, Cori had failed to sign any of the checks or to make any of the arrangements for his retirement benefits. She had written a letter insisting that Kit was alive. Until she had proof, she refused to participate in death benefits.

That was when Blake and the NOPD began to consider that Cori St. John was unstable. Of course, this information had to be kept secret. As one of the key witnesses in Ben DeCarlo's retrial, Cori's stability could not be questioned.

But was she losing it? Joey had thought she might be. Then again, she'd seemed perfectly sane. Just wounded and hurt. Most people had to let the scar tissue build to survive, yet Cori kept the wound wide open, kept looking for Kit and insisting he was alive, and had come to New Orleans to launch her own investigation. Now, that was crazy. Deliberately stepping into danger wasn't the footwork of a woman with good sense.

He flipped through more pages. In all of the notes and reports on Kit Wells and Brently Gleason, now Cori St. John, there was no mention of chocolate candies. Relief was his first emotion, and then disappointment. Deep in the back of his mind he had thought that just possibly the chocolate kisses were part of the record, something that someone could find and use against Cori. Now he was back at square one. Either Cori had made up the business about the candy—or someone who had known Kit was taking advantage of personal knowledge to manipulate Cori into danger.

He closed the folder and got up. If he followed procedure, he'd fill out the paperwork noting that Cori had abandoned the WP program and put herself in extreme jeopardy. To safeguard his job, he should do so immediately. But something held him back. Hefting his keys, he went out the door as fast as he'd come in. The black sports car spun loose gravel as he tore out of the parking lot and headed back to the French Quarter. Perhaps he could pick up her trail once again.

THE AFTERNOON LIGHT slanted down across the French Market, giving the bundled vendors a golden glow. Cori was not deceived by the light. The day was growing colder and colder. Christmas was often a time for shorts and T-shirts in the South, but this year Jack Frost had come for a visit and dug in his heels. It was going to be cold enough for a fire. For those lucky enough to have a fireplace.

All afternoon Cori had waited, getting up to stroll around the area, to buy a croissant or a cup of hot coffee, or a paperback to pass the time. Now her book was half read and she was cold to the bone. Several possibilities came to mind. Since she'd blown her cover completely, she could also call her sister Lane and make one human contact that would work against the depression and disappointment that was becoming all too familiar to her. But there were practical matters with more immediacy. Such as finding a hotel room. It was Christmas, and the hotels in the Quarter might be packed. That would mean moving to another section of town, which was something she didn't want to do. She and Kit had lived their life in the Quarter. This was where she'd find him—if he was here.

She pulled the heavy red sweater up and around her neck and ears and snuggled down into it. What she needed was just a tiny nap. The idea of sleeping on a park bench near the river made her smile. Had it come to this? Sleeping like a derelict on a bench? Yes. But the golden sunlight struck her face and forced her eyes closed, and she drifted deep into the warmth of the sweater, glad for the promise of sleep without the terrible dreams that often awakened her. Here, with the bustle of the market around her, she felt as if she'd come home. She could rest for a moment before she continued her search.

The last thing she remembered was the sound of a child crying in excitement at the puppets on display not fifty yards away. The vendor was fairly adept at managing them and was giving a small impromptu show. Exactly the kind of thing she loved to watch. She had fallen asleep with a smile.

When she woke, it was to stare into the face of a little girl. Fake fur earmuffs in a leopard pattern gave the child a comic look, until Cori sat up and took notice of her dark stare.

"Are you hurt?" the child asked. "My mother will help."

Cori shook her head and smiled. "I'm fine." The little girl was a true beauty. Dark eyes, dark hair. She looked something like Joey Tio's sister. "What's your name?" Cori looked around to find the mother.

"Kayla." The little girl did a curtsey. "And yours?"

"Bren ... Cori." In the two years she'd been in the WP program, Cori had never messed up her name. She had put aside her old self and become Cori. Now the name seemed to fit her far better than her old one. So why had she almost slipped? It probably didn't matter, anyway. She was out of the program. She could call herself anything she wanted.

"Can I have a piece of candy?" The girl bit her bottom lip.

"I'm sorry, honey, I don't have any."

"Yes, you do." She pointed to the seat beside Cori. "That man put it there."

Cori turned slowly to look at the bench beside her. Resting so close to her thigh that they almost touched her were three kisses. Three little silver kisses. She felt herself swallow and knew she could not scream or she would terrify the little girl.

"Can I have one?" the child asked.

"Sure." Cori's voice sounded strained even to her. Kayla looked up at her in mid-reach, a question in her eyes.

"Mama says I shouldn't ask people for things."

"Take the candy." Cori forced a smile. "All three. I think the man must have meant to leave them for you, anyway." She took a breath. "Tell me, Kayla, did the man look like Santa Claus?" She tried to put a note of teasing in the question. If she frightened the child, she'd never get any information.

"Oh, no." She unwrapped a candy and popped it into her mouth, looking over her shoulder to be sure her mother wasn't watching the illegal candy consumption.

"Well, he must have looked like one of the elves, then?" Kayla laughed, sucking the sweet chocolate. "No. He looked like Uncle Adam." She reached for another.

"And what does Uncle Adam look like?" Cori glanced around for the child's mother. Where was she? Surely she'd show any second and demand her daughter not do anything so foolish as stand and talk with a stranger.

"He's tall." Kayla nodded, then focused on the next candy.

"Go ahead," Cori said. "Have it."

Kayla reached for it. "He works on the oil rigs."

"Does he have dark hair?"

"Oh, no." Both little cheeks bulged, one slightly larger than the other where the freshest candy resided.

"Then he has blond hair?"

Kayla considered. "Not really blond. But kind of. Except this man had longer hair. And he stood and stared at you for a long, long time. I thought he was going to wake you up by staring."

"And then he put the candy down?"

"He took it out of the pocket of his coat. And he put it down...." Kayla imitated the very precise placement of the candy while at the same time snaring the last piece. "Just like that. He almost touched you but didn't. Is he your boyfriend?"

Cori felt her smile falter. "I don't know."

"But he left the candy for you. A Christmas kiss." She grinned impishly as she popped the third and last chocolate into her mouth.

The thought came to Cori so fast, so totally formed and filled with ugly possibility that she acted without thinking. She had eaten none of the chocolates left for her. What if they'd been poisoned? "Spit out the candy, Kayla." She grabbed the child's shoulder and shook her. "Spit it out!"

"What?" The little girl cried. "Mama!"

"Spit it out." Cori grabbed her jaw and forced it open, using her fingers to find the chocolates, one almost melted, and drag them out and onto the ground.

"Mama!" Kayla's eyes were wild and she broke free of Cori's grip. "Mama!"

Out of the crowd, a short, dark-haired woman came running. She scooped the child against her and then began to survey the crowd, her expression a fierce mask of fear and fury. She crooned to the child as she looked for the offender, determined to do terrible damage.

Kayla pointed to Cori, who remained on the bench.

"What have you done to my daughter?" The woman came at Cori like a mad dog. "What did you do?" She turned back to the marketplace. "Call the police! Call 911. This woman has hurt my child!"

Several men came out of the crowd and shifted closer, just in case Cori tried to make a break for freedom.

"I can explain." She spoke aloud but no one heard. Kayla was screaming against her mother's leg, terrified by Cori's abrupt behavior. The mother was guarding her and yelling instructions into the crowd. Cori sat on the bench, her thoughts centered on a tall, sandy-haired man who had crept up on her in her sleep and put three chocolate kisses by her thigh. The child had seen him. He wasn't a figment of her imagination.

"You are going to jail," the woman spat at Cori.

"Your child found some candy on the bench beside me. She ate it, and it suddenly occurred to me it might be poisoned. I made her spit it out." Cori spoke softly, staring directly into the woman's eyes. At last her words penetrated and some of the fury left the mother's face.

She turned to the child and spoke in rapid French, which Cori had never learned to follow. The child looked at Cori, her eyes still filled with tears but no longer screaming, and nodded her head.

The mother knelt down and examined the little girl's mouth. Traces of chocolate were clearly evident.

"I shouldn't have let her have the candy," Cori said. "I wasn't thinking. But she saw it here, and I didn't care. But then I realized I had no idea where it had come from. That maybe someone had, you know, put something in it."

Cori's words raised another fear in the mother's face, but she was calmer now. She spoke to the child again. This time the little girl shook her head. The mother turned back to Cori. "She said the candy fell from your purse."

Cori felt as if she'd been slapped. "It didn't come from my purse. She told me a man left it on the bench."

The mother consulted with Kayla once again in the heated rush of French. She held the little girl's face so that she could not look away. At last she turned back to Cori. "She said it came from your purse, that it fell out on the bench."

"A man left it. Kayla saw him. She described him perfectly. She said he looked like her Uncle Adam."

The woman gave Cori a strange look and spoke to the child in French once again. Placing her hand on her daughter's shoulder, she slowly shifted her away from Cori. "Kayla made up the story of the man."

"Why?" Cori felt her boost of confidence fade and her fears grow as she watched the woman's face fall into an expression of pity. "Because you looked so sad and alone. She wanted you to have a boyfriend. She said the candy fell from your purse." The woman backed away from Cori. "Kayla doesn't have an Uncle Adam."

Cori sagged against the bench.

"The candy she ate, where did it come from?" The mother was still worried that the candy might be contaminated.

Cori looked up. "I don't know."

Something in her vague and troubled stare made the woman pull her daughter against her body. "We'll wash out your mouth, Kayla." She got a Kleenex out of her purse and picked up the candy from the pavement.

In the distance was the angry wail of police cars approaching at a fast clip.

Chapter Four

Joey was drawn to the sound of sirens and the whirling blue lights of the black-and-white units that had congregated at the north end of the French Market. His gut told him that something bad had happened and that, somehow, Cori St. John was involved. He got out of his car and ran, dodging cardboard boxes filled with crafts and treasures. He saw four officers standing in a circle around a woman with dark hair and a big red sweater. Off to the side was a woman and a crying child and a gathering of sightseers that grew larger by the minute.

He stepped forward, flipped his federal commission to the cops and put a proprietary hand on Cori's arm. "Come with me," he said, smoothly pulling her through the tangle of black leather police jackets.

"Hold on." One of the cops grabbed Cori's other shoulder. "We've had a little problem here."

"You're going to have a bigger problem if you don't back off." Joey stepped between Cori and the policeman. "This woman is protected." He leaned forward. "Don't make me spell it out for you," he warned in a harsh whisper.

"This woman has been accused of accosting a child." The policeman, who was not as tall as Joey but several pounds heavier, was not budging. "We've made a report, and we have to file it."

Joey looked at the child, who was standing beside her mother. The mother looked less than certain. "Ma'am, are you filing charges?" Joey asked.

"I don't know," she said. "Kayla said the woman didn't really hurt her. She gave her some candy and then forced her to spit it out." She looked behind her as if she wanted to disappear.

Cori finally spoke, her voice soft and her words directed to Joey. He seemed the only one there interested in hearing what she had to say. "The candy was left on the bench. I didn't care if Kayla had it, but then I realized I didn't know where it came from. I guess I overreacted. I did make her spit it out." Her voice dropped to a whisper as she confronted a hard possibility. "I was afraid it might be poisoned. I haven't eaten any of the other candy."

"What candy?" The policeman wore a badge that identified him as Officer Lewis.

"Someone left candy on the bench while I was asleep. Some kisses." Even as she said it, Cori realized it sounded suspicious. Or at least deliberately dumb.

"This woman was attempting to protect the child." Joey eased Cori a little farther away. "I don't see where there's a problem."

"Ma'am, are you pressing charges?" Lewis asked the mother.

"No, no." She ran her hand through her child's hair. "But I am going to have a talk with my daughter. She knows better than to accept candy from strangers. It could have been poisoned."

"That's true." Lewis nodded at her. "Okay, then." He turned back to Cori, his pale eyes boring into her. "Aren't you..." He stopped and looked at Joey, obviously putting two and two together. "Well, I'll be. I thought you'd been moved out of the South."

"This really isn't the time." Joey nodded toward his car.

"Oh, yeah, the retrial." Lewis nodded sagely. "You know, Mr. Tio, it would be better if you kept your clients out of the middle of public disputes." His grin was shark-like. "I wouldn't exactly call this protection."

"I, uh, I'm not in the..."

Joey tugged her so hard she lost her train of thought as she tried to keep from losing her balance.

"Let's go now," Joey said.

Irritated at his strong-arm tactics, Cori shook free. "Since you know me, did you know my husband, Kit Wells?" She looked at Lewis and then the other officers, one by one. Three shook their heads, but Lewis nodded.

"Yeah, Kit and I used to play cards. Before he met you." His grin was quick. "He sure cleaned up his act after he started going out with you. When he told me he was getting married, I didn't believe it. Kit was never the kind to settle down. He was a guy who liked the action, the party."

Cori felt the knot in her stomach cinch tighter. She'd never heard this side of Kit. All of the officers she'd met acted as if he was a quiet man. One who had yearned for marriage and a home.

Joey saw her pale. "I think we need to go." He didn't like the public spectacle Cori had managed to create, and he didn't like standing around in the open jawboning with a guy who was having a good time revealing hurtful information.

Cori ignored Joey and spoke to Officer Lewis. "Do you believe Kit's dead?"

"I never figured old Kit to go out without a bang." He shrugged. "Then again, Kit had made some serious ene-mies. The talk on the street was that you wouldn't have testified if he hadn't insisted. He'd turned in his papers to resign, said he was going into the WP program with you. Everyone knew about how he supported you." He paused a beat. "Some folks like to keep the score sheet settled."

Cori felt his words like tiny flames of guilt. "Yes, everyone knew that." Her indecision had been headline news for two days. One of the television tabloid news shows had even done a story about the woman with the photographic memory who didn't want to testify. A retired judge who served as legal commentator for the show had pointed out that the justice system was falling apart because citizens like her wouldn't do their civic duty.

All along, though, Kit had urged her to listen to her heart. To do only what she felt comfortable doing. With him by her side, she'd found the courage to testify—and lost everything.

"So you think Kit is dead." Her voice was hollow, defeated.

"I didn't say that. We turned the city over looking for him. We never found a clue. Usually, a hit on a policeman can't be kept quiet. Not for two years."

"You're a very helpful man." Joey was mad enough to strangle Officer Lewis with his bare hands.

"It isn't like she hasn't heard this before." Lewis grew defensive at Joey's tone. "She knows."

"Yes, I do know." Cori turned away.

"Later," Joey said as he took her elbow and led her to his car. The word was a promise to Lewis.

"Where are you staying?" Joey asked her as he steered her. She was as lifeless as a rag doll.

"I don't know." She tried to think about places she had once wanted to stay. Not a single one came to mind. "I thought I'd get a place when I got here."

"This is the holiday season. Hotels are going to be booked." Joey felt himself sliding deeper and deeper into the mud hole that Cori St. John was digging for herself.

"I'll find some place." She shrugged. What did it matter? She wouldn't sleep, anyway. "Maybe over toward Slidell."

"I know a place uptown." Joey couldn't stop himself. She was so defeated. "It's a safe place."

"Won't your relatives get tired of you dragging me into their homes?" She gave him a brief smile.

"It's not a relative." Joey found himself smiling in return. She had a sense of humor. And she was quick-witted. He liked that. "It's a bed and breakfast. An old high school friend of mine runs it. She doesn't advertise at Christmas because it's her home." Joey's acquaintance with Jolene had begun long past high school, but he didn't think Cori needed to know the details.

"Then maybe she won't appreciate a guest."

Joey opened the door and handed her in. "She'll do it for me. And then I'll be able to sleep because I'll know you're safe."

Cori put her hand out and blocked the door before he could close it. "I'm out of WP, Joey. Really out. I'm not testifying, and I'm not hiding anymore. You have no need to protect me any longer."

He hadn't intended to get into the issue now, but she'd opened the door. "Cori, what happened with the candy?"

She shook her head. "I fell asleep. I woke up and this child was staring at me. She asked if she could have some candy, and when I looked down, there were three chocolate kisses right beside my leg."

"Did they fall out of your purse?"

She shook her head. "Kayla, the little girl, said a man had put them there while I was asleep. She said he was tall with sandy blond hair."

"Acute powers of observation for a girl who couldn't be more than eight." Joey saw her look down at her feet. "What is it?"

"When the mother asked her, she said the candy fell out of my purse."

Joey closed the car door and went to his side. As he slid behind the wheel he felt a terrible sense of foreboding. Cori St. John was likely on the edge of a total breakdown. And she had no one in the world to help her. "You'll like Chez Jolene." He started the car and realized that dusk had begun to fall.

Along the levee the sky was an electric pink that faded to mauve near the dark horizon. They pulled into traffic and rode through the neon streets of the Quarter before they reached the business district and, finally, the quiet of the huge old oaks and houses of uptown. The graceful limbs of the trees canopied the street and cut the vivid sky into an intricate quilt of shifting shades of pink and purple.

"Winter was always my favorite time in New Orleans." Cori spoke to break the silence. She was too aware of Joey beside her. Too drawn to his profile and the way his hand gripped the gearshift.

"Some of these houses really do the decorating up right." He pointed to a big white mansion whose entire yard was filled with the twinkle of tiny lights. As darkness fell, more and more of the Christmas decorations were brought to life.

"I've missed this." Cori stared out her window and exhaled on the glass, creating a tiny circle of fog.

"I'm sure they have Christmas lights in Houston."

"They do. But they don't have the homes and the trees and the...total abandonment to decorating. Houston is more restrained."

Joey laughed out loud. "So Houston is not like The City That Care Forgot."

Cori turned on him. That phrase had always been one of Kit's favorites to describe New Orleans. "I don't suppose I ever really thought of New Orleans as a carefree place. But it is alive. There's always music and food and laughter." She laughed self-consciously at herself. "I sound like I should work for the state tourism commission."

"And abandon your art?" Joey was teasing, but he instantly sensed that Cori had not taken his question as banter.

"If I could go back in time and never have entered Augustine's. If I could make it so that Kit and I were both thirty minutes later. If I could change that one day, I'd give up my talent. I'd be happy to give up..."

Joey put his hand gently against her mouth. "Don't ever say things like that, Cori. You tempt fate when you offer your talents as if they meant nothing to you." He lowered his hand. "You can't change what happened. None of us can. What you have to do is decide to go forward."

"I will. When I find out what happened to Kit."

Joey knew better than to press the issue. He made a left, then a right and finally pulled down a long shell drive that was lined on both sides by oaks.

"Somehow, I don't think this place is in my price range." Cori did okay, but she didn't have five hundred to spend for a night's lodging.

"It's okay. Jolene works with the program."

"But I'm not in the program," Cori reminded him.

"I didn't turn in the paperwork. I was hoping that by tomorrow you'd change your mind and go back to Texas. I was hoping I could convince you to wait in Houston until you're called for the retrial."

"Someone put candy beside me while I was sleeping. I saw a man who looked like my husband. Those things happened today, Joey. Not weeks from now. Today. This is the closest I've come to finding out anything about Kit. Do you really think I'm going to leave New Orleans now?"

Joey parked the car, got out and went around to her side.

"Damn." Cori got out. "I left my overnight case in my car." She had been brain dead to allow Joey to drive her here. Now she was stranded. Without a car or clean clothes. Probably just as he had planned it.

"I'll run it by tomorrow, early. Until then, Jolene can loan you something."

"What makes you think Jolene would want to loan her clothes to a perfect stranger?" Cori was amazed at the way people fell into line for Joey. His sister opened her home, this Jolene woman would loan out her clothes.

Joey put his hand on the small of her back and guided her down the brick pathway beneath the giant oaks. "Jolene's had her share of rough times. She understands."

Cori hesitated. Was Jolene one of Joey's relocated witnesses? She knew she didn't have the right to ask. And when it came right down to it, she didn't want to know.

Joey led her up the steps of the brick cottage-style home and to a beveled glass door that shimmered with the multicolored lights of a Christmas tree. A petite woman with hair the color of flame opened the door.

"Joey!" She threw her arms around him and hugged as hard as she could. "Come in, come in," she said as she stepped back.

"Jolene, this is Cori St. John."

As Joey made the introductions, Cori found herself under the intense gaze of the smaller woman.

"Welcome," Jolene said. "I have some hot mulled cider in the kitchen. Let's have a cup."

She led the way, not asking any questions of Joey.

When they were all seated at the table, Joey spoke. "Cori needs a place for tonight. A safe place."

"Of course." Jolene turned a smile of warmth and sympathy on Cori. "There's a cottage in the backyard. You'll have perfect privacy for as long as you need."

"And some clothes," Joey said. "She left her bag in her car until tomorrow."

"Let's see. About a size eight?"

"That's right." Cori should have felt ill at ease, but something about the woman made her feel welcome, and indeed, safe. The long day was wearing on her, and the hot mulled cider was potent and soothing. The idea of a bed was beginning to take priority in her mind.

Jolene spoke to Cori. "There's a clean nightshirt on the bed and a few things hanging in the closet that should come pretty close to fitting." She turned to Joey. "Why don't you see Ms. St. John to her room? I'll send a tray over when dinner is ready. I think our guest might like some privacy."

"It's been a long day," Cori agreed. She had left Houston at midnight after only a few hours' sleep. Now she was genuinely worn-out.

Joey led the way out the back door, flipping on small floodlights that made a wonderland out of the lush backyard. "This is beautiful," Cori said. "Extraordinary."

"Jolene took an old house and completely remodeled it. She's handy with a saw and drill. Not to mention plaster, electricity and plumbing."

"She looks too fragile," Cori said.

"Only goes to show, you shouldn't judge a book by its cover." Joey unlocked the door of the cottage, which was a miniature version of Jolene's house. He handed Cori the key but stepped inside and turned on the lights. As a precaution he went through the tiny house, checking the kitchen and bath, opening closet doors.

"Is this a standard service of WP?" Cori asked. The fact that Joey did those things without being asked made her remember Laurette's harangue about his manners.

"Habit, I suppose," he said. "But everything looks cozy here. No one should know you're uptown. You'll be fine until tomorrow, when you head back home."

Cori was too tired to argue. She sank down on the bed.

Joey walked over and picked up her purse. "How many chocolates did you have?" he asked.

"Six. The six that were left. Three each time."

He upended her purse. Amidst the lipstick and pens, the compact and billfold, were three glittering kisses.

The reality was like a slap. "Maybe they did fall out of my purse." Cori picked one of them up. "Silver bells. Christmas kisses. They couldn't have fallen out on their own."

"Are you certain?" Joey still held her purse in his hands. "Maybe the little girl . . ."

Looking up at Joey's worried face, Cori felt unsure, and she shook her head. "I'm not certain of anything anymore. Good Lord, I scared that little girl and her mother almost to death."

"Even if the candy came out of your purse, you don't know where it came from. It was a good precautionary move."

Cori knew he was trying to smooth over the event, to put the best face on it he could. For her sake and his own.

"When I fell asleep, my purse was closed. When I woke up, it was closed. And why did that little girl say she'd seen a man watching me?"

Joey gently put her purse on the bed. He knelt down and took both of the hands she held in her lap. "We'll worry about this tomorrow. Get some rest. There're spare tooth-brushes in the bathroom. Toothpaste, shampoo. Jolene keeps the cottage stocked. In the morning, things will look better.''

"Thank you." She knew there was nothing else to say. How could she convince Joey Tio of anything when she couldn't even convince herself?

Watching him walk to the door, she felt an impulse to call him back. But there was no logical reason to delay him. He'd given enough of his time. More than enough to a woman who'd done everything but cooperate with the rules of his employment. Still, when he turned back to her and gave a brief smile before he closed the door, it took all of her willpower to smile back. And then the door closed and she was alone.

The cottage was cozy and laid out in the design of the original French cottages. There was a bedroom, a tiny kitchen, a dining room-living room and a bath. The entire structure was thirty feet wide, and all the rooms had doors and or windows on both south and north walls to allow for the cross ventilation that would prove necessary during the summer. The design also gave Cori a view of the magically lit garden to the north, and of the backyard, which was lit by lights skillfully hung in some of the biggest oaks she'd ever seen. The effect was delightful. Weary to the bone, she decided to slip into the lavender-scented flannel nightshirt that had been left and crawl into the bed. Her brain was too tired to work anymore.

Just as she slipped beneath the cotton sheets, she heard a tap on the door. Jolene entered with a tray holding black bean soup and thick, crusty bread. A gingerbread cookie man was on a Christmas dish. "There's a stocked bar in the kitchen, and soft drinks in the refrigerator." She put the tray on the bed. "Will you be okay?"

"I can't thank you enough...." Cori felt as if she were a guest in this woman's home, not some stranger thrust upon her.

Jolene waved a hand. "I owe Joey a lot more than I can ever repay him. This is a small thing. And you look as if you need a port in a storm."

"An understatement." Cori lifted the tray onto her lap.

"Eat the soup. Have a glass of wine and sleep." Jolene moved back to the door. "I'll lock this behind me."

"Thank you," Cori called again to the sound of the lock sliding into place.

She was almost too tired to eat, but she finished the soup and rinsed the dishes in the sink before turning out all the lights and falling into the bed. The hodgepodge of the day's events flitted behind her closed eyes, a nightmare of bad decisions and worse actions. But she could not deny the powerful need for sleep, and she felt herself drifting into blackness that was strangely peopled with the eerie shadows cast by huge oak trees.

Cori was uncertain how much time had passed or where she was when she opened her eyes. The rapid drumming of her heart soothed her while at the same time she realized she was afraid. Trying to get her bearings, she kept herself perfectly still. The high ceilings of the house shifted with the shadows of the oaks as the wind moved gently through them. From her bed she looked north and saw the twinkling garden and remembered where she was.

Though she had never been a heavy sleeper, the past two years had robbed her of even a pretense of getting eight hours. She was lucky to get four, and then maybe another two somewhere between the wee hours of the morning and time to get up.

The pattern of shadows that lay across her bed shifted again, and she felt a chill. The oaks were beautiful, but they were also creepy. As a child she'd never liked the darkness. Only with Kit had she found the sweet, velvety nights to be a place of pleasure and enjoyment. Now, in a strange place, she watched the dancing shadows shift across her body, warm beneath the covers, and knew her life had been touched by darkness. She felt as if the shadows had laid a claim on her soul, tugging her gently after them into the blackness of the night.

It was foolish to indulge such thoughts, but she couldn't help herself.

In the pattern on the bed she could see the graceful branches bend and sway. But there was one shadow that didn't move. She sensed the danger before she could even comprehend what it was. Slowly, very slowly she turned to look out the large window that covered the south wall. She knew what she would see before she looked, but she had to look.

The man standing at the window stared in at her. He wore an overcoat that hid his body, but a gusty wind whipped his medium-length hair about his head. In the illumination cast by the lights in the oaks his hair looked silvery, but Cori knew it was sandy, with a bit of a curl.

Kit had somehow managed to follow her from the French Market. Fear held her in a viselike grip of paralysis. She could not see his face. It was in shadow. Light fell on the top of his head and across his shoulders, hiding all other features.

"Kit?" She whispered the word, unable to do more.

The figure stood, watching her as if she could not see him.

"Kit?" She sat up in bed, turning to face him directly.

He stared a few seconds longer, then backed away.

"Kit?" Cori got up and went to the window. Her fingers fumbled at the lock that would open it wide enough for her to slip through. "Kit?" She called out to him, louder now.

He was leaving, fading among the enormous oaks, a shadow lost among the deeper shadows of the trees.

"Kit!" Cori cried his name as she broke a fingernail on the lock. It was jammed. She pounded on it, first with her fist and then with a shoe. When it wouldn't give, she went to the door. Frantic, she searched for the key that would open the dead bolt lock. Where had Joey put it? She had a clear picture of him holding it in his hand, but she'd been so tired, so preoccupied. Maybe he'd given it to her. She finally found it on the dining room table and ran to the door. It took her shaking hands several tries to manage the lock. When it was open she threw the door wide and ran into the darkness. The grass, crisp and frosted, crunched beneath her bare feet as she ran toward the oaks where Kit had completely disappeared.

"Kit!" She screamed his name. "Kit! Don't go! Please, don't go!" She ran toward the trees. "Kit!"

The lights in the main house shot on. Every room, every window, bloomed with light. In a moment the back door opened. "Cori?" Jolene's voice was afraid. "Cori, are you out there?"

Cori stood in the midst of the trees, whirling one way and then another as the breeze shifted the tree limbs overhead and played with the shadows. Her feet were numb and moisture froze on her face. "Kit." His name was barely a whisper.

Jolene rounded the corner of the cottage with a flashlight in one hand and a deadly nine millimeter semiautomatic pistol in the other. She held the gun as if she knew how to use it.

"What is it, Cori? Was someone here?"

Cori turned slowly to face her. "It was my husband. Kit was here." She spoke almost as if she were asleep. "He came up to the window but he didn't say anything, and when I woke up he disappeared.''

Jolene shifted the light among the trees, searching for any sign of life. When she was certain no one else was in the backyard, she hurried to Cori and wrapped an arm around her. Easing her back toward the cottage, she kept the gun ready and the flashlight moving over any areas where an intruder might hide.

Cori watched the trees where a ghost from the past had hidden, watching and waiting for the moment he sought.

Chapter Five

Cori was still huddled in a blanket when Joey arrived. Jolene handed him a cup of coffee and drew him into the big kitchen of her house.

"She claims it was her husband." Jolene's brow was furrowed. "I didn't see anyone." She shrugged. "It was dark. He could have been there."

Joey looked down into the steaming cup of black liquid. "She might have seen someone, but it wasn't her husband. Kit Wells is dead."

"Oh." The word rushed from Jolene's lungs. "She was so certain. She saw him so clearly." She rubbed her arms and refilled her own cup. "She hasn't spoken a word since I brought her in here."

Joey sighed. "We need her testimony, Jolene. And I'm afraid she's going to break apart before the trial." He stopped himself. There was no need for Jolene to know the details of Cori's plight.

Holding her cup, Jolene stared at her friend. "It's the DeCarlo trial. I've already figured it out. But is it just her testimony, Joey? I saw the way you looked at her. It occurred to me it could be something more."

He turned and walked to the doorway where he could watch Cori. Her coffee cup sat on the table, untouched. "I can't let it be anything else. My job is to protect her and to make sure she's able to take the stand when DeCarlo goes up for retrial. Any other feelings will only get in the way of my job."

"You can't help your heart, Joey." Jolene put her cup down and went to him. Her hand on his arm was light, comforting. "I've known you for four years. There was a time when I hoped you might look at me the way you look at her. Then I worried that you'd never look at any woman, that you'd chosen a life alone. You have feelings for this woman, and no matter what else you do, you shouldn't deny your heart. Love is a gift, Joey. Don't turn it aside when it's offered."

He sipped his coffee. "Love is a gift only if it's returned. Cori is in love with a dead man."

"There's a lot of guilt there. Perhaps she's begun to mistake guilt for love." Jolene hugged Joey lightly and stepped back. "Enough of a lecture, Joey Tio. You didn't come here for a lesson in love."

"Sure enough, I did not," he answered, letting his speech fall into the natural patterns of his childhood. Growing up in New Iberia, he'd learned the easy rhythms of the French Acadians. Unlearning those patterns had been difficult, but a necessity to advance in the U.S. Marshals. At times, though, and with close friends and family, he allowed himself the luxury of drifting into the familiar ways. "Did you see anyone last night?"

She heard the slight half note of hope. "No one. But dawn is breaking. We can look for tracks or some signs."

Jolene was right. If Cori had seen something other than a shadow cast by the trees, there would be physical evidence.

"I'll talk to her." Joey took his coffee and went into the den. He sat on the hassock facing Cori. "Can you tell me what you saw?"

Without even looking up, Cori repeated the story exactly as it happened. As she talked, the sun rose, casting a slanting light into the room that touched the crystal ornaments on the Christmas tree and made them glitter. Jolene worked in the kitchen, humming audibly so that both Joey and Cori knew she was not listening.

"He left again." Cori finally looked up, at the end of her tale. "Why did he leave? I tried to open the window but the lock was broken. I couldn't find the key to the door, but when I finally got it open and ran outside, he was gone. Why didn't he wait?"

Joey touched her cheek with his palm and caught the tears in her lashes with his thumb. Very gently he brushed them away. He had no answers, and he felt an unpleasant ache in the region of his heart as he looked into her grief-stricken face. To be left over and over again by the one you loved, even if it was only in the imagination. It was a torture, and he felt pity for her and sorrow for himself. It was clear she loved Kit Wells, dead or alive. Whatever he felt for her, there was no soil for the seed to grow.

"I'm going outside," he said. As he started to rise, he felt Cori's hand on his. She clung to his hand, and for a moment he felt his chest constrict with a band of hope. But when he looked down at her, he knew it was not him she reached for but Kit.

"Find him, Joey. Please." Her voice broke.

At a loss for words, Joey nodded as he disengaged his hand and walked out into the sunlight. How had he allowed himself to begin to care for Cori St. John? He had not planned it, had not even acknowledged it to himself until Jolene had forced the issue. But care for her he did. Whatever he could do for her, he would, though he knew his feelings for her were hopeless. Cori St. John was caught in a time warp. He might finally provide for her the evidence she needed to escape, but he wasn't certain she wanted to. Or had the strength to try.

Pushing those thoughts aside, he went to the cottage and began to examine the ground, doing the job he did best. If only he could find evidence that someone had managed to tail him to Jolene's. And that someone was using the past in a very cruel way to push Cori over the brink into insanity— and to destroy her testimony. He had to believe that was the case, because the other alternative was that Cori had already slipped beyond reality to a place where not even all his considerable law enforcement skills could help her.

Making the first move she'd taken since sitting in the chair in Jolene's living room, Cori walked to the window. She watched Joey as he moved among the trees, forming a pattern as he walked carefully along the backyard, working his way to the cottage and the sloping lawn beyond where the giant oaks kept their many secrets. He had to find something. A print. Something. There had to be some trace of Kit that would prove that she'd seen him. That he was alive.

But instead of joy at that possibility, Cori felt a slowly growing dread. If Kit was alive, if he had been standing at the window staring in at her, why hadn't he talked to her? Why had he allowed two years to pass without even a sign that he was alive?

Why had he abandoned her?

She heard the sound of the morning paper thudding on the front porch and did not turn around as Jolene went to the door and retrieved it. Seconds after Jolene returned, Cori heard a soft exclamation of dismay.

"Joey is going to be furious," Jolene said as she finally drew Cori's attention from the window. She walked into the living room, the newspaper opened before her.

"What is it?" Cori knew it was not good news.

Jolene held the paper out to her. The headline was bold. One by One: Eye Witnesses in the DeCarlo Murder Trial Return to City. Beneath it was a photo of Cori at the French Market surrounded by cops and the woman and her crying child.

Cori studied the photo, hoping for a second that somehow Kit had been captured in the background. But the only hopeful note she found was that the picture had been taken before Joey arrived. He was not shown.

"Joey is going to be furious," she agreed, handing the paper back to Jolene. "And he has every right to be."

Jolene was scanning the story. "So the news is public that you're back in town and going to testify at the retrial. The other witness who was in New Orleans was murdered. Found in the trunk of his rental car." Jolene lowered the paper. "Why are you here, Cori? The trial isn't for another few weeks. Don't you see how dangerous this is?"

"It's a long story." Cori felt a sense of friendship with Jolene, and at the moment she didn't want to destroy it by proving she was crazy.

"How did that photographer happen to get your picture?" Jolene was looking at the paper again. "And how would he have identified you as one of the original witnesses in the trial? It was a sensational case. I remember it well. And I watched the television accounts and read the paper. I must have seen your picture, but that was two years ago. Two years and there have been many more murders, many more newspaper stories."

Cori suddenly remembered the cop. Officer Lewis. He had recognized her. And more than likely he had offered the scoop to the *Times-Picayune* reporter. "I think one of the policemen at the scene might have told a reporter." She walked over to Jolene's side to find the byline of the writer. Farris Quinn. The same person who had written the story about Emmet Wyatt's murder. The reporter obviously had a snitch in the NOPD, and it could easily be Lewis. Cori had not liked him.

"If that's true, that policeman is going to have to answer to Joey." Jolene folded the paper and dropped it on the coffee table in front of the fireplace. She stacked another log in place and signaled Cori to follow her into the kitchen. "How about some French toast? An old recipe of Joey's family."

"Sure." Since she'd snapped out of her dreamlike state with the arrival of Joey, she was feeling better and even hungry. Since she'd come home to New Orleans she'd found herself eager to eat. Before, in Houston, she honestly couldn't remember what she ate from one meal to the next.

Jolene waved her to the table as she heated the cast iron skillet. "Are you leaving New Orleans today?"

"I don't know." Cori's answer was honest. "First I'm going to pay a visit on an old friend."

Jolene dropped the battered bread into the sizzling skillet. "Who might that be?"

"Danny Dupray."

The bowl of batter slipped from Jolene's fingers. She caught it before it fell, but a splat of batter sloshed onto the burner of the stove.

"It's okay," she reassured Cori as she wiped it up and placed the bowl down. "It slipped. How do you know Danny Dupray?"

"He had a place beside my studio. The Twinkle, a sort of club." Cori couldn't help the distaste that touched her features. "He was always roughing up the girls who worked for him. That's how I met Kit. I called the cops one night when there was a real fight going on. I thought he was going to kill one of the girls." Cori picked up the napkin in front of her and smoothed it on the table. "Kit answered the call. He and Danny had a few words."

"So what do you think Danny Dupray can do for you?"

Cori ceased the motion of her hands. "Kit used to go to Danny. For tips and information. Danny always knew a lot of things going on in the city." She picked up the napkin and held it a moment. "I don't have anywhere else to go. The police have given up. I thought maybe Danny might have heard something. If I have enough money, maybe he'll tell me."

"What makes you think Danny Dupray would tell you the truth if you gave him your life savings?"

Cori looked up at the burst of emotion from Jolene. The redhead was standing at the stove, spatula in hand, face white with fury. "You're playing at a game that kills hard, well-trained men." Jolene shook the spatula. "Danny Dupray is no one to mess with."

"What do you know about Danny?" Cori was shocked by the change in Jolene.

"A lot more than I want to. I used to work for him. Until Joey came along and helped me escape." Jolene advanced on the table. "Stay away from Danny. I mean it, Cori. If he knew anything about what happened to your husband, he wouldn't tell you. And what he would do is turn around and sell the information about you to someone who might decide to put a bullet right between your eyes."

Joey stepped into the kitchen. "What's going on?"

"Cori was talking about visiting Danny Dupray, hoping he'd be charitable and sell her some information about her husband. I was disabusing her of Danny's charitable qualities."

"How do you know Dupray?" Joey's voice was calm but his eyes were dark and unreadable as he stared into Cori's.

"The Twinkle was right next door to my studio. It's how I met Kit."

Joey took the spatula from Jolene's hand and flipped the French toast. "Danny Dupray is one person you're absolutely to stay away from, Cori. He's bad news in a town full of bad news."

"Did you find anything? Any evidence of Kit?" Cori didn't want to argue with Joey or Jolene about her future plans.

Joey shook his head. "Nothing clearly identifiable as a footprint. The grass is thick." He walked around Cori so she could not see the speculative look he shot her. "Someone *could* have been outside the window, but there was no effort to gain entry. In fact, there was no need to force his way in. The window was unlocked."

"The window was locked." Cori held up her hand with the nail broken back to the quick. "I tried to open it. It was locked. And the door, too."

"I locked the door," Jolene said. She set a plate of steaming French toast before Cori and turned to put more in the pan for Joey.

"There was nothing outside." Joey hesitated. "But I did find this." He reached inside his jacket and brought out a small plastic bag. It glittered red, green and silver in the sunlight before he dropped it on the table. The chocolate kisses tumbled onto the wood and into the sudden silence of the room.

Cori reached out and touched them as if they were jewels. "Where did you find them?"

Joey sat down across from her and leaned forward, anger making his dark eyes hard. "A better question is what kind of game are you playing, Cori?"

Cori did not draw back from his anger. She picked up one of the chocolates. "Where were they?" The slight chill of them told her the answer. "They were in the refrigerator, weren't they?"

"As if you didn't know." Joey stood up so suddenly his chair scraped against the brick floor with a harsh sound. "What are you trying to pull, Cori? Has DeCarlo suddenly made it worth your while to get out of testifying by acting crazy?"

"Joey." Jolene tried to put a hand on him, but he shook it off.

"This has gone too far. I've been chasing my tail here, and I've had enough of it." Joey pointed to the candy. "This is your evidence that a dead man is haunting you. And suddenly I find the candy stash in your own possession. It appears to me, Ms. St. John, that *you're* leaving the candy trail."

Cori put the candy carefully on the table. "Yes, it would seem that way." She looked into Joey's eyes, forcing him to calm down enough to look at her. "But that isn't true. I didn't put that candy there."

"Right." The word was ugly.

Cori's smile was so out of place that for a moment Joey thought she had lost her mind. He watched as she picked up the candy again.

"You brought me into the cottage. You dumped my handbag. There were three chocolates in it then, right?"

"What's your point?" Joey was still furious.

"My point is that there were three pieces of candy there. Nothing else in the bag. I had no luggage. My sweater has no pockets. Where did I carry this candy? I don't have a car to go buy any." She looked at Jolene. "Maybe you should check your house to see if I slipped in here during the night and stole chocolate kisses from you."

Joey recognized the truth she spoke. There had been no way for her to get the chocolates into the cottage. "What in the hell is going on here?"

"That's exactly what I intend to find out." Cori spoke softly, without anger. "It isn't fun to be part of someone's game." She looked up at him. "I don't know what's going on, Joey, but I swear to you that I'm not doing any of this."

Jolene put the French toast in front of Joey, a plate stacked three slices high. "Just to set the record straight, I don't keep chocolate in the house. Too fond of it for my own good. Now, you two better eat. I've got to go to work, and I'm afraid you have other problems, Joey." She retrieved the newspaper and put it down in front of him.

"Oh, no." Joey slapped the story with his hand. "How did they get this?" He didn't expect an answer, so he was startled when Cori spoke.

"From that Officer Lewis, I'd bet."

Joey scanned the story, then looked at Cori. She *looked* sensible. "I'm sorry," he said. "I have to be honest, though. I'm not certain what to believe where this candy is concerned."

Cori thought she should be furious, but she wasn't. "It's okay. I don't know what I believe, either. All I do know is that candy didn't go in that cottage with me. Either it was there before I arrived, or someone put it there while I was out in the yard looking for Kit."

"Did you go back to the cottage?" Joey asked.

"No, I brought her here. She was . . . disoriented." Jolene sat down with her French toast and poured on some syrup. "I didn't check the lock on the cottage door, but I'm assuming Cori left it unlocked. Someone could have gone in while we were in here.''

"And opened the window," Cori insisted. "It was locked."

"Why, though?"

Cori knew this answer. "There are three possibilities. Kit is alive, which no one believes but me. Number two, someone wants to make me believe Kit is alive. Or someone wants to make me believe I'm losing my mind."

Joey nodded. "I'll vote for number two. The only thing I don't know is why. What possible good would it do to make you believe your husband is alive?"

Jolene put down her fork. "Possibly to use as blackmail to prevent her from testifying at the retrial."

The answer was so obvious that Joey slapped his forehead. "It could be, Jolene. It could be." He furrowed his brow. "How did you come to that conclusion?"

"You forget, Joey, I spent fifteen years working around lowlifes like Danny Dupray. I watched the wheels spin in their heads all day and all night, figuring the odds, calculating how they could use someone for personal gain. This sounds exactly like something he would cook up—for a substantial amount of money."

Joey turned to Cori. "You said Kit and Danny knew each other, that Danny was Kit's snitch?"

"In some cases." Cori thought back. She'd hated Danny Dupray, but it was a convenient source for Kit. Sometimes when Cori was caught late at the studio, Kit would check in with Danny to see if he had any good leads. There were times Danny would sell him something good, something that resulted in a big arrest or gave Kit the missing link in a case.

"Sometimes a snitch gathers a lot of information on the guy he's ratting to." Joey knew the dirty inside business of law enforcement would leave an honest citizen with a bad taste in his mouth. Like it or not, though, to get the truth sometimes an officer had to go through some pretty despicable people. "How often did Kit and Danny meet?"

"Twice a week." Cori shrugged. "Kit never liked to tell me much about his work. He didn't want me . . . tainted by the people he had to associate with." She suddenly remembered something. "But it was odd that Danny sent us a wedding present."

Joey felt the skin tighten near his hairline. It was indeed strange that a snitch would show enough finesse to send a wedding gift to a cop.

"What did he send?" Jolene asked, her contempt evident.

"A case of champagne. Good champagne, not cheap. An entire case. He had it delivered to . . . my . . . home." Eyes widened with fear, she looked at Joey. "Kit must have given him my home address."

"Maybe not." The more Joey heard, the less he liked Kit Wells and his method of doing police business. Surely he hadn't been foolish enough to do such a thing. "Maybe Danny just found out. I mean, the wedding was in the public square. You had a studio. You've lived there, you know the Quarter is like a neighborhood. People know a lot more of one another's business than you'd expect. Did you have a listed phone?"

"Unlisted." Cori looked at Jolene. "Artists call at all times of the day and night. Before a show, they lose their awareness of time or anything except their own insecurities. Unlisted is the only way to live."

Jolene got up and took her plate to the sink. "Danny could find an address. It wouldn't be hard at all. The question is why would he want to? Why not carry the gift next door to the studio? Why not give it to Kit when he was there? Why go to all that trouble and then have to pay extra to have it delivered?''

"Those are all really good questions." Joey pushed his plate back, too. "Ones I think Danny should answer."

Cori stood up. "I'm ready whenever you are."

"You're absolutely not going to the Twinkle with me."

Cori didn't back down an inch. For the first time in two years someone was asking questions that might lead to finding Kit. She had no intention of missing any part of it. "You can't leave me here alone. Whether you believe it or not, someone was in the side yard. Someone who was my husband or who wanted me to believe was my husband. Either way, someone knows I'm here. You can't leave me alone."

"No, but I can take you to the precinct headquarters and have your butt locked up for your own protection."

"They won't hold a person they think is crazy." Cori wanted to buckle under Joey's angry glare, but she'd buckled too many times in the past. "Besides, I'm out of the program. I quit, remember?"

Jolene slipped out of the room to get dressed for work and left them to fight it out between themselves. Neither of them saw the grin on her face as she hurried down the hallway to her bathroom.

"Witness or not, you aren't going to see that sleaze ball with me. Dupray is a very dangerous man."

"I'm not staying here."

For the first time Joey was aware of the flannel nightshirt she wore. It was red plaid and it came just past her thighs. Jolene had given her a pair of red knee socks to wear after she'd gone outside in her bare feet. He couldn't help the grin that touched his dusty features. "You're not dressed for the Twinkle. Or perhaps I should say you're overdressed."

Cori felt a sweep of embarrassment. The nightshirt certainly wasn't provocative or even slightly sexy. It was just the fact that it was night wear and Joey was staring at her. "I'll change," she said stiffly. "The Twinkle won't be open until lunch. I used to work beside it," she reminded him.

"You can ride with me, but you're going to wait someplace safe," Joey warned her.

"Fine." Cori got up.

"I put your bag in the cottage." Joey rose, too. "Let me make sure there's no one there." He wasn't sure what he believed about the candy, but he was not taking another single chance with Cori St. John. Things happened around her. Extraordinary things. Like double murders and disappearing husbands.

Before he could get out of the kitchen the telephone rang. He could hear Jolene's shower running so he picked up the receiver.

"Chez Jolene," he said.

"I'm looking for Joey Tio," a male voice said.

"You've got him." Joey was instantly alert. No one should know where he was. No one.

"This is Farris Quinn from the *Times-Picayune.* I understand you can tell me how to get in touch with Brently Gleason."

"Who?" Joey was taken aback.

"One of the eyewitnesses in the Ben DeCarlo double homicide trial. If you haven't seen the paper this morning, we had a shot of her in the French Quarter. She's in town and we want to know why."

"This isn't a good story." The very idea was deadly.

"Look, Mr. Tio, we've got one eyewitness back in New Orleans murdered. Then Ms. Gleason is spotted in some fracas in the French Quarter. We've talked to several witnesses, and what we're getting is a very, very interesting story. Something about her dead husband.''

"Ms. Gleason is a protected witness. Any stories about her could jeopardize her life." Joey tried to think of some threat he could use, but none came to mind.

"It would seem she violated her agreement by returning to New Orleans, unless there's some secret meetings going on with the district attorney. We know the D.A., Travis Shanahan, is determined to see DeCarlo remain behind bars, no matter what it takes. Are there some strategy sessions going on here that involve the original witnesses? Or should I say, what's left of them?''

"What did you say your name was?" Joey stalled. The reporter had caught him flat-footed.

"Farris Quinn."

"How did you get this number, Mr. Quinn?" He saw Cori start. She recognized the name from the morning paper.

"We don't reveal our sources. Is there something going on with the prosecution of DeCarlo? Some new angle?''

"I have no comment. But I have to know where you got this number.''

"Good investigative reporting, Mr. Tio, and Ms. Gleason hasn't exactly been subtle. That was quite a stir she caused yesterday. I understand no charges were filed.''

Joey knew he was walking through a mine field. The worst possible thing for Cori would be additional press. But Farris Quinn had a legal right to print whatever he could dig up. Consequences weren't the province of a free press.

"Quinn, the witness's life may be in jeopardy." He put it out there. The silence told him that he'd struck his target.

"That has to do with your job, Tio. My job is to print the news.''

Joey liked the defensiveness he clearly heard. Farris Quinn was a man who took his job—and its consequences—seriously. "You know the DeCarlo trial comes up in a few weeks. This witness is vital. There are compelling reasons for her to be in New Orleans, which I can't reveal. But I do promise you, as soon as I can, I'll let you know the details."

"I don't know that that's good enough."

"It's all I can promise."

"I've been told by other reporters that you're good for your word."

"I do the best I can." Joey felt that maybe, just maybe, he'd made it through the mine field without getting blown up. Of course, the boundaries of such a thing were never clear. There could always be one hidden bomb....

"Will you answer one question?"

"If I can."

"Is the witness here because she thinks her husband is still alive? You know there was never any evidence found that Kit Wells was murdered. Has something new broken in that investigation?"

Joey took a deep breath. "Off the record I can tell you there is absolutely no new information in the murder investigation of Kit Wells. Nothing at all. But it would greatly damage the witness if that issue was raised in print."

Farris sensed the hint of a story. "But if there is some new development, *you'll* call *me* with the facts, right?"

"You have my word," Joey said. He pulled a pen from his pocket and asked for the reporter's home number.

"Don't disappoint me, Tio," Farris said by way of goodbye.

Joey replaced the receiver and turned to Cori. "There's a leak as big as a fire hydrant in the NOPD. If you want to live, you'll stop calling there, and you'll stay as far away from Blake as you can.'' The barely controlled anger in his voice crackled. "Whatever harebrained scheme you've cooked up for finding Kit, you can forget it. If you want to continue to breathe.''

Chapter Six

By the time Cori had showered and dressed, Joey's hot temper had cooled. His anger was at the loose-lipped police officers who were either giving information to the press, or worse yet, selling it. But Cori had caught the brunt of it because her life was at risk—a fact she simply refused to accept.

"I'm sorry," he said gruffly as she came back into Jolene's kitchen. "If the press has your story, your face and name could be smeared everywhere. Your stability as a witness could be jeopardized."

"Not to mention my life. I'll put my things in the car." Cori was beyond being angry at Joey. She understood his position, the pressure to protect her and to make her fall into line so that the DeCarlo case was not jeopardized. She understood, but she had no intention of dropping her quest. She had to do what she had come to do, just as Joey had to do his job. They were on opposite sides of the issue. Looking into his dark eyes, though, she felt a flicker of disappointment at that fact. Joey Tio was a good man to have on her side. How long had it been since she'd found a man so compelling? One with a code of honor, and the principles to act on it.

Not since Kit.

The answer was so apparent that she stumbled on a crack in the sidewalk. She could not allow herself to entertain even the tiniest glimmer of interest in Joey Tio. Her husband was still alive. She was bound and committed to Kit Wells. The fact had sustained her for two years, and now the evidence to support it was stronger than ever. Whatever Joey thought, someone had put those kisses in the cottage. Someone had left them in her car and studio. Who else but Kit? No one else could have known the private candy code they'd used to communicate. Kit had to be alive, and she was going to find him. There were questions that had to be answered. Only Kit had those answers. Once she found him, she'd be able to figure out how to get on with her life. With or without him. Kit might not be a part of her future, but he was the past that held her chained in limbo.

She dropped her bag in the back seat of the black Supra and felt the crisp morning sun on her face like a blessing. The front door opened and Joey followed her out, and the reality of her thoughts struck her. Somewhere during the long wait for morning her thoughts had shifted from finding Kit as the primary goal to getting on with her life. She took a deep lungful of the cold air and felt it travel through her. She held it, feeling the wonder of it. Before, she'd begun to feel as if the air entered her lungs and leaked out of her skin, as if she were too porous to hold oxygen. Now, though, the air was bracing, invigorating. She couldn't stop the smile that grew on her face at Joey's approach.

"Whatever happens, I'm glad to be alive," she told him. As he slipped into the car seat she missed the expression of surprise, and happiness, that touched Joey Tio's face for only a fraction of a second.

They were out early, and for New Orleans the traffic was sparse. Joey pondered the problem of what to do with Cori while he made a visit to the NOPD and Captain Blake. He'd told Cori he would take care of Danny Dupray—and he fully intended to pay the owner of the Twinkle a visit. But Blake first. There were several issues that had to be resolved.

He would ask about the investigation into Kit Wells's disappearance, but his primary goal was to deliver a warning. Blake had to get his officers into line and shut their mouths—with whatever force necessary. Law enforcement officials were connected by webs and webs of state and federal laws. When one branch leaked, all the others suffered.

"Where are we going?"

Cori's question interrupted his brooding, and he glanced at her to find that there was a hint of expectation in the slant of her lips.

"I thought we might walk along the levee for a while. Watch the boats." The words surprised both of them. Was it really anticipation he saw in Cori's eyes before she lowered them demurely to her hands? He felt like a jackass. They had work to do and here he was pretending it was a lazy Saturday afternoon and he was out on a...date. "It's too early for any of the offices to be open, and Blake doesn't come in until ten. As you said, the Twinkle won't open until closer to noon." His excuses sounded paper-thin even to himself.

"I love the levee," Cori said softly. "I used to get up early when I'd spent the night at the studio and walk down to watch the sunrise. Could we stop by the Café du Monde and get some café au lait? I can't get coffee like that in Houston. It's one of the many things I miss about New Orleans."

If she could have bitten her tongue, she would have. As if coffee was the thing that drew her back to her home and the danger that surrounded it! Joey would surely think she was as idiotic as she sometimes acted.

Joey parked the car, and they walked in the brisk morning to the café and got two large coffees to go. Steam rising from their cups, they walked side by side up the steps and onto the levee. Mist rose off the river, creating a world of wisps and diffused light.

"It's like a dream," Cori said, stopping to sip the sweet, rich coffee. "The smells, the tastes, the sounds. I think I'll wake up back in Houston and find I've only dreamed of being here."

A riverboat blazing with Christmas lights churned through the fog. "Look," Cori pointed, excitement in her voice. "Christmas on the river right before our eyes."

Joey chuckled at her easy pleasure. She did love Christmas. That was one thing she hadn't lied about. "Where I come from, we decorate all the boats in town and parade down the Bayou Teche. And in Breaux Bridge, Santa drives a giant crayfish in the Christmas parade."

"It sounds delightful." The image pleased her. Santa's sleigh hooked to a mud bug! What a spectacle.

"Everyone decorates their houses. Of course, there aren't so many big homes like here in New Orleans, but even the small homes put up lights and a tree." He laughed. "Laurette says we all go a little crazy under the colored lights. And the swamp is beautiful. The trees are so bare, with just the moss and no leaves, and the water hardly moves at all."

Cori held herself perfectly still. Listening to Joey speak of his home made her realize that he, too, missed his family. His mother was dead, and what of the rest? She wanted to ask, but felt she didn't have a right. His life was personal, a closed door. Hers had become public property for everyone to poke at and explore.

"My memories of growing up are very good." He smiled at her, seeming to encourage her interest.

"You grew up in New Iberia?" Cori had never really explored that part of Louisiana. For decades that portion of the state had been cut off from New Orleans, isolated by the Atchafalaya Basin. She knew her history well enough to know that the French Acadian immigrants who fled Canada and settled in the area had lived in near isolation for decades, harvesting the riches of the Gulf of Mexico and the sugar cane, rice and salt that were the backbone of the agricultural economy.

"We were a very strong community, until oil and television." Joey spoke as if he read her mind. "Now things are changing. I sound like the old folks, but it isn't all for the best."

"Do you get home often?"

"Not often enough. It seems my work wraps around my ankles and holds me here." He pointed to a small tug headed through the fog. "Look, there's a band."

Cori saw the figures with their instruments on the deck of the barge just as four men struck a few chords and sent the rock 'n' roll reverberating off the fog and water. They broke into a rendition of "Proud Mary."

Joey groaned. "Every band in the world has to play that song."

"Especially when they're rolling on the Mississippi." Cori laughed at his mock anguish. "Do you play an instrument?" She knew that he did. She guessed guitar.

"Fiddle," he said, grinning with a streak of shyness. "My father taught me when I was younger. We used to play every Saturday night. For the dances." His face lit with the memory. "Everyone danced. My father was the singer, and he sang only in French. We never spoke English in our home, just French. When I started school, Laurette gave me English lessons in the afternoon."

"Your parents didn't speak English?" Cori found it fascinating.

"The whole community spoke French, mostly. Everyone could speak English, but it was a second language. In school we all spoke English, but the home language was French." He looked down at her and his smile gave him away as teasing. "We all speak French, and we all dance. The true prerequisites for being Cajun."

"Well, I can't do either," Cori confessed. "My tongue and my feet are clumsy."

In the soft morning light, filtered through the fog, Joey could not resist the softness of her cheek. He touched her, a feather-light brush. "I could teach you to dance," he said.

For a few seconds, Cori enjoyed the image that flitted into her brain. She could feel Joey's arms around her, holding her, guiding her in the lovely dipping and turning step called the Cajun Waltz. She had seen it performed, by octogenarians and grammar school children. It had always seemed so magical to her, a dance of laughter and fun where everyone seemed to have a good time. "That would be wonderful," she said.

"Let's start back toward town." He took her elbow and led her down from the levee. The intensity of his feelings for her had unsettled him. He'd always been able to differentiate between work and play. If there was any problem, it was that he worked all the time and played hardly at all. Now he was asking a witness in his program to dance. A widowed woman, to boot. He felt a wave of concern at his own emotional state. And he'd thought *she* was coming unhinged!

He checked the time. He'd fibbed about Blake. The man was in his office by now, but he didn't want Cori along. It was decision time. Since he knew she'd never agree to go back to Texas until he talked with Blake and Dupray, he had to think of something to occupy her time and keep her out of trouble. Unfortunately, he hadn't come up with a single thing.

"Joey, I know you won't let me go with you. Why don't you leave me at the federal building. I'll stay in the Marshals office while you talk to Captain Blake and Danny."

He glanced at her, seeing only sincerity in her eyes. This was a little too easy.

"When you're done, I'd like to walk down by my old studio." Cori looked up at him. "Not to go in or anything, just to see what type of work they're showing. I've heard, through the grapevine, the new owner is successful."

So, she still had plans to visit the Quarter. That was more in line with her character. "Let me talk to Blake and Dupray, and then we'll see about going to your studio. Maybe we could drive by." *Maybe* being the operative word. He had no intention of putting her at risk.

"You will press Kit's case, won't you?"

"You have my word on that."

She nodded. "Okay. Then I'll stay in your building." She brushed her hair back out of her eyes. "And I promise to stay out of trouble."

"If I talk to Blake, will you promise to go back to Houston until the trial?"

She shaded her eyes from the sun that had peeped over a building and was glinting directly in her face. "I can't make that promise."

"I'll check the files myself, Cori. I'll tell you everything that's in them. You have my word, but you have to promise me you'll leave New Orleans."

She had come here to find out the truth once and for all. What Joey offered wasn't necessarily the total truth, but it was more than she had now. "Okay." She could go back for a few more weeks—if she knew the truth about Kit.

They returned to the car and headed toward the federal building. "I'll meet you at twelve o'clock. That should give me plenty of time to strong-arm my way into the file and run down Dupray. Even if the club isn't open, he'll be on the premises."

"Thanks, Joey." Cori leaned back in the seat.

As they neared the building, Joey sighed. "I'll have to check in there soon, and I have a feeling there's going to be hell to pay when my boss, Clayton Bascombe, sees me."

"Because of me?"

"You haven't exactly made my job a piece of cake." There was no censure in his tone, just fact.

"I know. I am sorry about all the trouble."

"It's okay, Cori. I'll survive. The important thing is to make sure that you do."

"At twelve." She gave him a smile and a look of total innocence. They got out of the car, and he walked her to the door. "Stay in that building, Cori."

"I'll see you right here at twelve." She walked up the steps and went in the door.

Even as he walked away, doubt nagged at him. Cori St. John was a trouble magnet. He didn't feel great about leaving her, but the Marshals office was the safest place she could be—in New Orleans. If he took her into the PD headquarters, not a single officer would talk, and Blake would surely never open the file to a civilian. And there was also the little matter of Officer Lewis. Joey wanted him called in and dressed down, something that would never occur in front of Cori.

A sharp pang of longing touched Cori as she watched Joey's back. He disappeared into the crowd, and she took the empty coffee cups to a trash can and dropped them. The fact that she'd held her crossed fingers behind her back when she'd lied did not absolve her of guilt. She was going to the Quarter, and her destination was the Twinkle.

As soon as Joey was gone she hurried back to the curb and flagged down a taxi. In fifteen minutes she was cutting through the Quarter, among the thousands of tourists who hunted for bargains, liquor, sex or ambience. She had always enjoyed watching the tourists, though a lot of the Quarter residents generally felt anger toward the invading hordes. Without the tourists, the old French Quarter would have fallen into disrepair and ruin. And for an artist, the tourist dollar was survival.

She walked along, noticing the new stores selling furniture, clothes and jewelry, the restaurants and bars. The old familiar landmarks were still in place, but plenty of new businesses had sprung up in the two years since she'd been there.

At last she turned onto Dumaine and spied the marquee of the Twinkle. Though it was daylight, the running lights circulated around the letters advertising Buxom Babbette and Candy. The Twinkle had once been a movie theater, but it had long ago been converted to a bar with a runway where young girls danced and stripped. Even from a block away she could hear the music. So Danny was now open twenty-four hours a day. It disgusted her, but it served her purposes.

She stopped in front of the studio that had once been hers. A series of delicate watercolors were hung in the show window, and Cori judged they would be a good draw. The painting was fresh, filled with color and light. It was a good choice for the window, and she absently nodded her approval while casting an eye on the front door of the club. Now that she was here she wasn't certain exactly how to approach her mission. Her nerve faltered; only her desperation forced her forward. The cops had lied to her. No one wanted to bother with finding Kit. Danny was her only option. He was a dangerous man, but he had worked closely with Kit. He might know something. And he might tell her.

As she stood in front of the paintings, the door of the Twinkle opened and a man in a very rumpled business suit came out. He lurched slightly, found his balance, and tottered down the street, his tie in his hand. Cori shivered in distaste, then recalled that Jolene had worked in the Twinkle. Lots of bright young girls thought dancing was an easy way to make money. But it took a woman with a lot of self-confidence not to be eaten alive by that life-style. Jolene was obviously one who had survived.

With Joey's help.

Knowing that if she didn't act soon she'd lose her nerve completely, she pushed open the door and walked in.

The darkness of the room, the layers of smoke, the loud music from the jukebox stopped her in her tracks. She'd been in plenty of dark, smoky bars before, but in the Twinkle the only lights were focused on the stage. A young girl was doing a bump and grind on the runway while two men, almost too drunk to stay in their chairs, waved dollar bills at her.

It took a moment for Cori to notice that the entire runway was strung with tiny blinking white Christmas lights. Something told her that these had been in place a long time and were responsible for the establishment's name.

"You lookin' for someone?"

Cori turned around, trying not to show how badly she'd been startled. "Danny. I'm looking for Danny."

The guy was big, his T-shirt stretched across his chest and arms. "Who shall I say is calling?" he asked, his tone mocking her.

"He wouldn't know my name. I, uh, I used to live near here." Maybe she should just add she was the one who had reported him to the police for roughing up one of his girls out on the sidewalk.

"I'll tell him a mystery lady is calling. Are you looking for work?" His eye appraised her.

"No. Certainly not." She spoke before she thought.

"Right." The man laughed out loud. "You don't look like you've got enough flexibility for our requirements." He turned around and walked off.

Cori felt the fury whip through her. To be put down by a bouncer! Then she realized how ridiculous her reaction was. Who cared what a man who worked in a place like this thought? She looked up at the sound of approaching footsteps and recognized Danny Dupray. The lizard hadn't aged at all.

"Well, well, if it isn't Brently Wells."

Cori was completely taken aback. He did remember her. Right down to her married name.

"Mr. Dupray."

"You're something of a celebrity. I saw your photo in the paper this morning. What a ruckus you created down at the French Market. It appeared you were trying to abduct someone's child."

"Hardly." Cori found her tongue and her wits. "I'm surprised you remember me."

"How could I forget Kit's lovely bride? Bride is correct, isn't it? You were never really his wife."

"That's right." If he thought he could rattle her with a few ugly digs, he was wrong. She looked him squarely in his flat, blue eyes. His nose was sharp as a knife's blade, matching the narrowness of his face. His entire body was narrow. "In fact, it's Kit I've come to see you about."

"Old Kit. You know, I never believed he was murdered. Kit was far too smart to be caught like that."

At his words, Cori felt her heart racing. She had to be cool, not give away her intentions. "I don't believe Kit is dead, either. That's why I'm here."

"So you think I might know something about your husband?" Danny smiled, and even his teeth were narrow.

"I thought you might."

"Information always has a price."

"I'm willing to pay, if it's the right information." Cori felt as if she'd stepped into a movie. Behind her the music pulsed and the girl danced. The sound track seemed endless, and the smoky air was choking her.

"What might that information be?" he asked carefully.

"Proof that Kit is alive?"

"Merely proof. You wouldn't want a... reunion?" Danny's smirk was almost unbearable.

"No. Just proof."

"What, the romance is dead? And you never even got to enjoy the honeymoon. Maybe it's that marshal you've developed some feelings for. I hear Joey Tio is a handsome man. And some women, they just go from one uniform to the next."

Cori gritted her teeth and held back an angry remark. "Do you have any proof, Mr. Dupray?"

"Think about this, Brently Wells. Why should I help the woman who was always making trouble for me? As I recall, you repeatedly called the police to protest my business."

"I did, and if I were living next door to you, I'd probably still be calling. My concern is Kit, not our mutually antagonistic past."

"Well said." Danny pretended to clap lightly. "So how much would you pay for this proof?"

"It depends on what it is."

"Say a photo of him holding a newspaper with today's date. Isn't that what they do in kidnappings? They always get the little tyke to hold up a newspaper with the current date." He laughed. "I like that. I wonder if Kit could be persuaded to cooperate. You know if he's alive he's gone to great lengths to make you and everyone who ever knew him believe he's dead. Perhaps he doesn't want to be resurrected."

"I don't intend to bother him, I just want to know. So I can get on with my life." It struck Cori that she had made a transition from finding Kit to finding the truth. For two years she'd not been able to imagine a future without Kit. Now it was difficult to project him into her life. She only wanted to know what had happened to him—and why he kept lurking on the fringes of her life.

"Champing at the bit to be free of the past? Joey has caught your fancy, hasn't he." Danny gave his shark grin.

Danny Dupray was too astute to ignore. Reality struck home with a force that made Cori weak-kneed. She had changed. Even more than she'd thought. And part of it had to do with Joey Tio. She wasn't certain what her feelings were, exactly, but something in her heart had changed. Some cold, frozen place had begun to thaw and come to life, and Joey Tio was responsible for that.

"Tell me, Mrs. Wells, does the marshal know that you're out visiting the Twinkle?" Danny's eyes glinted as he shifted from her to the bouncer. A secret communication passed between them and Cori felt the back of her neck prickle with a whisper of fear.

"Of course Joey knows where I am." She intended to stand her ground.

Danny's grin widened. "I doubt that, Mrs. Wells. Not to call you a liar, but I seriously doubt that Joey or anyone else knows what you're up to. Surely a federal officer would recognize the danger of you being here. Surely he'd never allow such a . . . foolhardy endeavor.''

Cori had never felt such a rush of pure fear. Once she left the Twinkle, Danny had only to pick up the telephone and dial, and within five seconds, the entire DeCarlo family would know she was in New Orleans and on foot on Dumaine Street.

Joey had warned her about the danger. He had told her repeatedly about the eyewitness, Emmet Wyatt, who was shot in the head and left in the trunk of his rental car. *Gangland Murder.* She had read those words and they had failed to hold significance for her until this moment as she stared into Danny Dupray's soulless eyes. She had been foolhardy and worse than stupid to ignore Joey and Jolene.

She looked toward the dark wall where she knew the door had to be. If she got up and walked out, maybe she could dart into a shop and call a taxi.

Danny was watching her with the cool interest of a snake coiled and about to strike. He motioned the bouncer over. "Tell Candy to do her Christmas number next."

Cori wondered if it was some kind of code he spoke, some signal for the bouncer to call the DeCarlos while Danny detained Cori in the bar.

"I have to go." She turned abruptly.

"Kit and I became very close." Danny's voice was smooth in the vacuum left when the music finally stopped. He stepped in front of her. "We were close as only associates can be. I knew a lot of Kit's secrets, and he paid well for mine."

Cori wanted to tell him that Kit despised him as a stoolie and a lower form of life, but an outburst would only compound her already stupid behavior. "Thanks for your help,

Mr. Dupray. One day, I hope you finally reap the rewards of your profession.''

"Ah—" he smiled "—a message is hidden in there somewhere, and if I examine it closely, I don't think I'll like what I find.''

"I didn't come here to play verbal games with you. If you have any information about Kit, any proof, I'll pay for it. Otherwise, I'm leaving.''

Danny looked at the runway, which had darkened except for the constant twinkle of the tiny white lights. "Okay, Candy!" he called. "Let's see it." He turned to Cori. "You'll like this. A Christmas theme.''

The spotlight struck the black curtain that was flung open by a thin white arm. A blond girl with large breasts and slim hips strutted onto the stage to a very jazzed-up version of "Silver Bells." She wore a costume fashioned of silver foil-wrapped chocolate kisses that had been glued to some sheer fabric.

Cori felt the air expel from her lungs, as if she'd been kicked in the gut.

"Nice, isn't it?" Danny said. "Kit gave me the idea.''

Cori fled the club, not caring that Danny Dupray knew he had frightened her. She had to get out of that smoke-clogged hell and into fresh air. The nightmare version of Christmas playing out on the stage was a fantasy from the mind of a demented, evil man.

The panicked look on her face cleared a path for her through the tourists, street kids and drunks. Cori was completely unaware of the people she passed. Her mind was focused on what Danny Dupray had said. Kit could not have had anything to do with the noxious display she'd just witnessed. He had talked with Danny Dupray, had visited the

Twinkle because it was part of his duty. He had to hang out with lowlifes like Danny to get tips and information on people who were worse scum bags. But Kit would never, never have taken the token of their affection and suggested it for use on the costume of a stripper.

She looked up and found she had traveled four blocks through crowded streets without realizing it. She forced herself to slow down, to start glancing behind her to see if she was being followed. Yet everywhere she looked she saw the image of Candy dancing behind the glittering lights, the foil of her costume shimmering with each gyration of her hips. Silver bells. Kisses. Kit. One step led right to the next.

The conclusion was inevitable. If Danny did know about the chocolate kisses, if Kit had somehow slipped up and revealed her fondness for them, then it was also possible that the person tormenting her was Danny. He knew what Kit looked like. He knew well enough to find a near double. It was possible that Danny Dupray had been hired by the DeCarlo family to drive her insane, or to make her too afraid to testify.

Heart pounding, she stopped before a secondhand clothing store that specialized in fanciful gowns of lawn and lace. The faceless mannequins, draped in finery from decades past, gazed sightlessly toward the street. Cori pressed her cheek against the cool glass, hoping the pane would calm her heart, stop the ache that was pounding behind her ribs.

"Ma'am, are you all right?" An elderly lady stepped through the shop door and came to Cori's side. "Are you diabetic, or epileptic or something? Is there some medication I can get for you?"

Cori forced herself away from the cold glass and stood. "No," she answered. The woman was old enough to be her grandmother, and perfectly turned out in a red velvet dress and black choker with a cameo on it. A white lace shawl was pulled tightly around her shoulders, and her hair was silvery white, pouffed and tucked into a perfect Gibson girl. "I'm okay," Cori said.

"Would you like a cup of hot tea? It's a chilly morning and I have a nice fire in the stove. One of those old space heaters the city frowns on now, but the best ever to put your feet in front of and toast your toes."

What kindness had brought this woman into her life? Cori smiled, steadied by the compassion of a total stranger. "No, but thank you. I didn't mean to upset you. I just had a start and..."

"No need to explain." The woman took her arm. "Come into my shop and have some tea. It would do us both good."

Cori hesitated. She didn't want to impose on a total stranger. But she also didn't want to be rude, and the woman certainly seemed to want someone to visit. "Your clothes are beautiful." She drew the woman's attention to a hand-crocheted dress overlaid on a pale pearl sheath lining, which hung in the window.

The older woman stepped back. "Now, that's a dress for you. Artsy. It would suit you perfectly. Some of those dangly gold earrings. Stockings. Not those wretched panty hose things, but real stockings with a seam up the back." She nodded vigorously. "Maybe you'd like to try it on?"

The dress appealed to her, but Cori shook her head. "I really have to be going."

"And not even tea?"

Cori looked at the dress one last time. It was lovely. She was about to say goodbye when a reflection in the glass caught her attention.

The man wore a mahogany-colored overcoat, and the sun struck fully in his curly, sandy hair. The morning light slanted across the left side of his face, leaving the right in shadow. But it was enough for Cori to know that the man who watched her so intently from across the street was no one but Kit Wells.

Chapter Seven

The bustling police precinct that Willet Blake called home was in the heart of the French Quarter and one of the busiest station houses in New Orleans—but certainly not the worst. Normally the French Quarter crime ran from petty thievery to sex crimes with the occasional homicide thrown in on a more and more regular basis. But it was nothing like some of the districts with housing projects and street gangs. The Quarter had a kinky side, but it wasn't as lethal as other areas.

Settling in to his morning, Blake pulled the files on the top of the stack toward him, ready to get down to the business of a very busy day.

Joey saw the captain begin to work, and he opened the door without knocking. He closed it behind him and twisted the lock into place.

"I hope there's a reason for this behavior." Willet Blake was a third-generation policeman. He'd earned his captain's bars, had worked his way up through the ranks.

"I need a little of your time, without interruption." Joey wasn't certain what role Blake played in Cori's problems. Had the man made every effort, as he'd claimed? Or was he playing along by another set of rules?

"This better be good, Tio. I've heard from some of my men that you stepped all over them yesterday. I hope that's not an attitude problem you're developing." Blake tapped his pen on the desk for emphasis.

"The problem that's developing is the fact that one of those men, and my money is on Jake Lewis, dropped the dime on my witness. Someone identified her to the newspaper, thereby putting her life and also a big portion of the DeCarlo case in jeopardy."

"What's she doing in New Orleans? Isn't it your job to see that she remains safe, and anonymous, until the re-trial?" Blake didn't give an inch.

"It would be a lot easier to keep her safe if someone from the local PD wasn't *selling* information to the paper."

Blake came out of his chair slowly. "You better have proof to back that up."

"Look at the morning paper. Lewis knew the witness. He recognized her. The other three officers wouldn't have known her, but he remembered her. Call the paper and ask who identified the woman in the picture."

Blake's eyes narrowed. "I'll do that, and if it was one of my men, they'll find themselves suspended without pay."

Joey nodded. The only thing he could do was take Blake at his word on this matter. No officer liked to see another sell information, particularly one of his own men. It was a bad reflection on the entire force.

"If that's why you're here, you've made your point. And I've got work to do." Blake resumed his seat and picked up his pen. When Joey didn't leave, he looked up, pen in midair, as if he were about to execute a stroke of penmanship of the greatest importance.

Joey finally spoke when he had the captain's full attention. "What's the status of Kit Wells? Anything new?"

"That woman sent you, didn't she. She finally got someone to come over here and make sure we're doing our jobs. Well, you can repeat to her that the Wells case is closed. It has been closed and will remain closed. Period."

"I told her I'd ask. I have to get her out of town, Blake. For both our sakes she needs to get out of here. Her husband is the reason she's in New Orleans. She's decided to track him down herself."

The pen lowered to the desk and remained there. "Kit Wells is dead."

"How can you be certain?"

Blake reached to the side of his desk and opened a file drawer. After a moment he brought out a folder with Kit Wells's name on the tab. He held it a moment, then opened it on his desk.

"On December 24, 1993, Kit married Brently Gleason in Jackson Square. Half the force was at the wedding. Hell, *I* was there. The reception was held at Riches'. I saw Kit hand Brently into the limousine. He was going to pick up some champagne. Someone had given them some expensive stuff as a wedding present and Kit was determined to get it himself and put it on ice so it would be chilled for the toast."

This was all old hat to Joey, but he didn't interrupt.

"We all followed the limo to Riches'. The band started playing, and we were dancing and Brently was talking with the guests, making apologies for Kit being so long. No one thought much, until an hour had passed and no Kit. Brently was about to cry."

"I can understand that."

Blake nodded. "It was a bad scene. I thought he'd probably been in a traffic accident—one of those freak things that happen—and that he was probably in some emergency room waiting to get a few stitches or a leg set. It never occurred to me that Kit had been abducted."

"And that's what happened?"

"Yes."

"How can you be certain?" Joey asked again.

"There was an eyewitness to the abduction."

Joey's eyes narrowed. "There was never a report of any eyewitness or any abduction. The report I read showed Kit Wells vanished. No trace, no witnesses."

"That was the report we released."

Joey felt the anger building. "That woman, his wife, has been hanging on to hope for two years. Why was that information withheld?"

"There are other concerns greater than one woman's hopes." Blake's voice was terse.

"Such as?"

"According to our witness, Wells had compromised the force. He was playing both ends against the middle, and he got caught."

"What are you talking about?" Joey was beginning to see a bigger picture, and he didn't like the outline. The way it was shaping up would put Cori squarely in the role of sacrificial lamb.

"The night of the wedding, Wells was surprised. He went to pick up the champagne and was cornered unexpectedly by two men who have been affiliated with the DeCarlo family as enforcers. They took Kit at gunpoint, saying he had double-crossed Antonio DeCarlo and that they were going to make sure he suffered and that his body was never found." Blake closed the folder.

"Did your witness see the hit?"

Blake hesitated. "He heard a sound like a muffled shot, a silencer we figure, and Kit crumpled. He was shoved into the trunk. And that was the last anyone saw of him."

"This witness, you're sure he's solid."

"As solid as a source like that can be. He knew Kit. They'd worked together." Blake tapped his pen on the folder. "There was some evidence that Kit had met with some of the men associated with Ben DeCarlo. There is the possibility that Kit knew the DeCarlo hit was coming down."

"And had his fiancée there as a witness. The woman with the memory too good to be true." Joey wanted to find Kit Wells and feel his windpipe give under the pressure of his bare hands.

"Looking back at it, it was terribly convenient that Kit was in the bathroom at the moment DeCarlo was killed."

"So was Kit on the take from Antonio or Ben?" Playing it either way, it didn't make sense. One died and the other went to prison. It was a lose-lose situation for the De-Carlos. It didn't make a bit of sense.

Blake tapped his fingertips together lightly. "The way I figure it, he was aligned with one of the smaller competing families. D'Amatus, Giacosta, one of those. Of course we don't have any proof to support this. It's my personal theory."

A doubt, so bitter and so deadly, prompted Joey to step forward and grab hold of the captain. "You don't suppose Ben DeCarlo was actually set up, do you?"

"Now, I might believe he was voodoo-hexed and turned into a zombie, or hypnotized, or given mind-altering drugs that made him kill his mother and father without knowing he did it. But as far as the facts go, Ben DeCarlo pulled the trigger on that gun. There were five eyewitnesses, and Ben made no effort to hide his identity."

Joey paced the room for a moment. "That's exactly what's troubling me. Why *didn't* he hire a hit man to do it, or do it privately? Why do it in a restaurant with dozens of witnesses?"

"You want to ask questions like that, work for the defense lawyer." Blake picked up his pen. "Ben DeCarlo is guilty of double homicide, and Kit Wells is dead. Those two facts are indisputable. The motivations behind them are up for grabs. We never had any real proof that Kit was dirty, but we uncovered some things that weren't exactly on the up and up."

"Could you be a little more specific?"

"Evidence from cases that didn't get turned in."

"Drugs?"

"Sometimes. The stash would be a little short. Not enough to warrant an investigation, but some grams of coke here and there. You know. The junkie could have been lying about the amount. Anyway, Kit's association with that club owner and his girls, that was an avenue that no one pursued."

"I have a lot of sources and contacts on the seamy side of life. It doesn't mean I approve of their life-style, or that I'm participating in it, or providing recreational substances for my sources." Joey found himself defending a man he'd never known and didn't like.

"Kit's wife is another problem. Brently Gleason wasn't your typical cop's wife. Not by a long stretch. Some of the officers felt that Kit had betrayed them by getting involved with an artist." Blake held up his hands to ward off Joey's denials. "I know a man's wife is his business, but Kit was one of the guys. When he started seeing Brently, he changed. He started going to art openings and the theater. The officers felt like he was developing airs, and of course they couldn't blame him, so they laid it at the woman's feet. That's life."

"Would one of those men happen to be Jake Lewis?"

Blake nodded. "Lewis was one. He was at the wedding and very opinionated about the dim prospects for the survival of the marriage. It was almost as if he hoped it would fall apart so Kit could return to 'the brotherhood in blue.'"

"What about you? What was your opinion of the bride?" Joey found it disconcerting to refer to Cori as Brently or "the bride."

"Beautiful, talented, shy. Not exactly the best material for the wife of a detective. But she loved Kit. That was easy to see."

"And did he love her?"

Blake took a breath. "That's a harder question. Kit was always playing the angles. Every day. He liked to analyze and calculate. Maybe he really loved the woman. Or maybe she was a calculated addition to his life. I guess we'll never know, but I always felt it would be better to leave all of this buried. It won't help the woman to know Kit was possibly involved in something dirty."

"It would help her to know if he's dead."

"We have a witness." Blake held up his hands. "We have every reason to believe he's dead. But we still don't have a body. We may never find the hard physical evidence we need to prove this case beyond a doubt. She has to make her own choices, Tio. And let's hope she decides to make them out of New Orleans."

"Right." Joey unlocked the door. "Thanks for your time, Blake. And please don't forget to talk to Officer Lewis."

"Today." Blake lifted a hand in farewell.

As soon as the door closed behind Joey, Blake picked up the telephone and punched in four numbers. "Tell Jake to get up here to my office and do it fast. We've got a problem, and it all stems from his big mouth."

CORI HEARD THE OLD woman's sudden burst of concern, but her gaze was riveted to the man's reflection. She was afraid to turn around, afraid that there would be no one there. Then, certainly, she would have to accept that she was insane.

The old woman's hand on her arm startled her, and Cori looked down into a face wreathed in concern. "Child? Are you okay?"

When she looked back in the window, the man was gone. Whirling, she confronted the street where tourists streamed past, mingling with businessmen and women and kids. There was no tall man. Kit had escaped her once again.

"You're pale as a ghost." The old woman took her elbow and led her through the front door. They went to the back of the shop where a space heater burned before two antique rocking chairs and a basket of crochet and embroidery materials. "When the shop is slow I like to sit back here and mend some of the clothes. It passes the time." She patted Cori's arm as she installed her in one of the rockers.

Cori waited until the pounding of her heart had subsided. She had seen Kit. She was positive. This was no shadow figure or blurry outline. She had seen his face clearly, or at least half of it.

"Mrs...."

"Copperfield."

"Did you see a tall man in a dark coat across the street?" Cori had to know. Mrs. Copperfield had been standing at an angle that might have allowed her to see Kit.

"Indeed I did. He was just across the street, staring at us. I thought perhaps he was going to come over and buy something. And then it occurred to me that maybe you knew him. At any rate, he was staring a hole through you. Then you started acting odd, and I forgot about him."

"But you did see him?"

"Of course. Is there some reason I shouldn't have seen him?" She put a kettle on to heat and took the other chair.

"Some people think he's dead."

"Oh, a spectral visitation."

At her light, mocking tone, Cori looked up. "Ghosts don't frighten you?"

"Not in the least. Besides, that man was flesh and blood. Nothing noncorporeal about him."

"Thank goodness." Cori felt a deep need to call Joey. He had to hear this. He had to believe her. Maybe together they could track Kit down. He was somewhere in the French Quarter!

At the shrill of the kettle, Mrs. Copperfield got up and brewed the tea. "It won't be long. Now, tell me the intriguing story about you and the gentleman across the street. His interest in you is obvious. Why didn't he simply walk over?"

Cori found that she had no answer for that question. She looked toward the front of the shop. "Can you see if anyone comes in here?" It seemed dangerous for an elderly woman to be so trusting.

"There's a bell over the door. Jingles nicely. I think it has some Pavlovian use. You know, the shopper hears the bell, and based on other past shopping experiences, he believes it's time to spend money."

Cori laughed with Mrs. Copperfield. It was impossible not to be charmed by her. At the same time, she had a sudden thought. She rose abruptly.

"Please stay for tea."

The loneliness in the request made Cori decide that one cup of tea wouldn't hurt. She was torn between a desire to run after the man but she knew if anyone could hide in the Quarter, it was Kit. He would only be found when he was ready. "Just one cup," she said, taking her seat. She couldn't call Joey right now. He was with Blake, and disturbing him there wouldn't be smart, especially if she told him she was in the Quarter. She'd just have to wait until it was time to meet him.

"One lump or two?"

"Two." Cori was distracted by the jingle of the bell.

Mrs. Copperfield rose to greet her customers, a young woman and her little boy.

"There's candy in front of your shop," the boy said, holding out three silver kisses in his palm. "Can I have them?"

Before Cori could respond, his mother gently took them from his hand. "I'll buy you some candy, Chad. We don't know where that came from." She put them on the counter. "They were lined up, right at the door."

"I can't imagine," Mrs. Copperfield said. "Next time maybe they could leave money." They chuckled together as Cori gripped her teacup.

CORI SLOTTED THE QUARTER into the telephone and dialed the U.S. Marshals office. In a moment, her call was being transferred through to Joey's car phone. She'd left the clothing shop and gone straight to a phone booth to make the call. She'd been wrong to go into the French Quarter. Her encounter with Danny Dupray, and Kit's determined shadowing of her every move, had finally unsettled her. She was willing to concede the point to Joey—she was in danger and she was afraid.

"Cori?" Joey took the call with a feeling of dread. He knew before she told him that she hadn't stayed in the federal building. He never should have trusted her to do such a sensible thing.

At the sound of Joey's voice, Cori looked up and down the street. "I messed up, Joey. I'm on Bourbon, by the Jazz Club."

"Stay there." His voice was terse. "Don't you dare move. Just blend in with the crowd, and keep your eyes open."

Her head nodded up and down and she gripped the phone tighter. She had intended to tell him about Kit after they were in the car. She had planned on telling the story in clear, complete detail. No emotion, no outbursts. Just the facts, ma'am. Something his policeman's logic couldn't refute.

"Kit was following me again." Even as she said it she knew it was a mistake. It was all wrong. Her voice was high, breathy. She gripped the telephone cable and twisted it in frustration.

"Stay where you are." Joey took a corner too fast and almost hit a delivery truck.

"It's true, Joey. Kit was following me. I saw him in the window of an antique clothing store. The lady who owns the shop, Mrs. Copperfield, she saw him, too." The more she talked, the more desperate she sounded. Even the man waiting to use the phone was casting pitying looks at her.

"Easy," Joey said. "Take it easy, I'm on the way."

To Cori's utter dismay, tears blinded her. "But I did see him." Her voice was low but filled with determination.

"Everything's going to be okay," he reassured her, knowing his words were a terrible lie. He could hear the panic in her voice, the fear. It wasn't okay. She was having visits from a dead man. And since he didn't believe in voodoo or ghosts, there was only one explanation.

Cori wanted to yield to the release of her tears, to let out all the bitter disappointment and the hopes and dreams that had died so violent a death with Kit's disappearance. Even on the other end of the phone, Joey gave her a sense of protection. He listened to her. He'd tried to help her, and she had repaid him by lying to him and getting herself deeper into trouble.

She gathered herself and straightened up. "How much longer before you'll get here?"

"Three minutes. Hang on, Cori, I'm almost there."

The tenderness in his voice was almost her undoing, but she managed to lift her face and take a breath. "I can make it, Joey. I'm okay."

Joey felt the dagger of pain slice into his heart. She was so courageous. It didn't matter that her fear was not founded in fact. It didn't matter that she was imagining things. To her, Kit Wells was real. That made her courage even more admirable, and so very, very tragic.

He turned onto the side street beside the club and saw her. She was in a phone booth, clinging to the phone for dear life. A man waited impatiently for his turn, and Joey came too close to him when he pulled up on the sidewalk and signaled for Cori to get into the car. The expression on her face when she saw him made his heart thud. She dropped the phone without hanging it up and ran toward him.

THE RESTAURANT WAS OLD and quiet. It wasn't safe, but Joey knew he had to talk to Cori, and she'd needed the fortifying glasses of wine. Whatever she'd seen—and it hadn't been Kit Wells—had completely unnerved her. Now her color was looking better, but nothing between them had been resolved.

"Talk to me, Cori," he encouraged her.

"I know you think I'm nuts, but I saw him. Clearly, Joey. Not just a shadow figure or a possibility. The sun was full on his face and he was only thirty yards away. I saw him, and Mrs. Copperfield saw him, too."

"Did Mrs. Copperfield know Kit?" Joey spoke softly, still avoiding her direct gaze.

"Well, no, but she saw the man, and she described him. It was Kit. *I* saw him."

Because he knew he was going to hurt her, Joey reached across the table and took both her hands in his. He finally looked into her eyes and held her gaze. "Don't you want to know what Captain Blake said?"

Cori felt a surge of eagerness. "He knows Kit is alive, doesn't he? What did he say?"

Joey felt his lips dry, and his mouth filled with the taste of ashes. Why did it feel like a betrayal to tell this woman the truth?

"Joey?" Cori sensed something was terribly wrong. "What is it? What did Blake say?" The last held a note of accusation.

"He said that Kit was abducted. He was shot and killed. There was a witness. When they told you Kit was dead, they were telling the truth."

Cori felt as if she'd been slapped. It was clear looking into Joey's eyes that he believed Blake. Not her, but Blake. "How is it possible that I saw a dead man?"

Joey wanted to look down. He wanted to look anywhere except into the twin green pools of pain. "You didn't see Kit. Either you saw someone who looked a lot like him, or you didn't see anything at all. Except in your mind." There, it was out on the table.

She tried to stand but he held her wrists.

"Let me go, damn you." She tugged hard, pulling his chest into the edge of the table and upsetting the glasses. Wine, water and ice sloshed over the table, cascading down onto his boots and the floor.

"Cori, take it easy."

"Take your hands off me." Her eyes registered total, unforgiving fury.

"The witness saw Kit. He was shot once and pushed into a car trunk." He tightened his grip, expecting her to fight even more at the words. Already the maître d' was looking toward them and signaling one of the waiters.

"Is there a problem?" The man came up to the table, standing a little distance away, but close enough to give the spilled water and wine an imperious look.

"Everything is fine here," Joey said.

"Everything is *not* fine." Cori jerked her hands suddenly, almost getting free. Joey had to lunge across the table to recapture them. "This man is hurting me. I want to leave, and he refuses to let me go."

"Sir, the lady would like for you to release her." The waiter was clearly ill at ease. "If you don't let her go, we'll have to call the cops."

"I am a cop," Joey said softly, trying to hide that fact from the now-curious diners who had stopped eating and were watching the drama unfold.

"Take your hands off the lady." The waiter lifted a hand and made a signal in the air to the maître d', who instantly picked up the telephone.

"I can't," Joey said. "She'll be out of here in four seconds."

"If she wishes to leave . . ." The waiter didn't finish.

"Cori, you have to believe what I'm saying. You asked me to find out the truth. I said I would help you. Now you have to take my help."

"That isn't the truth. I don't care what Blake said. Either he's lying, or you are. I saw Kit." Her voice lowered to a hiss. "I saw him with my own eyes. Clearly. It strikes me as a little odd that I'm an eyewitness in a double murder and my word and memory are perfectly fine. It's only when it's my own husband in question that my vision or my sanity can't be trusted. Well, I saw Kit. If I didn't, then you're right, I'm insane. But I don't think so. I think someone is playing a terrible game, and I'm the pawn. Now, take your hands off me this instant or I'll have your badge and your career. You might be an officer of the law, but you have no right to touch me."

Joey let her hands go. To hold on any longer would do no good. She was not going to listen to what he said. He'd thought if he could hold her long enough to finish, the weight of the truth would finally make her believe.

Cori stood. "I'm out of your program, Mr. Tio. I'm not a witness for anything. My husband is alive, and I'm going to find him. I don't need you or anyone else."

"Cori, please..."

She turned away and stormed across the restaurant, oblivious to her surroundings, and to the man who fell into step some thirty yards behind her.

Chapter Eight

As Cori cleared the restaurant door, Joey pulled out his badge and flipped it open so the waiter could see. "It's business, man, don't interfere."

The waiter hesitated. "The police have been called. It's our policy...."

"Call them and cancel the summons." Joey stood. "Thanks." He walked out the door as several diners watched him with cold contempt at his manhandling of a woman. Just as he was almost out the door, he heard a young girl.

"Bully," she said, a word as clear as a Christmas bell. "You're nothing but a bully."

Joey didn't bother to refute the charge. He was feeling like a bully. He walked into the street and headed out the way Cori had gone. He had no intention of trying to catch her. It wouldn't do a bit of good. He'd had a chance, one chance, and he'd blown it. He should have taken her to the office and arranged for a counselor to break the news to her, someone who could have managed it with a degree of skill and compassion. But no, he'd believed he was qualified to do it. And he had messed up badly. If it would have done any good, he would have kicked himself all the way down the street.

He caught a glimpse of her dark chestnut hair as she bobbed around a corner. She wasn't jogging, but it was a gait a lot faster than a regular walk. Joey unfolded his legs a bit more and started after her in earnest. He had to keep an eye on her. And she wasn't going to like that one little bit.

For the first twenty minutes, he thought there was a pattern to her path, but he finally realized she was wandering. Aimlessly crossing and recrossing streets. Walking by places where she would stop and loiter at a storefront. When he realized what she was doing, he felt as if the marrow of his bones had chilled. She was using herself as bait. She was waiting for Kit, or someone else, to come to her. Too many people knew she was in town.

As he darted into the doorway of a small jewelry store, he saw another man and knew instantly that he, too, was following Cori. Joey's subconscious registered the man's patterned jacket—a jaunty combination of red, yellow and black. He walked with his hands in the pockets of the jacket, not an unusual sight on a brisk day, but he was definitely following Cori. He'd been on another corner, had angled across the street and now was behind her again.

Joey started forward, no longer caring if Cori knew he was behind her or not. As the man drew closer to Cori where she stood at a traffic light, Joey broke into a run. His heart pumped, blocking out the sounds of the city. His vision was locked on the man, the way the wind ruffled his thin hair. He was intent on Cori, and there could be no good reason for that interest.

The light changed and Cori started across the street, one woman amid a group of men and women, all moving at the same speed. Except the brightly jacketed man was moving faster—too fast for Joey to catch up. He was ten yards from Cori, and Joey felt more than saw him maneuver the gun in his pocket. It was going to be a hit. A murder right on the streets of New Orleans. In the confusion the gunman would get away while everyone looked down at Cori and saw the horror of deadly violence, helpless to stop what had already happened.

"Cori!" Joey called her name.

She halted and looked around, finally seeing him. There was a flare of something in her eyes, and then smoldering anger as she turned abruptly and started to walk faster. The man was working through the crowds, closer to her now, as Joey ran as fast as he could. Looking back, Cori saw that Joey was gaining on her, and she began to run, too.

Joey broke into the street, dodging a taxi and a blue Volvo as he gained the opposite curb and pushed past several nuns and a gathering of schoolchildren on a walking tour. He had his weapon, but the streets were too crowded. He could never get a shot off at the hit man without risking killing half a dozen other people.

"Cori!" He was gaining on the man, but not fast enough. The gunman would get to Cori before Joey could stop him.

Surprisingly, Cori stopped and turned. Instead of running away, she started back toward him, her face etched with anger.

He waved his hands. "No! No!" he called to her.

Puzzlement touched her clear green eyes, and he felt as if they had opened a line of pure communication that had nothing to do with voice or gesture. She looked from Joey directly to the jacketed man, and suddenly she read his intent as clearly as if he were holding a sign.

Still running, only a few yards away, Joey saw her hold her hands up to ward off the blow that her slender fingers could not catch or stop.

The sound of the gunshot came, as he knew it would. It was too loud, and yet not real. It echoed off the brick buildings and streets. He hurtled to Cori's side, too late, and pulled her down on the pavement and covered her body with his. *Too late, too late, too late.* His heart pumped the words, and he must have muttered them under his breath.

Above him a woman screamed again and again, a loud, pitching wail like a siren. Rolling off Cori, Joey surveyed her body, wondering where the bullet had entered and if he might possibly be able to apply pressure long enough for an ambulance.

The red sweater hid any sign of blood, and he grasped it, pushing it up, only to find pale skin, perfect, unmarred, and full breasts held by a satiny red bra. Beneath his hands, Cori began to struggle.

"Where are you hit?" he asked, looking into green eyes that were... furious.

"I'm not," she answered clearly. "Are you okay?"

Joey was up, his hand going to the gun under his jacket. He looked around, but the killer had disappeared. The woman still screamed, and Joey held a hand to indicate to Cori to stay down while he went to check.

He saw the jacket, a bright splash of color, in the gutter of the street. A wide circle of red had invaded the multicolored material, and Joey knew the man had been shot squarely in the heart. He was dead, but Joey checked his carotid to confirm there was no pulse. In the dead man's hand was a small, deadly blue steel automatic.

"Move back," Joey said, flipping his badge. "Move away from the body." He swept the crowd back.

"Can I help?" A shop owner had come out.

"Call the police and the emergency medical team."

The man nodded and ducked back into his bakery. Cori got up and went to Joey's side.

"He was coming after me," she said.

Joey ignored her as he tried to make sure no one touched the body. Squatting down, his gaze swept the street, shifting from window to window, from floor to floor. Whoever had shot the gunman could be sitting just across the street with another round in the chamber.

"He was going to kill me, wasn't he?" Cori insisted. When Joey didn't answer, she grabbed the sleeve of his jacket. "Wasn't he? Until you shot him."

Joey's focus had been on the crowd, on the windows and doorways all around them. There were a million places a sniper could hide.

"How did you know?" she asked, shifting closer to the curb.

Joey swung around on her. He pushed her against the wall of the bakery. "Stay away from the street." He gritted the words. "I didn't shoot him, Cori. Someone else did. And I don't know who or where they are." The stunned look on her face made him back off. "Go inside the bakery. Wait there, and don't do anything stupid this time. This isn't a game. Someone is trying to hurt you, and now another man is dead."

Cori pulled open the bakery door and stepped inside. She moved out of the line of the windows, but she stood in the center of the floor and stared out at the man who lay in the gutter, and at the man who knelt over him, waiting for the police.

JAKE LEWIS WAS NOT disturbed by the dead man. Not in the least. In fact, he was downright jovial.

"Yeah, it's Benny Hovensky. We've been trying to pin a hit on him for the past three years. He always comes up with an airtight alibi, even though we know he's done five hits in the past eighteen months. Good riddance to bad rubbish is my attitude."

Joey was surprised to see Lewis still in uniform and working. Blake had apparently not been able to prove it was him who leaked Cori's identity to the newspaper...or else Blake had never intended to discipline the man.

"Have forensics been able to determine where the shot came from?" Joey was feeling more and more nervous about the strange death of the man Lewis had firmly tied with the DeCarlo family. Benny Hovensky was one of the "paid retainers" of old Antonio DeCarlo. He'd been on the family payroll as chauffeur, gardener, pilot and general gofer. But his actual job had been to take care of people who messed up the lives of the DeCarlo family. Cori could very easily be seen as one of those people.

Lewis pointed across the street. "Down that alley. The angle of the bullet is straight in, right in the heart. That was some shot across a crowded street. Surprised he didn't take out a few pedestrians."

"Any sign of who the sniper might be?" Joey knew it was a hopeless question, but he had to ask. Even if Jake Lewis knew the answer, he wouldn't give him squat.

"Naw, nothing. No physical evidence at all."

"Since Antonio is dead and Ben's in prison, any idea who this guy might have been working for?" Joey pressed the issue.

Lewis shrugged. "Ben's in prison, but he's still calling plenty of shots, and don't ever doubt it. What with his case coming up for retrial and the woman being a key witness, it wouldn't be a long stretch to see his handwriting on the hit. But the truth is, Benny was acting more like a free agent. Some of the hits we're pretty sure he made, they were freelance. Anyone could have hired him." Lewis straightened his hat and gave Joey a knowing look. "Are you certain he was after the witness?"

Joey dropped his gaze. "Not certain."

"But you were chasing him?"

"I thought I saw a gun. My intention was to tackle him and pat him down." Joey moved out of the way of the ambulance attendants who had come to remove the body.

"Good intentions." Jake Lewis smiled, and it was not a happy expression. "You know what they say, 'The road to hell is paved with good intentions.' You and that witness better take care of yourselves. It would be a shame for either of you to become one of the big bad statistics of this old city." He waved the doors of the ambulance shut and moved away.

Joey waited until the ambulance and patrol cars were gone before he went to retrieve Cori from the bakery. She was sitting quietly, her shoulders rounded and her hands in her lap.

"Ready?"

"For what?" she asked. "Bedlam? Bellevue? What's the psychiatric hospital called here in New Orleans?" She stood up, her body tightly compressed. "A man was killed not five feet from me, and you and I believe he was trying to kill me. What am I supposed to do now? You think leaving New Orleans is the answer to all of my problems, but my husband is still out there somewhere, and I *can't* leave until I find him."

Joey looked out the plate glass window. Most of the witnesses had given a sketchy statement to the police and were gone—back to their errands and chores. The murder had been a tragic thing, a horrible event to witness, but it did not involve them. They were free of it and back in the swim of their lives. Cori, though, was trapped.

"Let's take a walk," he said.

"To where? Where can I go that I won't be a target, or where the people I care about won't die?" Cori pushed her hair out of her eyes. "I've been sitting here wondering what is left of my life, and I've come to a terrible conclusion.

There's not a single thing left of what I used to be. Or who I used to be." She pushed her hair back again. "And I don't know what to do now."

"Let's go outside." Joey wanted to get her moving. He thought for a second she was going to fight, but instead she pushed open the bakery door and stepped into the late afternoon light. Joey waved a thank-you to the baker and took Cori's elbow. "Across the street," he directed.

Cori held her arms stiff, but she didn't shake off his hand on her elbow as they crossed the street, darting easily between the cars, and stopped at the alley. "The sniper was here," he said. He looked down the narrow opening and saw only garbage cans. "Let's take a look."

Cori was surprised that he'd included her, but she stepped behind him as he entered the dark alley. "The officers who worked the case said there weren't any footprints. No spent shell casings. No cigarette butts. The weapon was a .38, a common gun that's easy enough to buy. The guy was a good shot, right through the traffic and crowd." Joey spoke as if he were tape-recording his observations and thoughts for some future reference.

Together they crept down the alley. They were almost halfway down when they came to a wooden gate. Joey gave it a rattle and the sound of a big chain and padlock on the other side told him he would need equipment and a court order to open it.

He went past, then returned to the gate.

"What is it?" Cori asked.

"Just curious." Joey signaled her forward. "If I lift you up, can you grab the top and look over?"

"What am I looking for?" Cori looked up at the top of the ten-foot privacy fence.

"Whatever is there."

"Sure." She moved up to the wooden fence.

Joey made a cup of his hands. "Step here, and I'll boost you. Grab the top, and I'll push you up the rest of the way."

"Okay." She braced against the fence and stepped into his laced fingers. With a mighty thrust from Joey, she rose in the air until her fingers found the top of the fence. Using her arms to hang on, she felt Joey shift so that he could press her bottom with both hands and lift her over his shoulders.

She found herself looking down into a garden on the other side. "It's someone's private patio."

"What building does it belong to?" Joey asked.

Cori looked to see if there was a clearly marked entrance. "I think it's the green building, about three over."

"Anything unusual?"

"Whoever owns it has a green thumb or owns a florist shop. The place is beautiful. Fountain, ferns, palmettos, thousands of flowers, and the thing is big. Really big. There are walkways, like a formal garden. It's truly beautiful."

"Coming down." Joey lowered her.

Though the alley was dark, she caught the look in his eye. "What is it?" she asked.

"I think we should find out who owns that garden."

"Why?"

"Because I think our shooter may have come from there."

"But it's walled. That doesn't make sense."

"Unless he knew what was going to happen and was waiting here. What if, somehow, he understood that someone was going to try to kill you?"

Cori felt dread tickle down her neck. "How could he know that?"

"Jake Lewis indicated that Benny whatever-his-name-was was a hired gun. A hit man. The sniper would know if he was the one who hired him." Joey took Cori's hand. "Let's get out of here." He led the way out and into the busy street. The thing that troubled him, and that he hadn't said, was how would the sniper have known Cori would walk the way she'd chosen?

CORI SIPPED THE HOT TEA, watching as Joey used the chopsticks to eat the spicy snow peas. They were across the river, far away from the Quarter and any part of the city that Cori knew.

"I went to see Danny Dupray this morning." She hadn't intended on telling Joey, but now it seemed like the right thing.

He put his chopsticks down on the edge of his plate. "You might have mentioned this earlier." He swallowed and waited. The events of the afternoon were too fresh in his mind. Now, along with the entire DeCarlo clan and their various factions, he could add Danny Dupray to the list of possible suspects. There was every chance that Kit had been taken not by DeCarlo, but by Dupray. Kit could easily have found out something major about Danny and his illegal operations. Cori had no idea that she'd just stuck her foot into a nest of vipers. Like snakes, sometimes these men didn't need a good reason to strike.

"I had to do it, Joey. I knew you wouldn't let me. Danny knew Kit." She rolled her eyes. "Far better than I ever thought, as it turns out."

"What do you mean?" Joey picked up the small, bowl-shaped cup beside his plate and drank the light, hot tea.

"It's the candy." She expected to see impatience in his eyes, but he showed nothing. "I thought that was special between Kit and me." She thought she'd be more emotional, but since the shooting, her emotions had been totally calm. "It appears maybe it wasn't the secret I thought it was."

Interest tugged at Joey. "What do you mean?"

"Remember I said we communicated with the chocolates?" She saw him nod. "That's why I thought Kit was leaving the candy for me. It was our old secret talk. Danny had a dancer wearing a costume made of chocolate kisses. He said Kit gave him the idea." Cori looked down into her teacup. "I guess Kit could have told some other people if he told Danny." It hurt to admit that what she'd taken as something very special between her and Kit had not been all that special to him.

"How did Dupray make this point?" Joey put down his cup and listened intently. In an effort to protect Cori, he'd called Captain Blake and checked on all reports filed on the shooting. There was no clue as to who the sniper was who had killed Benny Hovensky. Not a single clue. That fact troubled Joey, who knew that only the most professional killers could leave a scene without a single shred of evidence.

"Danny had the girl come out and dance. To 'Silver Bells.' I don't think that song will ever have the same imagery." She sipped the tea. "I know you're angry with me, but I wanted to tell you the truth."

"Since you lived to vocalize it." Joey was beyond being frustrated. He had actually accepted the fact that Cori was going to do exactly the opposite of what she should.

Cori was attempting to follow Joey's train of thought. "So... you think the man I saw was someone hired to pretend to be Kit."

Joey nodded. "That's what I think."

"This is aimed at frightening me out of testifying."

"That's the way I see it," Joey said.

"And you think whoever is trying to frighten me hired that Benny person to kill me, and then killed him...."

"Right in front of you."

"To frighten me even more. But why not just kill me?"

"The fat lady hasn't sung yet, Cori. One witness is dead. Murdered. There's nothing to stop them from killing you, except it would be better if you *refused* to testify. That way DeCarlo's defense attorney could imply that maybe you weren't so certain, maybe *you* were having second thoughts. And a second murder would have all the high-powered politicos throwing money all over the place to 'resolve the threat of danger to our citizens who dare to tell the truth.' It would be better if you simply didn't testify, but don't think they won't kill you if that's what it comes down to."

"That's pretty cynical-sounding."

"I'm a cynical kind of guy." After the talk he'd had with his boss, following his visit to Blake's office, he had to be cynical and tough as old boot leather. Bascombe had threatened to "skin him alive" if anything happened to Cori. He'd also given him a deadline of six hours to get her out of the State of Louisiana. Joey considered that by crossing the river for lunch, he was headed toward Texas, even if his pace was a lot slower than he'd hoped. If Cori found out he was gradually easing her west, she'd no doubt put on the brakes, or worse, bolt and run.

"I don't think you're cynical at all." Cori made the pronouncement as she put down her cup. "If you were really cynical, you would have turned in the paperwork on me and let me out of the program. You would have decided that I was going to do what I was going to do, and that you could have no effect on the outcome."

"And that's pretty much the way things have turned out." Joey couldn't help the self-deprecating smile he gave her. It wasn't a funny situation, but he'd never been so hornswoggled by a witness as he had been by this average-sized female.

"But you didn't drop me. You didn't give up. You didn't resign yourself to the inevitable. Therefore—" she reached across the table and picked up a fortune cookie from the tray "—you don't qualify as cynical."

Joey cracked his own cookie open and pulled out the white slip of paper. When he read it he smiled, his dark eyes burning with merriment. "'You are in control,'" he read, laughing. "Is that one ever off!"

Cori unfurled her paper. "'Do not sit quietly when the music plays.'" She looked at Joey, remembering for one brief instant his offer to teach her to dance, and the conflicting emotions that it generated in her.

"Now, that sounds like fate stepping in." Joey suddenly knew his next step. He knew exactly what he had to do, and how he was going to accomplish it. He picked up the check and reached for his billfold. "Are you ready?"

The look in his dark eyes warned Cori, but they also excited her. "Depends on where we're headed."

"New Iberia." He spoke the words casually, then let his generous mouth twist into a smile that could not quite hide his own excitement. "We're going to visit the family."

"I don't believe I can find Kit Wells in New Iberia."

"That may not be true." He waited for her to gather her purse. "Kit found you in Houston and again at Jolene's. Someone has been following you all over the city. There's a place near New Iberia. A place where we might be able to set a trap."

"Why not do it here, in New Orleans?" Cori had the distinct impression that Joey would do anything to get her out of the city, even pretend that he was setting up a trap.

He paid the check, pocketed his change and ushered her out into the evening. "I'll be honest with you, Cori. Our office is understaffed. We can only do a certain amount of protection, and you've made it very hard."

"I know that."

"Good, then you've also got a feel for Jake Lewis and some of the NOPD officers."

"Kit's so-called friends."

"They may be friends of Kit, but I don't think you should consider them your friends."

"I've come to that conclusion." Cori idled slowly by Joey's side through the parking lot and toward the Supra.

"I grew up in New Iberia. I have friends there. Real friends. If I wanted to set up a trap, I could count on them not to shoot me in the back."

She saw his point, but she also didn't want to leave the city. Kit was close. Joey didn't believe it was him, but she was still positive. "If you set a trap, who do you think you'll catch?"

"Maybe the people who are torturing you. Maybe the folks who killed Emmet Wyatt. Maybe someone who knows the truth about your husband's disappearance."

"Because you think it's all related."

"I do."

She paused when he opened the car door. "How can we be certain Kit will know where I've gone?"

"We'll go back to the French Quarter, and we'll leave a trail of bread crumbs. If Kit is out there, we'll leave him a clearly marked trail to follow."

The idea of another night filled with visitations by a man everyone thought was dead chilled Cori to the bone. But she had to find the truth. She had to. So she could have her life back, or whatever remained of it.

Joey saw her hesitation, and he covered her hand on the top of the door with his own. "We can do this, Cori. You want resolution, we can find that. But you have to be some place safe before I'm willing to risk helping you. It has to be a situation where I have control."

"Okay." She looked into his eyes and saw relief.

"You have to promise me you'll do whatever I say." He wanted the ground rules clear. If he was going to risk Cori and his friends, he had to make sure she would do exactly as he said.

"This time I promise." She held her hands out in front of her to show her fingers were uncrossed.

She looked so childlike, so vulnerable, that Joey couldn't resist. "Even learning to waltz," he said sternly.

Cori suddenly felt his arms around her, holding and guiding. It was only a fantasy, but she knew that she wanted that sensation, if only for one night. "You've got it."

Joey almost bent to kiss her, but he stopped himself. She was a woman near the edge. A woman someone wanted dead. His job was to protect her, to make sure she survived. Kissing her was out of line. Unprofessional. And damn tempting. Instead, he squeezed the hand beneath his on the door. "We can do this."

"Just remember what happened to Hansel and Gretel when they left a trail of bread crumbs," Cori said as she ducked inside the car and let him shut the door.

Chapter Nine

Joey parked the black car in deep shadow by the side of the Twinkle.

"You think Kit will contact Danny?" Cori asked, unsure now that Joey's plan was about to be set in motion.

Joey reached across the car seat and took her hand. "I'm going to be honest with you, Cori. I think Kit Wells is dead. But I do believe someone is imitating him and trying to frighten you out of testifying. Or trying to make you doubt yourself."

"And you think Danny knows who this person is?" It did not matter that Joey didn't believe Kit was alive. He believed *something* had happened. That was the important thing. He had finally conceded that she could not have smuggled the chocolates into Chez Jolene in her jeans or shoes. Someone else had put them there. Someone who *looked* like Kit Wells.

"Danny is my best bet." He'd given the report of the alleged abduction and murder of Kit a lot of thought. If Kit had been killed, as the report stated, then someone had to have tipped the hit man off as to where Kit would be. And everyone would have assumed he would be at his wedding reception. So the person who had set Kit up had been at the wedding. He had called in when Kit left, and the tipster had to know where Kit was going. There was no other way it could work. Jake Lewis and a lot of NOPD officers were on the scene, and they would very likely have known Kit's destination.

"Why Danny?"

"He's the easiest to manipulate. The most believable source. He's been a pimp for the police, selling information for several years now. People like Danny have no loyalties. They sell to the top dollar, so this information would be valuable to him. If I showed up at police headquarters and filed my travel plans with them, it would look very suspicious. With Danny, I can drop a few hints, and he'll know exactly what I'm saying. Once he puts it together, then he either gives it, or sells it, to his buyer."

"And who do you think that might be?"

"Ben DeCarlo." It was the most obvious answer. "He doesn't want you at the retrial. One witness is dead. If you won't testify, then he's only got three to work on."

"Whatever happened to the waitress?" Cori remembered her. She'd been pretty, in a hard kind of way. The shock of the murder had really upset her.

"She's safe, and a lot more cooperative than you are, I might point out," Joey said. He was ready to go inside, but he didn't want to rush Cori. In a short amount of time he'd come to know her pretty well. It was the set of her shoulders, the angle of her head, that told him of her fear. Danny Dupray had revealed some hurtful things to her. Was it more pain she feared? More revelations of a past that didn't exist as she remembered it? Or was she afraid Danny would hurt her?

"What about the other witnesses? Are they safe?"

"They're fine, Cori."

"They'll come back to testify?"

"They've indicated they would." What choice did they have? He didn't ask that question out loud. They were under the thumb of the federal government. Their lives had been taken, and they were hooked to a federal leash, just as Cori was.

"What would happen if none of us testified?"

He waited a few seconds before he answered. "I don't honestly know. The evidence against DeCarlo was so strong because we had five eyewitnesses to the crime. Five people, from all walks of life, saw a hideous crime committed, and they all gave up their lives so that justice could be done. That was powerful. The jury couldn't ignore it—that you witnesses believed enough to give up everything. That you braved the long reach of the mob to tell the truth."

"But it was the evidence that convicted him, right? The bullets..."

"It was the eyewitnesses who cinched the case." He did not want to downplay her role. They needed her testimony, and the testimony of all the other witnesses, if Ben De-Carlo was going to stay behind bars.

"Why did Emmet Wyatt come back to New Orleans?" This question nagged at her.

"I'd like the answer to that, too. He never notified us that he was coming here. We thought he was in Atlanta. In fact, one of the other marshals had taken a call from him the day before. It was routine, he wanted some travel documents for a vacation to France. He was chatty, informal, happy-sounding. He never mentioned that he'd booked a flight to New Orleans two weeks earlier."

"Why do you *think* he was in New Orleans?"

Joey looked at the back door of the club, which had opened. Two girls in scanty costumes came out. Both lit up cigarettes and puffed. "I guess they have to come out here to get some peace and quiet," he said.

"Tell me what you think about Wyatt." Cori wasn't willing to drop the subject, though she knew Joey would prefer to let it go.

"I think he'd been contacted in some way. I think he was at the docks to make some type of connection with someone."

"He didn't have a dead fiancée or wife who might be luring him back, did he?" Cori tried to make her tone light, but she heard her voice quiver.

"No. No, I don't think Wyatt's tastes ran to commitments of any kind with the opposite sex." He shrugged. "Just a passing observation."

"Who do you think he was meeting?"

Joey had a theory, but not a shred of proof. All he had was a gut reaction. "I think he was trying to take a payoff. I think someone from DeCarlo's family had gotten to him, and he was going to take a lot of money not to testify. We found out he had two one-way tickets booked to Paris. He wasn't planning on coming back."

"He had sold out." Cori spoke softly, tasting the words as if she couldn't decide on the flavor of them.

"We have no proof of that. It's a theory. My theory. Not the marshals' or anyone else's."

"And you thought maybe I'd been bought off, too, didn't you?"

Joey looked straight out the window, but his lips turned up slightly in a smile. "It crossed my mind. Until I met you."

"And now?"

"Now I think you're a victim of someone playing a very deadly game." —

Cori put her free hand on the handle of the door. Joey still held her left hand, and began unconsciously to massage it. It should have relaxed her, but instead she imagined his touch working slowly up her arm, moving closer to places that suddenly anticipated the pressure of his fingers. "Let's do this so we can get on the road," she said.

"Are you sure?"

The concern in his voice stopped her as she swung her feet to the ground. "I'm sure that this nightmare has to end. I'm not living, and it's not going to get any better until I take some action. Yes, I'm ready."

"Say as little as possible," Joey directed as he got out and locked the car. They went to the back door, and Joey pulled it open, unleashing a cloud of smoke and the reverberating noise of the jukebox.

Cori drew back involuntarily, pushed by a wall of noise. Joey looked at her. "Are you sure?"

"Absolutely." She walked through the door he held open.

She found herself at the edge of a room filled with men. In the darkness, only the stage was recognizable from her prior visit, the long strings of white lights endlessly winking. A few of the men had women with them, but most were alone or in groups. They watched the gyrations of the girl she recognized as Candy as she danced in an outfit made of fake leopard skin. The big bouncer materialized out of the smoke.

"At night there's a ten-dollar cover, each." He gave Joey a wolfish grin and offered a wink to Cori. "Back so soon?"

Joey handed him a twenty, but kept a grip on it when the man tried to take it from his hand. "Where's Danny?"

"I think he must be at church." The bouncer smirked.

"We'll wait."

The man walked away, and in a moment a young girl with tired eyes came up to them. "Danny's in his office." She turned around and led the way.

Cori was relieved to step inside the small room and close the door behind her and Joey. Danny Dupray sat at a desk, stacks of money in front of him.

"Make it fast, Tio. I've gotta make a deposit tonight."

"You know anything about a hit on this woman?" He nodded at Cori.

"I know she's an eyewitness against Ben DeCarlo. I'd say more than one party might want to see her dead." Danny counted out another stack of twenties.

"Benny Hovensky was killed this afternoon."

"Ah, too bad. Several of the girls will be sad to hear that."

"So you don't know anything about Benny?"

Danny looked up from his money, the overhead lights slicing down his nose. "You want to know who hired him or who hit him?"

Joey pulled his billfold from his pocket and put a stack of new twenties down on the desk. "Both."

"I don't have that information now." Danny reached for the money, riffled it with his thumb and added it to a stack on the desk. "I can get it. Or some of it." He looked down at the money. "Is there a place you can be reached?"

"She isn't safe in the city."

"That's a revelation." He looked up, his eyes flitting over Cori as if she were no more than another stick of furniture.

"We're going over to the bayous."

Danny's eyes snapped. "Does this place have a phone, or should I strap a message to an alligator's back and hope he delivers it before he eats you?"

"Funny, Dupray." Joey reached across the money and picked up a pen. He wrote a number on the back of a small card and handed it over. "You can get word to me here."

Danny tucked the card into his desk drawer.

"Keep that number safe," Joey warned.

"It'll go with me to the grave."

"If you roll over on me, Dupray, I'll see that you are permanently put out of your misery."

Danny stood up. "If you're done with your threats, I've got a business to run."

Joey motioned Cori out of her chair. "Stay in touch."

Danny saluted, but his eyes were hard.

Joey opened the door and Cori preceded him back into the music and the smoke. She focused on the place where the door had to be and walked straight toward it, aware that Joey was behind her, his broad frame protecting her from any threat.

Stepping out into the night, she expelled the breath she'd been holding. "He never even acknowledged me," she said.

"You're a part of a business transaction, Cori. Nothing more. Nothing less."

The fact was disturbing. Up until Antonio De Carlo's murder she had lived a safe, structured life where everything made sense. People operated within a prescribed set of rules. The Danny Duprays of the world were far removed, and never acknowledged as part of the circle of life.

"How long do you think it will be before he sells that phone number?" she asked.

"Oh, he'll make the call and then hold out until tomorrow."

"We'll be ready by then?"

"We'll have to be."

"IT'S NOT A LOT FARTHER now." Joey nodded at the sign for Breaux Bridge. The forty-mile stretch of raised interstate that gave access over the Atchafalaya Basin had ended. They were back on solid ground.

Cori felt as if her eyes had glazed over and dried. They burned with weariness, and she knew Joey had to be as tired. The drive had been long, the night dark, and anxieties weighed heavily on her.

She had not asked Joey for the details of his plan. He would tell her when he was ready, or he would not. She had left that in his hands. He had called his office and said he was headed to Texas to take her home. Then he had called his sister and told her he was going to New Iberia. There had been a whispered conversation, and Joey had ended with a soft, "I love you, sis."

Those words haunted Cori. Joey had put himself in danger to protect her. It was his job. He said that repeatedly. But if she had not come back to New Orleans, the danger might have been held at bay.

Except for the fact that someone had uncovered her identity. Someone who knew her past, and was using it to manipulate her.

Kit.

It all boiled down to that single fact. In the past hours she had begun to accept the fact that Kit was not the man she'd thought him to be. She had married an upright, honorable police detective who loved his job and cared about the city he protected. She had never known the dark side of Kit Wells.

She gritted her teeth and stared down the interstate illuminated by Joey's headlights. How deep did Kit's dark side go? Was he trapped in a situation he couldn't get out of, or had he deliberately set her up as a witness, promising to marry her and start a new life with her only to get her testimony? Two days ago the very thought of such a thing would have reduced her to tears. Her heart had been so wounded, so tender where Kit was involved, that the idea of such a betrayal would have devastated her. In a very short time she had toughened up considerably. She was not so much devastated as angry at the idea of having been played for such a fool. Angry at Kit—and at herself.

"Do you need anything? Cosmetics, that type of thing?"

Joey's question scattered her bitter thoughts. She glanced at him. "I have everything I need. But thanks for asking."

"I need a razor and a few things." He pulled into a small drugstore. "Will you stay in the car?"

"Yes." She smiled. "Word of honor."

He killed the engine and looked over at her. "With an attitude like that, you're going to make a great partner."

"You mean as long as I do exactly what you say?"

"You're a smart cookie." He chucked her chin. "Word of honor, remember."

She watched as he went into the store, a tall man with broad shoulders and lean hips. A man who was comfortable in his own skin. A skin he was all too willing to risk to protect hers.

He was back out in fifteen minutes with a shopping bag. At the pay telephone he stopped, slotted in a quarter and spoke for several moments. When he hung up, some of the anxiety was lifted from his face.

"Good news?" she asked when he got in the car.

"Very good. Aaron's home off the boat this week. He'll be waiting for us at Henderson. With his boat."

"I thought we were going to New Iberia?"

"Too hard to protect you there. This camp is perfect. The only way to get to it is by boat. And Aaron knows the way."

"How will they find us?" She was suddenly concerned that Kit would not be able to follow. She wanted to see him, but not for the original reason. She had plenty to say to him, and none of it was about how much she missed him. Whatever tender feelings she'd gone to New Orleans nursing, they'd been killed. The truth of Kit Wells and his machinations had destroyed any desires she'd clung to.

The man sliding into the car seat beside her was responsible for her changed emotions, though he'd done none of it deliberately. The truth had come to her slowly, by deed and example. How could she compare Kit to Joey and not see the differences? Right this moment Joey was creating a plan to save her life, at the risk of his own.

Her hand lifted an inch, wanting to touch his cheek, to thank him for his concern, his honor. She dropped it back into her lap and listened to what he was saying. Her life and his might depend on his words.

"We can't make the plan too easy or they'll know it's a setup. Don't worry, Cori. I'll leave plenty of clues."

She settled back into the darkness and tried to imagine the town around them as they passed through Breaux Bridge and headed for Henderson.

"We have to cross the levee." Joey gave that information just as the mountain of dirt loomed up in the night. The sports car seemed to soar straight up at a ninety-degree angle before it crested the top of the levee and came down the other side. The headlights illuminated a fairyland that could easily be inhabited by the darkest of creatures.

Cypress trees, huge old roots sunk deep, were surrounded by water. Their leafless branches clawed the starlit sky.

"Spanish moss." Cori identified the view caught by the headlights, an eerie landscape of stark trees growing in water, their branches hung with filigreed lace. She inhaled sharply. She had driven past swamps before, but this one stretched far beyond the car's lights. It was almost another dimension.

"Yes, Spanish moss." Joey sensed her sudden anxiety at the scene before her. The swamp could be a very intimidating place. In times past, many people had gotten lost in the turning canals and twisting bayous. Some had never found their way out. He focused on a lighter story, something to ease her mind. "Some of the old stories say it's the beard from the Spaniards who passed through this area. The old legend goes that a Spanish conquistador fell in love with a girl of the swamps. He climbed a tree to catch sight of her, and he lost his balance and fell. His beard hung in the tree and became the first bit of Spanish moss."

"It's beautiful, in an eerie kind of way."

"I love the swamps." Joey blinked his lights twice and then killed them. The silence of the night surrounded them as quickly as if someone had thrown a spangled blanket over their heads.

"Let's explore." Joey got out and Cori met him at the front of the car. The water was a constant presence, a soft whispering against the shore.

"Is it ever dry?"

"The tide affects the water level, but it's never dry." There was amusement in his voice. "This is a world unto itself."

"You grew up here, didn't you?"

"Yes. This is my home. I hadn't realized how much I've missed it."

She could hear a love for the area in his voice. There was also the distant sound of a boat motor. She knew without asking that their ride was on the way.

"How long do you think before they find us?"

"It'll take them a couple of days." He saw her shiver, and he put his arm around her, drawing her close. "I forgot how intimidating the water can be for someone who doesn't know it. I'm counting on that factor to work in our favor when we need it."

She could only hope that he was right. For the moment, she was content to shelter against him, a moment's respite from the events yet to unfold. A chain of actions that she had set in motion.

All too soon the small boat glided into view. The lean man steering cut the motor and slid against the shore. Joey held the bow steady as she climbed aboard, and then he pushed them back out into the water, stepping in without rocking the boat or getting his foot wet.

"What about alligators?" Cori asked. The sides of the boat were only inches from the water. One little lurch and she feared they'd take on water and sink. She glanced at the silent man who guided them. He was dark-haired, his muscles pulling his jacket tight across his back. She'd caught only a glimpse of him, enough to know that he was dark and unflappable.

"They're very big, those alligators," he answered her.

She could hear the teasing in the man's voice. His accent was easy, like a gentle rain.

"Don't upset her, Aaron." There was no reprimand in Joey's voice. "Whatever you do, don't tell her about the gator that tipped over that boatload of tourists last spring."

"Ate them every one," Aaron pronounced with satisfaction. "They was fat, too. Big ole tourists. That was one hungry gator. And he's still out there, waiting for another chance."

"I'm delighted to be your sport, since it's too dark to fish," Cori said. "Just to let you know, I'm not afraid of alligators. I like reptiles."

"Oh, this one, Joey, she's spirited. She *likes* the gators."

Joey's only answer was an easy laugh.

"You think we're kidding, don't you? When you go back to the city, you look in the old newspapers. May 12, 1995. Four tourists attacked and eaten by the swamp gator. They sent bounty hunters from Florida and Texas to get that big ole granddaddy gator. But he was too smart for them. He took the fattest tourist down to his den up under an old mud bank and he held on to him for days, until all the hunters gave up and went home. Then he came up and got him some sun. You watch for him. He's snoozin' on a little piece of land, waitin' for the next boatload of careless tourists."

Cori couldn't help chuckling. Aaron was a lively storyteller. But alligators or not, she found that she felt perfectly safe with Joey and Aaron once she adjusted to the boat. What was troubling her was that she had no idea which way land might be. They had slipped into the dark water, and there was nothing but the trees, each looking exactly like the last. "I hope you guys know where we're going."

"If she pulls out a map, Joey, I'm going to throw her overboard."

"No maps, Aaron. No maps and no directions. We're playing this strictly by ear."

Joey's serious tone dampened the banter as Aaron notched the motor up to a higher speed and they skimmed the glassy black water that was patterned with a reflection of the stars.

THE CABIN WAS BUILT on pilings, a construction that Cori found strange and charming. At the small dock, Aaron handed out their bags while he remained in the boat. "You sure you want the car left back at the levee?"

Cori heard the doubt in Aaron's voice.

"Positive." There was *no* doubt from Joey. His plan was made.

"I put three shotguns in the house. I know you wanted the rifle. It's there, too. But the shotguns, you don't have to be such a good shot, you know?"

"Thanks, Aaron."

"I also brought your fiddle. And a tape player. There's food and firewood." He didn't want to leave. "Maybe I should see about that wood. Maybe it's not dry like it should be. You never were much at making a fire."

"We'll manage." Joey reached into the darkness and grasped his friend's shoulder. "Bring them when they come, Aaron, but be careful. Remember how we planned it."

"I'm not likely to forget to duck to save my own hide."

"Do it just like we planned."

"How many, you think? Three, four?"

"Three. I think it'll be three of them."

"Maybe Kevin should come stay with you. That's two against three. Better odds."

"Don't tell Kevin. Not anything, okay?"

Aaron hesitated. "If your butt gets blown to bits, Kevin's gonna hold it against me."

Joey tightened his grip. "I'll be fine. Just do it like we planned."

"Okay." Aaron took the boat line Joey threw him. "Later, man."

"Later, Aaron." Joey waved goodbye, though his gesture was swallowed by the darkness.

Standing on the dock, Cori had listened intently to the exchange. Their mutual affection was clear.

"Why are you risking your friends?" she asked.

"Your life is at stake, Cori. And because I can trust them." Joey picked up the bags and led the way to the stairs. "Aaron is smart. I can rely on him."

He opened the door, which was unlocked. "There's not any electricity," he warned her. "Let me light a lamp."

Cori felt him leave her side, but she stood still, unable to see anything. She heard the match and watched the flame bloom, revealing a room that was unpainted. The walls and ceilings were made of beautiful natural wood.

Joey lit a hurricane lamp that did a fair job of illuminating the room.

"Won't they see the light?" she asked, wondering if Joey was deliberately baiting a trap for the killers.

"Not tonight. They can't possibly find us here without Aaron's help. Tonight is a bonus from the gods, a measure of safety." He walked toward her, catching her gaze. "You can rest here, Cori. Tonight, I'll keep you safe."

"This is wonderful," she said, trying hard to ignore the thump of her heart that his words produced. Realizing how silly she sounded, she added, "I only wish we could have come here under different circumstances."

Joey turned suddenly to face her. The lantern cast his face into angles and planes. "What circumstances would you want, Cori?"

The seriousness of his question gave her pause. Did she dare to answer him honestly? She had to. After everything he'd risked, she owed him that. She owed herself that. Somewhere in a very short span of time, the shy, painfully timid and insecure Brently Gleason had disappeared. She had become someone new. After two horrible years of trying, Cori St. John had finally grafted and taken hold.

"I would like it if you had invited me here so we could be alone."

Joey felt his body react to her statement. He reacted to everything about her, the way she stood, saying words he'd hardly allowed himself to dream he'd ever hear from her. But there was one thing he had to ask. One question that had to be brought out in the open between them before they both made a mistake that could ruin everything for them.

"What about Kit?"

"He's alive. I believe that with all of my heart." She knew she sounded bitter, but she had no reason to hide her feelings from Joey. He knew the worst about her marriage to Kit. He had seen her for the fool she'd been, and he had never implied by word or gesture that he thought less of her because she had given her heart to someone so callous. "Kit isn't the man I married." She hesitated, trying to shape her thoughts and words clearly. "That Kit never existed." She bit her bottom lip. "Whoever he really is, I don't feel I owe any allegiance to a stranger."

"You have to be sure." He forced himself to say it. He wanted only to pull her against him, to hold her close and feel the silk of her hair against his lips. But she had to be absolutely sure.

"I want to find Kit. So I can divorce him. That wasn't my original intention, but it's what I'm left with. And this has nothing to do with you, Joey. My feelings for you are aside from the past." She didn't wait for him to reach for her. She walked into his arms and lifted her hands to his face.

Joey's hands circled her waist, then slid to her back. Pressing her against him, he could feel the beat of her heart all the way through her, a rhythm that matched the beat of his own. "You're in a vulnerable position now." He eased away from her so that he could look into her eyes. "And so am I."

A terrible thought struck Cori. She had taken it for granted that Joey was not involved. But she had not asked him, she had only assumed. "Is there someone else?" she asked.

"No. Laurette was telling far too much of my personal business." He kissed her forehead. "And Jolene was predicting my future."

"Do women always fall in love with you?" The question was teasing, but there was a hint of concern in it.

"My sister and a woman who lived a life of desperation until I gave her a hand? That's not exactly a harem." His fingers moved over her back, sculpting her shoulder blades and the smooth muscles that covered her ribs and narrowed at her waist. She was firm yet rounded, her skin warm through her sweater.

Cori felt her body yield to his exploring touch. Nothing had ever felt so right. She let his fingers press her against him, her arms lifting to wrap around his neck and to draw him down to her lips. He was so tall, so undeniably masculine.

All of the fears that had held her in limbo for the past two years were seared away by her desire for him. They had no future together. If she lived to testify, she would be gone, placed anew in some city with another name and another identity. The only thing they had was the night, a string of iridescent moments that were shaped by touch and sensation.

His hands lifted her, pulling her up his body until their lips touched. Cori opened to his kiss and, in that second, cut herself free from her past and her future.

For the rest of the night there was only each other.

Chapter Ten

The sound of the boat motor brought Joey upright. Beside him, Cori tried to blink reality back into place. Joey's abrupt movement had shaken her from a cocoon of warmth and security and total peace. Waking up to the look of concern on his face was as effective as a slap.

"What is it?"

"Someone's coming." Joey found his pants and his gun. Barefoot, he stepped across the worn boards of the floor to check from behind the window shade.

Outside the cabin was a world of fog. Rising out of the dense mist, the cypress trees that grew close by were eerie sentinels.

Cori pulled the sheet around her and got out of bed. Her clothes were scattered around the room, testimony to the passionate stages of undress from the night before. The memory made her stop and look at Joey. No man had ever treated her so tenderly, or with such finesse. Perhaps it was that she trusted him. Not only with her body, but with her life.

"What can I do?" she asked, slipping into her jeans and sweater.

Joey watched the fog. The motor was just a dull throb, a premonition of company on the way. The route to the cabin was winding and hard to follow. He listened intently, trying to make certain the boat was traversing the correct channels before he hit the panic button. It would seem Dupray and his master had acted much faster than Joey had ever anticipated. They were taking no chances that he would move Cori again, which likely meant they were coming in with a lot of firepower, in broad daylight, and without all due preparation. He, too, was not completely prepared. He'd hoped to use the daylight hours to set up a few surprises. Now he would have to trust that Cori was as courageous as she seemed.

"Do you know how to use a gun?"

Cori had not expected that question. She had never even considered that she might hold a deadly weapon—much less use it with intent to kill. Could she? "I don't know how, but I can learn. Fast." The answer was unequivocal. She could do anything to protect Joey. Because he'd risked everything to protect her.

"Get one of the shotguns." Joey pointed to the corner.

Cori picked up the weapon, surprised at the weight of it. While Joey kept one ear attuned to the drifting sounds of the boat headed their way, he broke open the breach and showed her how to insert two fresh shells, loading both barrels.

"There's only a single trigger. It shoots one shell, then the other." He watched as she placed the gun against her shoulder.

"Pull the butt tight against your shoulder. It's going to have a lot of kick, Cori. Be prepared and don't get knocked off balance. Brace. Hold tight. The rifle doesn't have as much kick, but the shotgun has a broad spread of pellets. You don't have to be as accurate, and if you have to shoot this thing, I want you to hit what you're aiming at, because if they get close enough for you to have to shoot, I won't be in a position to help you.''

Cori did not allow the dread his words created to linger in her heart. She kept them in her mind, where they would motivate her to do whatever was necessary. But she kept her heart safe from them, refusing to envision what circumstances might prevent Joey from helping her.

"Whatever you do, once you raise this weapon, shoot to kill."

She nodded, holding his gaze with her own.

The sound of the motor was much closer now. The hope that it was a fisherman just passing their way died as the sound came closer and closer.

"They aren't using a bit of precaution." Cori went to the window, lifting the shade back as Joey had done. The sight that greeted her was startling. "It's like the entire world has disappeared. The fog is as thick as clouds."

"There's no need for them to be quiet. They aren't counting on surprise. They'll rely on superior firepower."

Cori felt a sense of gut-twisting anxiety. Looking out at the fog, she could anticipate a man, only twenty feet away, suddenly looming out of the mist, intent on killing them both. She would have to react quickly. She would not have time to assess the situation or even make a decision. She would have to kill or be killed. The gun weighed heavily in her hands. What if Kit was the one who stepped in front of her?

Joey knew exactly what was going through her mind. Kill or be killed. The fog diffused the early morning sunlight, and the glow rested lightly on Cori's pale skin. She stood in front of him at the window, and Joey could not resist. His hands touched her arms, moving up to her shoulders. He gently pulled her back to him so that she rested against his bare chest.

"It's not Kit." He knew exactly the path her thoughts must have taken. Any sane person holding a gun and intending to use it for self-protection had to think of the consequences.

"How can you be so certain?"

"Because I believe he's dead." He kissed her head, bending to her neck. "Cori, no man could have walked away from you. Kit Wells did not voluntarily leave the night of his wedding. If he were alive, he could not have stayed away from you."

The combination of his words and lips released the last self-doubt that Cori harbored about her past. She had always believed that somehow Kit had found her lacking. He had been unwilling to take her wherever he had gone because she had not been worthy.

Yet no matter how much Joey's words soothed her, she could not let go of the image of the man reflected back to her from a New Orlean's store window. It had been Kit Wells. Not an imitation of Kit. She put her memory to work and came up with the details, the evidence that had made her such a good witness in the DeCarlo murder trial.

Kit had been wearing a dark overcoat, very similar to one he had owned. One she had bought for him, as a matter of fact. The detailing on the coat was perfect, down to the black buttons. Beneath the coat had been the broad shoulders of the man who had often held her in his arms. She mentally placed her hand on his shoulders, knowing the familiar fit. She moved her memory up to the face, to the dip in the cheek below the cheekbone, the brow that protected his deep-set blue eyes. The hair was longer, a slight mixture of gray turned silvery by the morning light. Could a look-alike deceive her? She didn't think so.

"Whoever walks out of that mist, Kit will be with them." Her grip on the gun tightened.

Joey saw where she was headed, and once again he felt a rush of fear for her sanity. "If Kit Wells is alive, and I believe he's dead, then he's a liar and a crook. If he's coming here, it isn't because he loves you. He's coming here to kill you. If that was your ex-husband lurking around, dropping little chocolate kisses all over the place, he set you up to be murdered."

That was as plain as it could be spoken. Joey felt his own muscles tighten with anxiety, but he kept his arms lightly around her, giving her plenty of room to step away from him if she needed.

"I know." It was all she answered, and she made no attempt to move away from the comfort of his body. "I've come to some hard truths in the last two days. Maybe deep down I always knew them, but I didn't want to accept them. I just drifted around in limbo, hoping that I'd never have to confront the truth."

"But you did." And now he fully understood why she had come to New Orleans. She wasn't chasing a fantasy, she had finally come to face the truth. She was even more courageous than he'd thought.

The abrupt cessation of the boat motor halted further conversation. Joey gathered her tightly in his arms, holding her close a moment longer before he let her go, and then he picked up his shirt. In a few seconds he was fully dressed, gun in hand. "Wait here. When I come back, I'll whistle like this." He gave a low, mournful whistle. "That way you'll know it's me, and you won't shoot me." He tried for a lighthearted note. "If anyone else comes up, shoot first and ask questions later. This is your life, Cori. Don't think they won't kill you. Emmet Wyatt is already dead. Remember that. I'm sure he didn't expect to be killed."

She lifted the gun to her shoulder, pulling it hard into the place where her arm met her body. "I've got the shells." They were in her pocket. "I'm ready."

He kissed her then, a long, desperate kiss that spoke of a future that hung in jeopardy. Then he was gone. Cori watched from the doorway as he went down the stairs and disappeared into the fog in the general direction of the boat landing.

The fog seemed to muffle ordinary sounds. There was the gentle slap of water against land. She thought it was louder, possibly a result from the wake of the boat slipping silently toward them. It seemed like hours had passed, but she checked her watch and found it was only minutes. Was Joey okay?

The low, mournful whistle came out of the fog, and she felt her fingers seize on the gun and then relax. She'd expected something horrible, a gunshot or a scream. Carefully she put the shotgun on the floor and then she flew out the door, down the steps and into the fog in the direction Joey had disappeared.

He heard her footsteps pounding along the dock toward him, and he turned from the boat to catch her in his arms.

"Joey!" She buried her face in his chest. Whatever else happened, she would never let him walk into danger alone again.

From the boat came the sound of a low, feminine chuckle. "I think maybe my timing was not so good." Laurette stepped out of the boat and onto the dock with the grace of someone who had grown up making that unsteady transition. She reached back and brought out several guns, a large net and a knapsack of other provisions.

Still in Joey's arms, Cori was almost too shocked to speak. "Laurette, what are you doing here?" she asked.

Laurette's grin was just visible in the dense fog. "I heard my little brother had left for the swamps with a lady. I've come to defend his virtue and good name."

Joey's laughter mixed with his sister's, and Cori joined in. "You just about scared us to death," she finally said.

"So Joey was telling me."

Joey released Cori and looked at the things his sister had brought. "You're a genius." He lifted the net. "Perfect. How did you know?"

"I've spent too many years with you fishing these swamps not to know exactly how your mind works."

Joey pulled his sister to him for a kiss on the cheek. "Thanks, sis. Now, you'd better get out of here. I don't know when they'll come."

"You think I'm leaving?" Laurette slapped his arm. "Think some more, little brother. I'm here to help."

"Not this time. It's dangerous."

"Who's the best shot in this family?" She didn't wait for an answer. "No one's been by the landing yet. There's time for some practice for Cori if the fog lifts enough to see a target. Then, tonight, we'll be ready for them when they come."

"You can't stay here, Laurette."

She put her arm around Cori and started toward the cabin. "I can't leave, Joey. This is what family is about. Besides, if anything happens to this woman, I don't think I'll ever get to see any nieces and nephews. It's taken you more than thirty years to find this one." She squeezed Cori's shoulders. "I knew the moment I saw you that you were the one. When you got out of that car, with your leg bleeding, I saw the way he looked at you. The big galoot, he didn't even know it then, but I did. And Jolene, she knew it, too. Everyone knew it but you two. I always heard Cupid's arrow could cause blindness. Now I know it's the truth."

Ignoring Joey's protests, she talked on and led Cori back to the cabin.

BY TEN O'CLOCK, THE FOG had burned away, and Cori stood behind the cabin, shotgun to shoulder while Laurette directed her to aim at a makeshift target they'd hammered to a tree.

"Pull it into you," Laurette directed. "Tight. Sight down the barrel, yes. Now pull."

Cori pulled the trigger and felt as if a cannon had smacked into her shoulder. She rocked back but did not lose her balance. In a few seconds she had the gun back in place.

"Excellent." Laurette's smile was wide.

"Joey said it would kick, but he didn't say it would knock me down."

"Well, he's usually a very truthful man." Laurette arched an eyebrow at her brother. "One more time, but let me check the target." She hurried to the target and returned. "You were a little to the left and too high. You just caught the corner of it."

Cori resighted and pulled the gun harder into her. This time the blast was not so bad, and she had the satisfaction of seeing the pellets pepper the target.

"Excellent!" Laurette said, nodding. "Remember, this is close range. It's harder to aim over a distance." She went to her brother, who sat on a stump. "I brought some food. Maybe Cori could make us some sandwiches?"

Cori knew Laurette had something to discuss with her brother. "Sure. Let me reload." She broke the breach like a professional and inserted the new shells. Without being told, she carried the gun with her as she walked back to the house.

She had the cabin picked up and smoked turkey sandwiches on the table, complete with chips and soft drinks, when she heard them coming up the steps. There was a tension between them she sensed instantly.

"Laurette refuses to leave." Joey's dark eyes smoked with frustration. "You have to be here, Cori. Laurette doesn't have to involve herself."

"My brother is in danger. I'm supposed to go home and cook lasagna for Angela's lunch box?"

"What about Cliff?" Joey had a sudden vision of his brother-in-law showing up.

"Angela's with Connie. Cliff's over in Georgia, making a delivery." Laurette grinned. "There's no one to report me to, Joey. Even Papa can't make me mind."

Joey tried hard to suppress it, but he couldn't help the answering grin. It faded, though, with his next words. "Laurette, if anything happened to you, I'd blame myself forever. This isn't fair."

"If I left you here with Cori, knowing someone meant to harm you, I could never forgive myself." Laurette shrugged.

Cori listened to them, envying the closeness that made them fight to protect each other. "You are two lucky people," she said softly. "And I'm lucky, too, because I've met you both. Let's eat."

"A woman who knows how to end a sibling argument." Laurette took her place at the table. "We have a lot to do before dark."

JOEY'S HEAD POPPED OUT of the black water, and Cori could see there was a bluish tint to his olive complexion. He was freezing.

"One more time," he gasped, then ducked beneath the water again.

"He is one stubborn man," Laurette said, pacing the dock. Cori stood with the heavy towel in her hands, waiting for him to finish and climb out.

"Why is he putting the net in the water?" Cori had watched the process, but she still didn't understand the reasoning behind it.

"Aaron will bring the men in." Laurette had come up with the plan almost at once when Aaron told her what Joey faced. "He'll come in pretty fast. The motor will tangle in the net and it will jerk the boat." Laurette made a whiplash motion with her hand. "If luck is with us, they'll tumble into the water. The shock of the cold should incapacitate them for a few seconds, and it will certainly mess up their weapons. That will give Joey the advantage."

"And Aaron?"

"He expects it. He'll be prepared. Either he'll hold on to the boat and stay in, or he'll jump away. Aaron grew up with us, he's very able to take care of himself."

Cori could visualize it—three or four mobsters all sputtering around in the water. And then what? That was the part that concerned her. Would Joey try to take them prisoner?

"Maybe they won't come," she said.

Laurette started to speak, then thought better of it. "Maybe they won't, Cori. That would be the best thing for all of us. Still, it's better to be prepared for the worst, don't you agree?"

"Will it be tonight?"

Laurette sighed. "Probably tonight. Aaron will guide them in. He can say the darkness will work to their advantage. Actually, it will help us."

"I hope it's not foggy when they come."

"Me, too." Laurette watched as Joey surfaced, this time with success evident on his cold face.

"Done," he called. He'd had to run a cable from the dock to one of the cypresses. The swim was a snap in warm weather, but the cold water was inordinately fatiguing.

"I'm going to the cabin to see to some things." Laurette beat a hasty retreat, leaving Cori to fold the shivering marshal in the big towel she held out to him.

Cori rubbed his back, concerned that he felt cold to the bone. "Maybe we should go inside and build a fire," she said.

Joey turned in her arms, hugging her against him. "Maybe we should start a fire right here." He kissed her, feeling the warmth of her body begin to heat his own.

Cori pulled away. "Joey, your sister..."

"Would highly approve," he finished. "Don't think it was my hide she came all this way to save. She likes you. She didn't trust me to take care of this on my own." His dark eyes teased her. "Always the big sister. While I was under the water, did she try to plan a wedding?"

Cori laughed. "No. She was nice to me."

"Hah, just wait. In a few weeks she'll be bullying you around the way she does me."

A few weeks. Cori heard the words and clung to them. In a few weeks this would all be over, she hoped. Until the retrial.

"If we get out of this, and I find out about Kit, I promise you that I'll go to Texas or California or even Massachusetts. Wherever I'll be safe, and you won't be in danger."

"We'll get out of this." Joey wiped away the water he'd left on her cheek. "We have to. Then we'll take it day by day. When you went to make the sandwiches Laurette told me that I'm in some difficulties at work. If they can find me, they're probably going to fire me."

"Joey." Cori felt a wave of guilt.

"I lied to them about going to Texas, and then I didn't call in, because I didn't want them to tell me I couldn't do this. It's one thing to set a trap when you're an officer of the law. It's another when you're a citizen. I needed the authority that comes with the badge.''

''But it could cost you your career....''

''You did something two years ago that cost you your career and family. It was a risk I felt I had to take.''

The wind that had finally blown the fog out had steadily increased in strength all afternoon. Even though he was wrapped in the towel, Cori could feel him shiver. ''Let's get you inside.''

''Good idea. I think I have a promise to live up to. I would have done it last night, but we got... distracted.''

The teasing note was back in his voice. Cori looked up at him as they walked down the dock, his arm around her shoulders. ''Is that what you call last night, a distraction?''

''A *wonderful* distraction.''

She punched his arm. ''I would hope it would fall under life-changing events.'' She slipped her arm under the towel and around his waist, hugging him. ''I think it may have changed my life.''

Joey halted, bringing her around to face him. ''No serious talk for the rest of the evening, okay?''

Cori tried to read his intention in his eyes, but there was nothing there except tenderness, and a whisper of sadness. ''Why?''

''Call me superstitious, but I don't like to challenge the future. We have today, these few hours right now. We have to get through tonight. Then we can make plans for whatever comes next. For the good things that are waiting.''

''So, a superstitious cop.'' Cori tried to keep her tone light. She couldn't talk about the horror that lay just beneath the surface of his words. ''What promise are you about to live up to?''

''You'll see, because you have a corresponding one to fulfill.'' He held open the door and ushered her inside.

After he was dressed, he led Cori to a chair and placed her in it with great ceremony. Laurette's laughter was as mysterious as Joey's behavior, but she refused to reveal any Tio family secrets, no matter how Cori pressed her.

With Cori's gaze following every move Joey made, he found the fiddle case in the corner and brought out the old fiddle. In a moment he had it tuned and tucked beneath his chin. Laurette retrieved an old accordion from the closet.

To Cori's delight, they played a few of the old Acadian tunes that had her feet patting the floor. As the tempo slowed slightly, Joey broke into a song with Laurette picking up the harmony. The words were in French, and she had no idea what they meant, but the music spoke to her. It told of dark, velvety nights and the pleasure of the company of the man she loved. There was the sound of water in the songs, and work, and beneath it all the simple pleasure in being alive.

"That's wonderful." She applauded at the end. "I can't believe you both play so well."

"Music is part of life," Joey said, putting down his fiddle and sweeping her out of the chair. "We're given only this moment, Cori. So now you'll dance."

Cori turned to Laurette. "I don't know how."

"Then it's time you learned." Laurette retrieved the tape player from a corner. She checked the batteries and inserted a tape. "I'm going to catch us some fish for dinner. Joey is an excellent dancer. You're in good hands."

"But shouldn't we be doing something about tonight?"

Joey eased her into his arms before answering. "We have done everything we can, Cori. Every precaution has been taken. Laurette will keep watch for us while she fishes, and she'll hear any approaching boats long before they can hear us. Now we can enjoy the moment." He started moving forward so that she had to step backward. "The Cajun

Waltz,'' he whispered in her ear. ''Listen to the music, feel it. Your body will know what to do.''

After a few awkward moments, Cori gave up trying to anticipate what to do next. Joey's strong arms held her, moving in the three-beat succession of steps that were at first plain and then quickly became gliding swirls of motion as she gained more confidence in herself, and in Joey's ability to lead her.

One song bled into the next with hardly a moment for Cori to gain her breath. The dance was fast, but it wasn't exertion that made her heart pump too hard. It was Joey. He was as graceful as a cat, and his strength lent her grace.

''That's it,'' he said, encouragingly, ''and you said you couldn't dance.''

Cori had no response. She only wanted the music to go on and on forever. She was Cinderella at the ball. No matter that she wore jeans and a sweater that had seen cleaner days. She saw herself reflected in Joey's eyes.

''This is wonderful,'' she whispered.

''I think so. I believe every child should be taught to dance in the first grade. I think we'd have fewer criminals.''

He was kidding, but Cori knew there was a grain of truth in what he said. ''Maybe you're right. Maybe I'll give up my art studio and open a dance studio. Of course, you'll have to work as an instructor.'' She laughed. ''Then again, I'm not sure I'd like that.''

Joey guided her around the entire cabin, circling the sofa and chairs, moving through the kitchen. ''In our family, we danced in the yard or the kitchen or the hallway. My mother and father didn't care where, just as long as there was music and they had each other.''

Cori was about to answer when she heard footsteps on the stairs. They were running.

Joey heard them, too. As he pushed Cori down on the floor behind the sofa he switched off the music. He took cover beside her, his arm snaking out to capture his gun.

The door flew open and Laurette dashed into the room, eyes large with concern.

"Someone's coming, Joey. It sounds like Aaron's boat, but I can't be certain."

"Damn." Joey stood up. He reached for the rifle and handed it to Laurette. The shotgun he gave to Cori. "Remember the signals."

"I didn't think they'd come in daylight."

"Neither did I," he said. "It'll work against us, I'm afraid."

Cori tasted metal in the back of her mouth, and she realized it was pure fear. She had never been so afraid in her life. These men had come to kill her, and Joey and Laurette stood in danger because of it.

"Remember the plan." Joey looked at each, waiting for them to nod. "Okay. I'm going out to take my position. Laurette."

"I'm headed for the tree." She hefted the rifle and made sure her pockets were bulging with shells. She hugged Cori quickly and gave Joey a kiss. Then she was gone.

"Cori?"

She nodded, patting her pockets to show she, too, had shells.

"Shoot to kill, no matter if he looks like Kit or not."

She nodded again, unable to speak. Nothing in life had prepared her for this moment.

Joey brushed her silky hair back from her face. He kissed each cheek softly, then her lips. "Things will work out." He went out the door and down to the small island of land that would afford him the best shot when Aaron's boat hit the snag he'd constructed.

Chapter Eleven

Cori shaded her eyes against the setting sun. An hour had passed, an eternity in hell. The boat motor had been cut, and there was nothing, only the knowledge that they were out there, waiting, biding their time. An eerie quiet had settled over the cabin and surrounding swamp. She could hear the second hand of her watch twitch the slow minutes away, and she could only imagine the torment Joey was going through. Aaron was on that boat. If anything happened to him, Joey would never forgive himself for involving a friend.

From her vantage point at the window of the cabin she could see the boat dock. Joey had placed her as far from the action as possible; she knew that. The shotgun would be necessary only as a last resort. Still, she could see the scene. With the sun dipping behind the stark cypress trees, the swamp was impressive. There was a wild beauty to the place that touched her, while at the same time it reminded her that she was totally removed from the world she knew. If anything happened to Joey and Laurette, she wouldn't have the vaguest idea how to get home.

A shaft of golden light pierced her eyes and she drew back. The truth struck her with such force that she started toward the door, then stopped herself. The men who were after her were not stupid. They were planning on using the sun to their advantage. They could come in with the light behind them, giving them a clear view of what they were attacking. Joey and Laurette would be staring directly into the blinding light. And there was nothing she could do. Her first impulse was to warn Joey, but that was foolish. Surely he'd come to the same conclusion long before her.

As if her thought had kicked the boat motor to life, she heard it crank. And then came the sound of a boat moving toward the cabin at breakneck speed.

Although the boat was too far away, Cori lifted the shotgun to her shoulder and sighted down the barrel, ready for whatever might come.

In the distance, the boat was a speck of black illuminated by the golden sun. She blinked, trying hard to distinguish how many men were in the boat, but the sun was too intense. She blinked again and lowered the gun. It was almost impossible to stare into the sun long enough to draw a bead. Determined, she lifted the gun again. This time she could see a man who looked like Aaron sitting in the back, steering the boat. Someone stood in the prow, and there were other figures, shifting even as the boat raced toward her, the wake a V of molten gold. She counted three, aside from Aaron. She could not tell if one of them looked like Kit.

The boat came in straight, not angling in as Joey had expected. Cori watched as Aaron neatly avoided the net that Joey had so laboriously set.

"Damn," she whispered as she lowered the gun so she could press her face to the window. "Damn!" The boat completely avoided the trap and then angled so that Cori could finally see. The man in the prow stood facing Aaron. In his hand was a gun, and it was pointed at Aaron's chest. One bump, one false move, and the man's finger would automatically pull the trigger. As the boat sped by, Cori got a good look at Aaron's face. He was afraid, and ashamed that he had failed his friend.

Instead of attacking the cabin, the boat moved behind it, circling like a shark. Cori heard Laurette's lighter footsteps pounding on the dock, and she ran outside to meet her.

"What's happening?" Cori asked.

"There's no entrance from the back. It's all marsh. They can't get through. Trust me, with what's back there, they won't get through. They'll have to come to the front, but Joey's worried about Aaron. He's afraid they'll kill him." Laurette was breathless.

"They'll need someone to lead them out of here, and my bet is they'd rather keep Aaron alive than Joey, and they don't know about you."

"That's comforting." Laurette rolled her eyes. "I have to get back. They'll have to come this way, and now we've lost the advantage of surprise, and we're handicapped by the sun. Stay in the cabin, Cori. Stay safe."

"Right," Cori answered to her retreating back. "I'll stay really safe while everyone else gets blown to bits."

On the far side of the cabin, the boat motor was still audible, but it was farther away. Cori peered out the kitchen window but could see nothing but the waving grass that Laurette had told her was aquatic. Only an airboat could traverse that terrain. She hoped Laurette was right about that.

Feeling as if her nerves had been stretched too far, Cori went back to the front window and waited. Like Joey and Laurette, she could do nothing else.

This time the drone of the boat was no surprise. It came around the shallows that surrounded the cabin and, without warning, came straight in toward the dock.

Cori heard the opening gunshots before she realized that the men in the boat had set up a fusillade of bullets, and the guns they carried had a lot more firepower than anything Laurette or Joey had. The shotgun she carried was an antique compared to their weapons. Her first impulse was to put her hands over her ears and run to hide under the bed, but she kept her post at the window. Running would do no good; she'd tried that for two years. At last she had taken a stand.

The gunfire was heavy out at the dock, and Cori found that she was trembling as she aimed the gun. Laurette's scream almost made her pull the trigger. The cry was a spiral of pain, a woman hideously injured. "No." Cori spoke the word, then punched open the door and stepped outside.

She had given Joey her word that she would do what he told her. Without exception. And he had told her to stay in the cabin where she could shoot anyone who tried to enter. But Laurette was hit, and though she couldn't see him, she was fairly certain Joey was pinned down on the small island where he'd taken his stand. Laurette might be bleeding to death. Surely Joey would want her to try to help.

Still holding the gun, she started down the steps. She was at the bottom and ready to dart down the dock when she felt something staring at her.

The skin on her neck prickled, and if she had been a dog, she knew her hackles would have risen. The stare was as intimate as the touch of a cold hand.

"Brently?"

She turned into the dripping face of Kit Wells.

"Kit?" Cori didn't believe it. "Is that really you?"

His smile was tired. "Unfortunately for you, it is."

"What are you doing here?"

"I've come to finish some business that I should have finished two years ago."

Cori had the advantage of the sun, and she used it to study Kit's face. It was him. Older, more haggard, the fine edge of robust physical fitness and masculine power had been worn a bit, but it was still the handsome police detective she'd fallen in love with—and married.

There were a million things she had wanted to tell him. Not a single one came to her mind. She could only stare, her body numbed by the final truth.

"I'm sorry," he said. "You'd better come with me."

"Where?" Another burst of gunfire out on the dock made her flinch, but she didn't take her eyes off Kit. He had been so elusive, so unreal, that she knew if she turned around for a second he would disappear, and than all she would be left with was more evidence that she was losing her mind.

"Let's go." He brought the gun up from his side.

The gun was wet, and it occurred to Cori that it might not work. She held the shotgun casually at her side. Was she quick enough to lift it and get off a shot? Staring at Kit face-to-face, could she? Her fingers twitched but that was all.

"There was a time I would have followed you to hell, Kit, but I'm not going anywhere with you now." She surprised herself. She was calm, and deadly earnest.

"I've been in hell, Brently. In ways you'll never appreciate. I made a bargain with the devil, and he called in my ticket." Kit shook his head. "This wasn't my idea. I just don't have a choice."

"Everyone has a choice. You just want the easiest way. For you."

He reached across and took her arm. His grip was firm but not angry. "Let's get this over with." He pulled her beneath the cabin and toward the swamps.

"How did you get here? There's no way."

"There's always a way, Brently. I had to walk through the swamps, which isn't exactly my idea of paradise, but at least we had the daylight."

Cori balked. "If I go with you, if I follow you out of here and don't give you any trouble, will those men leave without hurting Joey and his friends?"

Kit's smile revealed a harshness she had never seen before. "They don't want to kill a U.S. Marshal, but they will. If I get you out of here, they'll leave. Tio has no way to follow. We've got his buddy and the boat. He'll be stranded here, and we'll be long gone."

Cori put the shotgun down. Her decision was made. Joey and Laurette could hold them for a little longer—if Laurette was still alive. But the men had more firepower. A lot more. The end was inevitable. The only thing she could change was whether Joey had a chance at survival or not.

"Why do they want me?"

"That's a question you don't want me to answer."

Cori felt the finger of death touch her lightly on the spine. They were going to kill her. Joey had been right.

"How did you find me in Houston?" She had to know for certain it was Kit all along.

"We've known where you were since the very beginning. I thought I could make you doubt yourself. Maybe upset you to the point that you wouldn't testify. I tried, Brently, I..."

"My name is Cori." She lashed out with the words. "Cori St. John. The woman you tricked and married is long dead."

"It doesn't matter to me what you call yourself. The outcome is going to be the same, I'm afraid." Kit pushed her ahead of him down a narrow, barely visible trail toward the back. Cori stumbled over clumps of weeds, and when they

were only a few yards from the cabin, her shoes began to
sink in the thick grass that was saturated with water. Kit had
indeed walked in through the swamps. But Laurette had said
it wasn't possible.

And Joey had been certain Kit was dead.

The long marsh grass snatched at her feet, tangling
around her ankles. When she started to slow, Kit gripped her
arm and thrust her forward, pushing her through grass and
water that was now knee-deep.

"You want to save Tio, you better hustle. The longer it
takes you to get through this, the more chances they have of
blowing him away."

That inspired Cori to lift her feet higher and trudge deeper
into the swamp. She focused on one step at a time, and on
the curious fact that she felt nothing but contempt and hatred for the man behind her. Had she ever loved him? It
didn't seem possible now. She couldn't even remember why
she had let his disappearance cause a ripple in her life. She
should have been glad to see him gone. She should have
turned to her new life and begun to live. The fact that she
was going to die seemed inescapable, yet somehow distant.
What bothered her was that she was going to die a fool.

"Go left," Kit said. He nudged her that way for good
measure.

"Don't touch me," she said. She knew it sounded ridiculous. He wasn't going to touch her, he was going to shoot
her. She stopped abruptly. "Why don't you shoot me here?
Why go through all of this slogging through the swamp?
Shoot me now and you could move a lot faster without me."

Kit drew a breath. "Believe it or not, I'm not wild about
killing you."

"So why prolong my torment?" She held up her hands.
"Just get it over with." There had to be a reason Kit hadn't
shot her. He had become a man who did whatever he had to

do to survive. Killing her would be one in a long list of atrocities. Why was he hesitating? Had he actually cared, a little, for her? Could she use this to her advantage?

"They want to be certain you're dead. If I kill you, I'll have to drag the body out. It's easier if you walk on your own."

Cori's plans crumbled into dust. There was no sentiment in Kit's unwillingess to kill her, only practicality. A body that could push itself along was far preferable to having dead weight to carry. She turned to the left and started forward. If he touched her one more time, gun be damned, she'd claw his eyes out with her fingers.

Cori's right foot shot through the grass and water, plunging her waist-deep in mud. She was so startled by the way the ground gave beneath her that she didn't react when Kit tugged her out.

"Keep moving. This whole area is riddled with those holes."

She slogged on, trying to see through the water to the firmness of the ground beneath, but it was impossible. She hit another hole and cursed.

Kit pulled her out. "I could have used you coming in to find the holes," he said.

Cori thought she had despised him before, but his comment made her boil. She turned to speak when a movement to her right froze her. The marsh grass had begun to shimmy, and not in a way that indicated wind. Something big had slid into the water, and she could see it coming her way.

"Alligator." She spoke because in her heart she knew it was true. Now Laurette's statement about no one making it in through the swamp took on new meaning. She wasn't talking about the water. She had known there were alligators here.

"Where?" Kit spun around, and he too saw the rippling grass begin to part as the creature came toward them. "Run!" He tried to push Cori forward, but she was frozen. She couldn't take her eyes off the grass that marked the alligator's rapid approach. Every gruesome Tarzan film and natural science show that she'd ever watched held her prisoner in the wet grass.

Kit did not wait for her. He darted past her, his longer legs giving him an advantage in the thick grass and mud. Not five feet from her, he went down in a hole, pulled himself up and kept going. Cori stood perfectly still.

Movement in the tall grass ceased completely. Then the alligator shifted directions. It had forsaken her and moved after the thrashing, floundering Kit.

Turning some thirty yards from her, the reptile headed for open water, where Kit would be an easy target. Cori watched, unable to move and barely able to breathe. As the alligator passed, she caught a glimpse of it through the grass. It was at least ten feet long, deadly. When it was gone she started back to the camp, making as little noise as possible. There were bound to be others.

When Kit's scream pulsed in the still air, she put her hands over her ears and tried to block it out. As she found her way back to the shallower water, she began to run. The gunshots at the dock had ceased, and she knew only that she had to get her shotgun and see what had happened to Joey and Laurette.

She found the gun exactly where she had left it. Her fingers lifted it just as the sun sank below the rim of the swamp, giving a last, beautiful glimpse of the open swamp and the circling gun smoke that was left hanging in the still air.

Darkness was the cover she needed. When she could dart from tree to tree with some degree of safety, she made her way to the dock.

"Laurette?" Cori whispered her name, praying there would be an answer.

"Laurette?"

"Over here. I'm hit."

Cori followed her voice "How bad is it?"

"In the shoulder. I've managed to stop the bleeding, but I can't move or it starts up again."

"Joey?" Cori tried to sound strong.

"I don't know." There was desperation in her voice.

"Aaron?"

"I don't know what happened to him, either. They came out of the sun, and all we could do was fire blindly."

"Where are they?"

"They pulled back, but I don't know where. They could be out there, waiting again." Laurette's voice sounded hopeless. "What do these men want? Why are they so determined to kill all of us?"

Cori hesitated "I testified in a mobster's trial two years ago. But what I don't understand is, why kill me now? Why didn't they do it then when I was in New Orleans, unprotected?"

Laurette's answer was a groan as she tried to shift positions.

Cori inched forward until she found Laurette's leg. Joey's sister had managed to drag herself into a small depression where she was safe. As Cori felt in the darkness, she found the ground beneath Laurette's shoulder sticky with blood. A compress bandage was what she needed.

"I'm going to the cabin for some towels. Don't move, Laurette. You're still bleeding."

"Okay." Fear edged Laurette's voice.

"I'll be back. Listen for Joey. I'm sure he's okay." Cori didn't believe it, but Laurette needed something to hang on to. If she gave up, if her will deserted her, she might die, too.

Cori couldn't allow herself to think of Joey. She had to focus on saving Laurette. Bandages. That's what she had to think about. And after that, she would tackle the next physical task. She could think of anything except Joey.

Cori crept back to the cabin, found the towels and tore a sheet into strips. She was back at Laurette's side in less than fifteen minutes.

In the darkness, it was hard to construct a compression wrap around a shoulder, but she made the best of it until she could get Laurette into the cabin. She was almost finished when the gentle slap of the water against the dock intensified.

Automatically, Cori's fingers reached for the shotgun. She brought it up, swinging blindly in the night. At this point, anything that moved was a likely target.

The low, mournful whistle came to her. For a moment, she didn't believe her ears. Then she gasped. "It's Joey. Laurette, it's Joey!" She lowered the gun and whistled softly back, imitating the sound of a marsh bird as best she could.

She heard the water slush as he made the dock, and then there were the slight sounds of him easing from the water. Cori whistled again, directing him toward them.

He slipped beside her, dripping and freezing, but his voice was calm. "Are you okay?" In the darkness his fingers found her face, touching, assessing, even before she could voice her answer.

"I'm fine. It's your sister." Cori found his hand and placed it on Laurette's shoulder. "She's shot. She's lost a lot of blood."

"I'm okay, Joey," Laurette assured him, but her voice had grown weaker.

Without a second's hesitation, Joey scooped his sister into his arms. "Get both guns," he urged Cori. "And hurry."

Carrying the shotgun and the rifle, Cori followed behind Joey as he made his way silently up to the cabin.

"IT'S AN INFECTION." Joey pressed the cool cloth on Laurette's forehead. It was almost midnight, and Laurette's fever had come on her with terrible speed. There were no antibiotics in the cabin, nothing to deep clean the wound, and Joey had determined that the bullet was still lodged in the muscle. "We have to get her back to town."

How? Cori didn't bother to ask the question. They weren't certain Laurette's boat was still tied to the tree where Joey had hidden it, and they had no idea where the killers might be hiding in the swamps. With Aaron as their hostage-guide, they could have set a trap anywhere.

Joey sat back in his chair. "We haven't talked about Kit."

Deep within her mind, Cori heard the horror of his scream. She saw again the grass shifting as the alligator made its way toward him. "There's nothing to say. He came to kill me, and an alligator got him." She felt nothing. Absolutely nothing. In time, her numbed feelings would awaken, but right now she wanted them to stay dead. She didn't want to think about Kit, or talk about him. He had intended to kill her, and he had died. If he had lived, she would have died. It was a simple equation of survival. Later, much later, if she lived that long, she might want to explore the betrayal, the loss, the rationalization of Kit's actions, and her own. Not now, though. Now she wanted only to cool Laurette's fever and figure out a way back to Henderson and help.

"There's nothing to say," she repeated.

"You were right, he was alive." Joey shifted so that he could look at her fully. They had risked the lantern. They needed the light to care for Laurette. There was also a fire in the fireplace for warmth. Laurette's fever shifted periodically to chill.

"*You* were right," she said. "Those chocolate kisses were a lure. Bait in a neat trap to draw me back to New Orleans where they intended to kill me on the street. Just another unfortunate homicide."

"But why?" Joey pondered the question. "If Kit found you in Houston, why not kill you there if that was the intent? It could have been done successfully, and perhaps without drawing suspicion."

Cori understood. "They *wanted* to draw attention to the murders. Emmet Wyatt was lured back to New Orleans and shot. I would be the second witness pulled back and killed. It was meant to be a warning to the other three eyewitnesses. Come back to New Orleans, and you'll die."

Joey knew what she said was true. That put all of the other witnesses in dire jeopardy. Somehow, he had to relay this information back to his office. There was another matter, though.

"At first, Kit set you up as a witness. He wanted you to testify against Ben DeCarlo. Now it seems he's switched allegiances. Did he say anything that might explain that?"

Cori thought back to what had been said. There was nothing to explain Kit's sudden change of heart where Ben DeCarlo was involved. "Maybe the pro-Ben forces offered him a bigger paycheck." She felt as cynical as she sounded. There had been a time when she'd thought Kit was a force for justice, a man who lived out his convictions every day. For a woman who lived in New Orleans, Louisiana, where the sun shone hot year round, she had certainly fallen victim to a snow job.

"I can't seem to let it go," Joey admitted. "There has to be an explanation, and if we could just figure out how the forces have shifted, then maybe we could figure out a way to escape." His shoulders drooped. "I thought I was so smart bringing you out here. I had the greatest plan. I knew I could protect you. Now my sister is wounded and in danger of dying, and I can't find a way to get us to a safer place."

Cori had to distract him. Joey's confidence in his own abilities was a key to their survival. If he began to doubt himself, the results could be disastrous. "Did you recognize any of the men in the boat?"

"Yeah, Aaron. The one with the gun to his chest." Joey was bitter at the knowledge that his friend was in danger because of him.

"Anyone else?" Cori pressed gently.

"There were four of them, not counting Aaron. When they circled the cabin, I wondered what they were up to. I thought maybe Aaron hadn't told them about the alligators."

"Apparently he didn't, or Kit would never have tried it."

"I'm amazed he made it safely in. The cold weather has made them sluggish, I suppose. When the boat came back around with only three of them, I wasn't worried. I can see that's another area where my strategy didn't pay off."

"In the long run, it did." She blocked out the scream, the grass shifting, the slide of the reptile not far from her. She didn't allow the fact to translate into feelings. She could not risk such turmoil. "Is there any chance of someone coming out here to stay in the cabin?"

"No, Aaron would have made sure none of the guys would even think about it. He knew how dangerous it would be."

Cori left the fire and went to the stove. "I'm going to make some soup. At least we can have something hot and nourishing to eat. They're stuck on a boat, guarding the exit. Do you think they found Laurette's boat?"

"I don't know. I imagine they think we're stuck here."

"True, but they can't be one hundred percent sure. They can't risk leaving, so they're as stuck as we are. And they're cold and hungry. We're warm and soon to be fed. Laurette might be able to take some of the broth. We need to keep her as strong as possible. She has to fight that infection with her own resources until we can get her help."

In the dim light cast by the single lantern, Cori built a small fire in the wood-burning stove and used the items Laurette had brought for sandwiches to make soup. Aaron had also brought in a few vegetables, and in fifteen minutes she had what she thought was a healthy combination ready to go. The busier she kept her hands, the better she felt.

She paused long enough to stare into the room where Laurette was stretched out on the only bed. They had moved the bed closer to the fireplace, and Joey sat at her side. She could hear his occasional low murmur, spoken in French, as he tried to comfort his sister.

A flash outside the window of the cabin made her start. The loud boom of thunder followed. The fact that it was going to rain gave her grim satisfaction.

"They'll be drenched," she said. "And miserable. Maybe they'll freeze."

Joey put a fresh compress on Laurette's forehead. "Can you manage Laurette for a little while?"

Instantly she was afraid. "What are you going to do?"

"With the lightning, I may be able to spot them."

"How? Where? They could be anywhere. They won't be within sight of the cabin. And if they were, you could see them better from the window here."

"I've always been a strong swimmer. Maybe they're just around one of the turns. It would help us to know."

"Maybe the alligators will eat you, or you'll die of hypothermia in the cold water. No, Joey! You're the only chance Laurette has. If anything happens to you, they'll swarm up here and kill both of us without batting an eye.''

Joey knew she was right about the last part, but he also knew he could no longer sit and wait for his sister's fever to rise, for the inevitable end that would come then. Or wait for the sound of the boat motor as they came to attack. He was almost out of ammunition. Laurette could no longer shoot. He had to take the initiative. He'd always been taught to attack when defending wasn't feasible.

"I have to do this," Joey said. "It's our only hope."

"If you go, you take my only hope with you." Cori turned back to the stove to hide the fear on her face. If Joey left, she would be alone with Laurette—and her own guilt.

"I'll be back, Cori." He walked to her, pulling her stiff body into his arms. "I have to do this. I can't sit here and wait."

She understood that. And from deep within her she found the strength she needed. "Be careful, Joey. I'll be waiting here for you. Me and Laurette." She kissed him, holding tight to him for a moment, trying to use her strong memory to imprint every nuance of him, every smell, every sensation, into her mind.

"I will be back," he promised her as he slipped through the door and into the night.

Cori walked to the window and watched him. A flash of lightning, a jagged fork of pure light, illuminated the dock. She watched as Joey zigzagged across the bit of dry land that sustained the cabin and headed toward the black and deadly water.

Chapter Twelve

Cori pulled the old rocking chair so that she was beside the window, yet close enough to Laurette so that she could hear the slightest murmur. The shotgun was across her lap, the rifle at her feet. Joey's departure had taken much of her hope for survival. What kept her sitting in the chair, guns at the ready, was the determination to survive as long as possible—and to make them pay dearly for victory.

Outside, the storm had built to a pyrotechnic wonder. Lightning sizzled over the swamp. In two instances it had struck cypress trees, creating Roman candles against the blackness of the water.

She prayed that Joey was still alive. With the water temperature, she couldn't help but worry. During the day he'd almost frozen. At night it would only be colder. But he was a very strong swimmer, a man in terrific physical shape. She had to think positively.

Laurette's murmur drew her forward in the chair. The fever seemed to have leveled. It had not gone down, as far as she could tell, but it no longer seemed to be climbing. Although she knew it was painful, Cori had mixed table salt and warm water and gently soaked the wound. It was the best she could do to fight infection.

She had also managed to spoon half a cup of broth from the soup into Laurette. Cori had not been able to eat.

The rain started with a burst of noise like bullets assaulting the cabin. At first startled, Cori quickly became entranced by the loud and droning patter of the drops. In a way, it was soothing. She'd always liked rain, especially the gentle afternoon showers of New Orleans. During the summer, it often rained every afternoon, leaving the streets a wash of hues. Corals, reds, browns, traces of the sky picked up in a pale blue. Those rainy streets and the reflection in the puddles of old bricks that made up so many of the French Quarter buildings had been among her favorite subjects to paint.

She had not used watercolors since she'd left New Orleans. Houston had not provided the same inspiration. She had put her talent on hold just like the rest of her life, and Cori felt a sudden, intense regret that she had not painted more. How right Joey had been when he warned her against bartering her talents away. She had done worse, she had squandered her gift.

If she ever got out of this mess, she would not be so quick to let her abilities languish. She would use every minute to its utmost. Make every day count. She vowed to herself that she would face life squarely—head on. No more dodging and weaving; instead, a frontal attack.

She got up and checked on Laurette. Joey's sister had gone into a deeper sleep. Maybe the worst, for Laurette, had been reached. That was, of course, assuming that no one appeared at the cabin to kill them.

Cori returned to the rocker and pushed it back for a better view out the window. There was only rain. More rain. Thick rain, and the continued dazzle of the lightning.

In the quick flashes she could make out the dock, the water, the cypress trees near the dock, the...

Kit's face loomed in the window, his eyes staring hard into her own.

A scream caught in Cori's throat, a lump of fear so large she couldn't let it out.

She swung the gun up to the window, her finger on the trigger and ready. In the next burst of lightning, there was nothing. Just the dock and the trees.

Cori felt her heart pumping. Her hand unsteady, she lowered the shotgun to the floor. Virtually paralyzed by fear, she leaned back in the chair, pushing the floor with her feet until her face was almost pressed against the window. Two minutes passed before the lightning came again, revealing only the old familiar scene. There was no one staring in at her. She had imagined it.

It had to be her guilty conscience. Kit was dead. He could not have been standing there, staring in at her, weeds in his wet hair and on the shoulders of his coat.

"Kit is dead." She whispered the words aloud. "Kit is dead."

The fury of the rain escalated until it was a deafening drum on the tin roof of the cabin. Cori buried herself in the sound, hid in the excess of noise. She chanced a look or two out the window, but the rain was so heavy she couldn't even see the dock. She was isolated in the cabin with Laurette, who slept on.

The hypnotic sound of the rain finally lulled her into a light daze. While her eyes focused on the place where the dock should be, her mind drifted among memories of the past, days centered around Kit and his once-powerful influence in her life. There were snippets of past events, split seconds of time blended with other seconds, a jumbled home movie of her last year in New Orleans.

Lightning smashed into the cypress closest to the dock, and the resounding noise and flare of white-hot illumination made her nearly jump out of her chair. Turning to survey the damage, she again looked straight into the eyes of Kit Wells. He stood on the other side of the glass, drenched and holding a gun directly at her face.

His left hand came up slowly, as if it were being pulled by strings. He motioned to her. "Follow me," the gesture said, while the face was expressionless. A thin line of blood seeped from a wound in his temple.

Heart pounding, Cori didn't move. Kit looked less than alive. Like Frankenstein's monster, the lightning had brought him back to life. He *was* a monster, a member of the walking dead. And he was after her. Cori swallowed the scream and forced her mind back to a more rational track. She had to wait for the next bolt of lightning. She'd imagined him before. Maybe she had been dozing and made up his image in the window, the blank stare in his pale eyes.

Bright light burst outside the window, and Cori stared into Kit's gaze. She couldn't tell if he comprehended what he saw, or if he had any notion of who was on the other side of the window.

"Kit!" Cori could not move. "Kit!" Her whisper was harsh.

She could not hear him, but she could see his mouth form one word. *Goodbye.* He looked directly at her.

JOEY COUNTED THE STROKES as he made his way along the route he knew by heart. The water was freezing, but he thought his body had adjusted. Maybe he was kidding himself. Maybe he was slowly numbing and had simply lost the ability to feel the cold creeping up on him. It didn't matter. He could only swim. He had no choice, since Laurette's boat was gone. They'd either taken it or cut it loose to drift away on the slow current.

There was land throughout the swamps. Not dry land, but land only knee deep in water. During the winter, before the spring floods and summer rains, there were areas where a person could set up a camp. He and Aaron and several other friends had explored the region thoroughly. Even in the blinding rain he could not get lost. His concern wasn't direction, it was endurance and his ability to effect a change in the situation.

He had not told Cori that he suspected the men were camping close by because he didn't want her to panic. The fact that he was storming the enemy alone would make her desperate with worrying—and guilt. Cori was a very complex person, and he recognized that guilt had played a large role in her quest to find Kit alive.

And, by damn, she'd been right. He could only hope he was as right that Aaron had taken the men to some dry land and established a camp. It would be the sensible thing to do. And Aaron was sensible. And smart. He would be thinking of ways to escape, and the only possible route was to get the men out of the boat.

Using a breast stroke, Joey surveyed the dark horizon, looking for the trace of grass that signaled shallower water. In the darkness he was almost on it before he could see it. He slowed his movement, not wanting to disturb the vegetation—or alert any nocturnal creatures that he was bait on the edge of the marsh. Now he would have to be careful.

He'd brought his gun, not certain what good it would do after such a thorough soaking. He hoped he didn't have to rely on it, but at least it *looked* effective. It was a sad state of affairs, but he was down to counting on appearances for help.

He made his way through the darkness to the spot he knew would be solid enough for a boat to pull up onto dry land. As he recalled, there was a slight depression in the center of the island, a good place to shelter from the wind.

In the darkness he almost bumped into the boat before he saw it. Hands braced along the wooden side, he eased toward land and the low murmur of men talking. He could only pray that Aaron was still safe.

Joey felt a lump of affection for his childhood friend. Aaron was willing to risk his own life to protect Joey and the woman he was sworn to keep safe. Joey had to make sure his friend didn't suffer too cruelly for his big heart and loyalty. At the sound of voices he ducked lower in the water.

"Hey, it's going to rain."

The voice came to Joey clearly. The men were exactly where he thought they'd be. The accent was from New Orleans.

"You ain't sugar. You won't melt." The guy sounded mean.

"I ain't no Boy Scout, either. I didn't come here to camp out and sing around the camp fire. I came here to kill the witness. I say we do it and get back to New Orleans. I've got other business to take care of."

"Kit may have taken care of her for us."

"Yeah, and Santa Claus is a real person. Get a grip on reality. If Kit was coming back with her, he'da been back. They got Kit. I guess that little witness was surprised when she found her bridegroom was alive and kickin'." He laughed. "I hear she was determined to find him. She still believed he was alive."

"I told the boss that she was trouble. We shoulda popped her before the first trial."

"You woulda thought," the first man agreed. "Nobody listens to us, though. They wait until things come to a head and then send us in to clean up the mess."

Joey eased forward, taking care not to disturb the grass that fringed the land. He had to find out where Aaron was before he launched his attack. If at all possible, he wanted to make sure his friend had a chance to duck for cover.

Lightning popped and he flattened himself on the ground, but not before he saw the campsite. There was no fire. Either the knoll had not offered any burnable fuel, or the men were being more cautious than they sounded. Joey inched forward in a crawl. He had to spot Aaron—without getting spotted himself.

The men were twenty feet from him, ringed together. One smoked, and though he tried, Joey couldn't identify him in the glow of the ash. These men were hired guns. They could be anyone. He only knew they were local by the way they talked—that strange blend of Brooklyn and Louisiana that sounded European at times, and yet always Southern.

"When are we going in?"

"Just before dawn. There's only Tio and the witness. We hit the other woman and she's down. Tio will have to stay up all night standing guard. He's already tired. He won't be a problem."

"I wish we didn't have to kill a marshal. A lotta crap's going to rain down on us for that. The boss won't be pleased."

"The boss will send us to Mexico for a little vacation. It'll blow over, like always. Our man has got the right connections."

"I still say Kit should have killed her."

"Kit should have done it when he was paid to do it." This was the voice of the third man, the one who had not spoken yet.

"Yeah, well, spilled milk is a mess, but whining about it won't fix it."

There was laughter from the other two men. "Bailey, you couldn't pour piss out of a boot if the instructions were on the heel."

A flash of lightning gave Joey the brief glimpse he needed. The three men were dressed in dark clothing, their bodies illuminated only a moment. They were lean, young hired killers. Aaron was sitting to the left, his arms behind his back and his legs in front of him. Not a comfortable position, but then the killers weren't necessarily concerned about their victim's comfort.

Anger made Joey even more cautious. Whatever he did, he couldn't risk Aaron. Since his friend couldn't get up and run to safety, Joey knew he'd have to construct a diversion.

Easing backward, he felt his way to the boat. The little skiff was Aaron's joy. Joey would see that he got another one. He checked the gas tank. It was half-full. When he cut the gas line, he allowed it to seep over the seasoned wood. Jerking the loose knot free, he cut the boat adrift. When she was easing out into the deeper water, Joey found the lighter in the waterproof pack he carried. Striking the flint, he tossed it into the pooling gas.

The explosion was so fast and so hot that even though he ducked beneath the surface of the water, the sound deafened him. The water rocked over him, a heated blaze of liquid fire. Joey held his breath and swam until he thought his lungs would explode with the same force. When he dared to lift his head and draw in oxygen, he was outside the area illuminated by the burning boat.

"My boat! My boat!" Aaron's voice carried across the water, a cry of terrible loss.

"Shut up!" one of the men ordered. He yelled back at the others. "Stay with him. Somebody's out there, and I'm going to find him." There was an edge of fear in the man's voice.

Joey eased along the edge of the knoll, following the man. When he was as far away from his friends as he could get, Joey tossed the bullet into the still water only ten feet from him.

The gunshots blasted into the swamp only feet from Joey. There was no point in ducking; the shooter couldn't see him. He was firing blind, shooting at anything that moved on the off chance that it might be life threatening.

"You okay, Bailey?" One of the men yelled.

"Yeah, it was nothing." Bailey's voice held embarrassment. "Musta been a turtle."

"It wasn't a turtle that set our boat on fire. Now, how are we going to get out of here?" The man sounded more annoyed than upset.

"We're not going anywhere until we finish our job. I'd rather stay out here and be alligator bait than go back and admit that the witness is still alive."

"Right," Bailey grumbled. "There's nothing here that I can see." He started back.

Joey threw another bullet. The plop was audible, a challenge.

Bailey edged closer to the water. He listened, waiting for the lightning that would give him a chance to see. Joey knew he had to act before that very lightning gave him away. When he heard Bailey turn as if to go back to camp, Joey flung himself out of the water. Before Bailey had a chance to do anything but struggle, Joey pulled him down into the water, holding him under as he fought to get up to air.

Lifting the butt of his gun, Joey brought it down as hard as he could. Bailey ceased to struggle, his body going limp in the cold water.

Joey knew the smart thing would be to kill him, but he dragged him into the shallows and turned him on his back. He was out, but only for a limited time. Joey used the tie line from the boat to secure him. It was a thought that it might be kinder to kill him. Left alive, he could attract an alligator. Joey pulled the knot brutally tight. It was a chance old Bailey would just have to face.

"Hey, Bailey?" Another of the men approached. Joey grabbed Bailey's gun and tucked it in his pants.

Using the same ploy, he subdued the second man. Now there was only one left. Joey walked out of the water and toward the place where the lone killer guarded Aaron.

"Where's Bailey?" the man asked without looking up. He was sitting on his haunches before an old army pack, eating out of a bag.

The night was terribly dark, and Joey had counted on the fact that the man would not recognize him. He walked straight up to him and lashed out with his foot, catching the man just under the chin. He went down like a sack of flour.

"Joey!" Aaron's voice held a real note of relief. "I knew you'd figure out a way to save me." His face darkened. "You didn't blow up my boat, did you? That wasn't you who blew up my *Antoinette?*"

Joey untied his friend's hands. "It was the boat or you. I really liked the boat a lot, but I picked you, anyway."

As soon as Aaron's hands were free he shook them vigorously while Joey untied his feet. "Couldn't you just have cut her adrift?" Aaron asked.

"It would have lacked the visual effect," Joey said. Using the same ropes that had bound Aaron, he tied up the third killer.

"We should shoot them." Aaron wasn't kidding. "They were going to kill us."

"I know. It would be the smart thing, but the way I figure it, they wouldn't dare swim. If they have any brains at all, the thought of what might await them in the black water will keep them on land. I want them alive so I can question them.''

"Are you sure?'' Aaron wasn't ready to let them off so easily.

Joey patted his friend's back. "Find their guns and let's go.''

"Go where? The boat is blown to bits.''

"To the cabin.''

"You want me to swim?'' Aaron made a motion toward the swamp. "The gators will eat us alive.''

"I made it here.''

"Well, we should stay here.''

"Laurette's been shot, and Cori's all alone with her. We have to get back.'' He could picture her, standing at the door, watching for him to come back. It was powerful motivation to make the long, hard swim. That was the image he had to keep focused on. Something positive. Cori St. John.

"Is Laurette hurt bad?''

"She could be if we don't get out of here and get some help.''

"You really want to swim?'' Aaron looked toward the water as if he could make the boat reappear.

"It's going to rain, anyway. If we stand here we'll get just as wet.''

The lightning popped and the sky rumbled. Fat drops peppered the water in front of them.

"Damn, it's cold.'' Aaron shivered. "I guess we might as well swim for it.'' He waded into the water with Joey at his side.

The rain was so hard that Joey swam by instinct. All of the landmarks were obscured by the pelting rain, and at times he had to tread water until he felt Aaron beside him. They did not waste energy talking. Joey knew that he had pushed past the edge of endurance in the cold water already. He could think only of getting to the cabin, of the fire and the hot soup, and the healing warmth of Cori's sweet kisses.

When at last his fingers found the dock, he fumbled before he could get up. Only Aaron's gentle pushing got him up the ladder and onto dry land.

"You're freezing," Aaron said, putting an arm around his friend. "Let's get inside."

Together they lurched up the dock and to the cabin door. Joey knocked lightly, calling Cori's name as they entered.

The fire in the fireplace was out, just a bed of dying embers. The stove was cold, the smell of the soup still in the air. Joey's gaze swept the room. Laurette was sleeping soundly, her chest moving gently up and down.

And Cori was nowhere in sight.

"Where is she?" Aaron asked.

"I wish I knew." Joey felt a sickness in the pit of his stomach. There was no boat, no way for Cori to leave. Where had she gone? Better yet, how had she left? And why?

"What are you going to do?" Aaron asked.

Joey closed the cabin door. Still dripping, he went to the fireplace and built up the fire. Then he felt his sister's forehead. "Her fever is down." At last he picked up a towel and threw it to Aaron while he found one for himself. "I don't know what to do. I don't think Laurette knows where Cori went. I suppose I'll look for her." He didn't have a clue where to begin to hunt. The patch of land was barely a quarter of a mile wide, and a half a mile in length, depending on the tides. It was surrounded by marsh on the west side, and the north end was a jungle of small trees. There was no place Cori could go, and no reason for her to leave the cabin.

Aaron looked out the window. "You won't find any tracks left after this storm. We don't even know how long she's been gone."

"Joey?" Laurette's strained voice silenced anything Joey might have wanted to answer.

He was at her side. "Are you okay?"

"Dreams. Strange dreams." She smiled. "I need some antibiotics."

"And we'll get them." Joey brushed his fingers over her brow. "Where did Cori go?"

Laurette tried to look around the room, but the effort was too much. "She was here. She gave me soup." She smiled. "She's a good girl, Joey. You picked a good one."

"I did." Joey smiled down at his sister. "Now, rest, Laurette. Aaron and I are going to think of a way to get us back to town. Just rest and dream of being at home with Cliff and Angela."

She was asleep before he finished speaking.

Joey stood, acting as calm as possible. He could not show that he wanted to beat the walls down with his fists. He turned to Aaron. "I have to go."

"I'll watch Laurette. Don't worry about your sister. I'll take good care of her. Just find Cori."

THE THICK MUD SUCKED at Cori's shoes, and the rain blinded her. She had given up any attempt to listen for wild beasts in the marshy land she traversed. If an alligator came to eat her, she wouldn't be able to see him coming. Rain, mud, bitter cold and Kit Wells were the only realities.

He was alive.

Somehow, he had managed to survive the alligator attack. He had come back.

By the time she'd gotten to the door, he was gone. The only evidence he'd been there was a trail of blood that was rapidly being swept away by the rain. Using the lantern, she'd examined the bloodstain. She'd touched her finger in it, drawing back the redness. It was real. Kit was real. Her teeth chattered as she clung to that thought. He was real. She had not imagined him.

Leaning against the door, she fought the demons of self-doubt. After weeks of believing that Kit was alive, she'd finally discovered that he was. She'd come for evidence, and she'd found it. Now he was dead. She'd seen the alligator go after him with her own eyes.

Except he'd been standing at the window not two minutes before. Dear God, the man had come back from the dead again. And this time she didn't believe it.

From the closet she borrowed a rain slicker. Gun in hand, she went out the door and into the driving rain. At the bottom of the steps she hesitated, torn between loyalty to Joey and his sister and the image of Kit. It had to end. Kit could not possibly have been there. He was dead. But she had to prove it to herself.

Had the horror of Kit's face begun to unravel the edges of her sanity? She looked at the fingers she'd dipped in the blood. There was no trace of anything except cold rain.

"Kit!" She called his name as she moved steadily away from the cabin. She had never asked Joey how large the tract of land was that the cabin stood on. She turned to look behind her and saw nothing but the driving rain. The lighted window of the cabin was totally hidden by the gray curtain of water. And Laurette? Cori could not leave her for long.

Only long enough to prove to herself that Kit was dead. She would not spend the rest of her life catching glimpses of him out of the corner of her eye.

The heavy pounding of the rain made her dizzy. Leaning against the trunk of a tall, slender tree, she fought for deep breaths. She considered turning back. She knew that she was not acting in a rational manner, and that frightened her more than the thought of seeing Kit's ghost.

She struggled forward through the copse of slender trees, the rain blinding her. The shotgun was slick in her hand, the metal slightly oily. Stumbling forward, she grasped another tree as she went down on her knees. The futility of her search struck home.

In the downpour, she'd lost her direction. The swamp around her was empty. There was no movement, no sign of any other life. Gradually the rain began to lesson.

It stopped as abruptly as it had begun. The sky was still overcast, a roiling gray that spoke of more bad weather to come. The only sound was the rain dripping into water and mud. The ground was covered in dark leaves and sticks. There were no tracks, no trail to follow.

Once again, Kit Wells had led her to a total dead end.

"Cori?"

She swung around to find Joey standing not ten feet from her. His look was strained, pushed to the limit. She couldn't tell if the water on her face was from the rain or her own tears.

"Cori, are you okay?" Joey approached her slowly. She looked broken. When she didn't try to dart away from him he pulled her against him, both of them shivering. He kissed her forehead and her cheeks, and lastly her lips. "What happened? What are you doing out here?"

Cori grasped his hands and pushed away from him. "Did you see him?"

"Who?"

Her voice was panicky. "Kit. He isn't dead. The alligator didn't get him. He was here, I saw him."

Joey finally understood her shivering was not completely from the cold. He'd never felt that Cori was in greater danger.

Chapter Thirteen

"Well, we're one sorry group." Aaron threw a wet log on the fire and let the hiss conclude his commentary. He looked at Cori, who stared sightlessly into the flames, and at Joey, who watched Cori with the intensity of a hawk.

"Laurette's fever is down even more." Aaron shrugged when he realized he was talking to himself. Ever since Joey and Cori had returned, soaked and silent, there had been an air of tension in the cabin that was palpable. They were drier now, but no more talkative.

In the short amount of time that Joey and Cori were together, something had happened, and from the way it looked to him, neither of them knew exactly what it was.

"Joey, why don't you and Cori get some rest. I'll keep watch for a while. When it gets daylight, we're going to have to make some decisions." They had left three men hog-tied on an island that could submerge with a strong tide. According to Cori, there was another man, perhaps severely wounded, somewhere outside the cabin. Laurette was better, but the bullet needed to be extracted, and soon. There was no boat, and Aaron wasn't certain when a fisherman might happen by. There were a lot of things that demanded priority.

"I'll bring in a bit more wood," Joey said. "We can stick it in front of the fire, and maybe it'll dry out a little."

He left the cabin without looking back. The rain had stopped, and the hovering clouds seemed to have trapped some warmth. Dawn was just around the corner, and he could tell already that the day was going to be much warmer. That, if nothing else, was good news. He angled under the cabin and went to the pile of wood that had been carefully gathered for fuel.

They didn't really need more wood, but he hoped the exercise would help clear his thoughts, which had been very confused since he'd found Cori was safe. The feel of her in his arms had been one of the most intense pleasures he'd ever hoped to feel. That was before he started to wonder why she was out in the swamp.

Three days before, she'd been a woman who wanted desperately to believe her husband was alive. Apparently, that hadn't changed. He'd seen the desperation in her eyes. She wanted Kit Wells alive, no matter that he'd tried to kill her.

When he'd first sighted her, slumped against a tree, he'd thought she was mortally wounded, but the wound had been only to her heart. He had seen the look on her face. She was still in love with Kit.

He hefted the ax and brought it down with all of his might. The slender log snapped in two and both halves leaped into the air. He chopped another and felt the beginning of the physical release he needed.

Cori St. John or Brently Gleason. Who was this woman who had crept under his skin? Did he have any idea? Could the past drive her away from him? He brought the ax down with tremendous force. The log snapped and the blade of the ax dug deep into the muddy ground.

AS SOON AS THE CABIN DOOR closed, Cori stood. She paced the room a moment, then made her decision. "I'll go help Joey." She picked up the shotgun as if carrying it were second nature to her.

Outside the cabin she saw the first fingers of dawn streak the sky pale pink. *Red sky in the morning, sailors take warning.* It was something her sister Lane had said as a child. When they had shared a room together and were planning a picnic or swim, Lane would predict the weather. *Red sky at night, sailor's delight.* Cori was sure there were a million variations of the saying, but that was the one Lane had taught her. She made a vow to herself. As soon as she got back to civilization, she would telephone her sister and arrange a visit.

Witness protection be damned. She was going to see her family.

But first she was going to talk to Joey. There was a lot unsaid between them. Too much. She'd been emotionally wrung out and terrified when he'd found her in the woods. Fear for her sanity had made her back away from Joey. Now he'd put up a shield between them, an emotional barrier that she didn't fully understand.

The sound of an ax hitting the solid logs came to her, and she followed the noise to the woodpile behind the cabin. He was a solitary figure against the pinkening sky. Stopping, she watched him heft the ax and bring it down to cleave the slender logs.

She couldn't tell if he saw her or not. He didn't break the rhythm of his work. Carrying the shotgun in the crook of her arm, she walked closer to him. So close that he had to acknowledge her presence.

He let the ax fall beside his foot and leaned on it. "You've got a little more color in your face. That's good."

"I'm okay." She tried to read his expression, but he was careful not to show what he was thinking. What had changed between them so suddenly? She was in his arms one moment, and the next . . .

"I think if we can get out of here, Laurette will be fine."

"I think so," she agreed. "And you? Will you be fine?"

Joey lifted the ax and acted as if he were going to ignore her question and split more wood. Slowly, he lowered it to the ground. "I'm worried about you."

Emboldened by the tone of his voice, she walked up to him and put her hand on his face. "I'm going to be okay, Joey."

"Eventually, maybe." He turned away and lifted the ax. "This business with Kit . . ."

"I know." There was nothing else she could say. She knew that her actions had made her look insane. Standing beside Joey, she didn't believe she'd seen Kit. It had to have been her imagination. There was no way he could have survived an alligator attack. Yet . . . yet she *had* seen him.

"No, I don't think you do know. It's not the fact that you think you saw him. It was dark, storming, your eyes could have played tricks on you. I won't say it doesn't concern me, because it does. This obsession you have with Kit Wells concerns me greatly. But the heart of the matter is that you went out after him. A man who tried to kill you. A man who could have killed my sister. You left Laurette unprotected while you chased after the past."

"Not the past!" Cori needed to make him see. "I had to make certain, Joey. Kit is dead, or he's not. I saw him killed, and then I saw him again in the window. Don't you understand? I can't go on having him pop out of every dark corner, peering through every window when the lights are out."

"I have a lot of concerns. About you. About us. It isn't the past that troubles me, it's the future." He kicked several pieces of wood out of the way. "Maybe when the re-trial is over we can see what's between us." That wasn't what he wanted, but Cori was too close to the edge. Way too close. He'd seen it in her face as she stood in the rain in the middle of the woods. Hunting a dead man. The last thing she needed was pressure from him.

She nodded. So, Joey had come to the conclusion that the night they'd shared together had been a mistake. She was a witness, someone who would testify and then . . . move on. When they relocated her out-of-state again, there was no telling where she'd end up. Joey would manage to get his job back and his life would resume. With his friends and family, his work.

Their paths had crossed for one brief period of time. She'd seen the handwriting on the wall; she'd just refused to read it.

"It's okay," she said, trying to force a smile that would not materialize. "You don't have to think up an explanation. I think I know all the reasons."

He looked at her. "The reasons?"

"We're traveling in different directions, et cetera, et cetera. I thought of all that, too." She found a smile, even though it was small and sad. "I guess I just didn't want to accept the truth."

"So that's what you think." Joey gripped the ax handle, knowing that somewhere Kit Wells played a role in her thoughts, whether she would admit it or not.

"I've gotten pretty good at accepting some hard facts lately. The man I married set me up and used me and then tried to abduct me so he could kill me. I had to give up the way I wanted the past to be and look at it straight on. I see a lot of things about myself that I don't really like. I was afraid to confront the truth, I think. I never asked Kit the questions I needed to. It was enough that he wanted to marry me. I should have asked why." She looked down at the wood Joey had been chopping. "I went after Kit because I didn't want to live like that anymore. I don't want to hide my head in the sand and hope for the best. I wanted to find him, dead or alive. To be honest, I didn't really care which."

Joey let the ax fall sideways. A smile lifted the corners of his mouth. "You weren't chasing after him, clinging to some hope that you could follow him back to the past?"

Cori shook her head. "A life with Kit is the last thing I'd want. I want to live, with a real future, not just a tragic past."

Joey touched her cheek. "Are you sure you're okay?"

His touch, the concern for her, blanketed her in what might have been. She closed her eyes for a few seconds, savoring the feel of him. When she opened them, she knew she had really changed. "I'm okay, Joey. I'm fine."

"When I got to the cabin and you were gone, I was terrified that someone had taken you. Not because it was my job to protect you, but because I've come to care about you. Maybe too much. That's a problem for me, Cori."

Those words were the warning. Cori recognized them for what they were. She'd been living those words for the past two years. Life had required too much. Too much risk, too much energy, too much desire to live. So she had avoided living. Avoided risk and all of the attendant potential heartbreaks.

"I was sick with worry about you, too," she said carefully.

"I know." He let his thumb trace her cheekbone. "Oh, I know." He took another breath. "Anyway, I found that you weren't hurt. That you followed a known killer into the swamps." He hesitated. "I guess it crossed my mind that maybe you'd chosen to go with him, that you were running away from me, and from testifying."

"Is it that important to you that I testify?"

Joey dropped his hand. "That's what this is all about. That's why Laurette was shot. They want to prevent you from testifying."

"And if I decide not to testify?"

"Then all of this will have been for nothing. But it's your choice."

"So that's the bottom line. I testify, and you've done your job. I'll be free to assume a new identity."

He heard the anger, but he didn't understand its source. He was telling her that she had a choice. Three days before, he wouldn't have considered giving her one. His job had been to protect her until she was due on the witness stand. A clear-cut job. Her happiness hadn't figured into it.

"What do you want me to say?" he asked.

"Nothing." She turned away. "I'll take some of that wood inside." She picked up an armload and walked back to the cabin. She could feel his eyes on her back as she walked. She held herself erect and her head high.

With her arms loaded with wood, the climb up the stairs required some effort, but she managed to kick the door and alert Aaron to open it. She put the wood down in front of the fire and went to the kitchen.

Aaron paced in the living room area. "Did Joey say anything?"

"No." Cori had to struggle not to sound sharp. "Nothing about *his* future plans." She cracked eggs in a bowl and stoked up the fire in the stove. "He'll be in soon. There's not enough wood left to keep him busy much longer."

Aaron heard the tension and chose not to ask. He returned to cleaning the guns. "I'll do this for you," he said, picking up the shotgun. "Next time, I'll teach you."

"Let's just hope there isn't a next time."

The sound of a boat approaching hushed them both.

"It's fast," Aaron observed. "Nobody I know."

She took the gun he handed her, loading it with an expertise she'd never suspected she possessed. Snapping the breach shut, she went to the window. Joey was coming up the stairs, fast.

The door burst open and he was inside, checking his own weapons.

"What's the plan?" Aaron asked.

"We'll wait it out here. We can look out for one another better from this vantage point."

Aaron picked up a rifle and took a position in the window opposite Joey. Cori stood backup, her lungs banded by a grip of iron as the boat came closer and closer.

"Look, there's some guy in the front waving at us." Joey motioned for Aaron and Cori to lower their guns. "It looks like . . . Ken Applewhite."

"Who?" Cori and Aaron asked simultaneously.

"Ken. He's from my office."

"Well, damn if it's not the cavalry," Aaron said as he recognized the official lettering on the blue jackets the men wore. "We've been rescued."

CORI STEPPED INTO THE BOAT, taking care not to rock Laurette any more than she had to. She sank down beside the injured woman, taking her head in her lap. "Okay." She looked up at the U.S. Marshals. "We're ready."

"Take care of Laurette," Aaron said as he waved from the dock. "Me and Joey, we'll be along." He smiled but he couldn't hide the concern. Joey was not on the dock to say goodbye. He was in the cabin plotting the roundup of the killers with the three officers who had remained behind to help him. Aaron would stay also, waiting for another boat to be sent from Henderson.

Cori looked behind Aaron, hoping that Joey would at least wave to her from the cabin. There was no face at the window, no sign of him in the doorway. He had turned her over to the system. She was now back in custody in the witness protection program.

Whether she was going to testify or not was an issue she had not come to a clear determination on. The fact that she had been lied to about Kit's fate nagged at her. What other facts had been withheld?

She felt manipulated and used, and at this point, she wasn't certain who was the mastermind behind it. It could be the legal system as well as the men who'd hired Kit to kill her.

And Kit. No matter how she tried to convince herself that she'd imagined his face at the window, she still believed he was somewhere on that tiny little patch of land that contained the cabin. Joey and the deputies would find him soon. And then? The questions that had burned in her a week ago no longer seemed important.

Would Kit's answers help her decision about testifying and rejoining the witness protection program?

Whatever she decided, she couldn't allow herself to be influenced by the hurt she felt at the thought of Joey. He'd turned her over to his associates without batting an eye, almost as if it were a relief to be rid of his responsibility for her. He had not asked them where they would take her. He had not asked if he could see her. The exchange had been silent. No one viewed her as a creature with needs and emotions. She was a witness, plain and simple. A regurgitator of facts.

The boat motored through the swamp, guided by a fisherman who knew Joey, Laurette and Aaron. The old man kept casting worried looks at Laurette. Each time she moaned, he notched the throttle a tiny bit higher until Cori finally put aside her tormenting thoughts and concentrated on keeping perfectly still in the boat. One slight movement might tip them all over.

When the boat pulled into the landing at Henderson, Cori was met with the flashing light of an ambulance. The siren was blessedly silent, but the attendants were on the dock with a stretcher, waiting for Laurette. As Cori started to climb into the ambulance with her, she felt a hand on her shoulder.

"We're going back to New Orleans."

She shook off his hand. "I'm going to the hospital with Laurette. She's alone. Her brother is still out in the swamp, doing his job. Laurette needs me."

"Her family has been notified. Her husband is flying in from Atlanta." The grip tightened. "I'm sorry, Ms. St. John, but you have to come with us."

The flat voice held the tone of an arresting officer. Ken Applewhite had not a flicker of personality. And Cori suspected that he was not a friend of Joey's.

"I don't have to do a damn thing." She put a foot in the ambulance and started in.

Applewhite's hand jerked her backward and spun her so that she was facing the side of the ambulance, his hand on the back of her neck.

"Sorry it has to be this way, Ms. St. John, but you've caused enough trouble." He clicked the cuffs into place. "Now, we have a patrol car waiting for you. You're going to get in the back seat, and you're going to ride back to New Orleans without making trouble, is that understood?"

She gritted her teeth. "You had better take your hand off me."

"You forget, Ms. St. John, you're not in the business of giving orders here."

"I am a protected witness."

"Not anymore. You are a witness in protective custody. That puts you about one rung higher than an arrested criminal." He pulled her away from the ambulance and twisted her so that she faced him. His teeth were clenched together and his green eyes were hard as unpolished stone. "You've caused enough trouble. People are getting hurt because of you, and I for one have had enough of handling you with kid gloves. You're about to see the other side of law enforcement."

"Believe me, I've seen it." Cori felt a tidal wave of fury, but she knew she had to keep her cool. "Can I simply ride to the hospital with Laurette?"

"No."

"Then let me tell her goodbye."

Applewhite led her to the back of the ambulance. "Make it fast."

With her hands cuffed behind her, Cori couldn't climb into the ambulance. "Laurette, I've got to go back to New Orleans. Joey will be here soon. And your husband is on the way."

"I'll be okay." Laurette's voice was weak, but she managed to lift her head. "Are you okay?"

"Fine," Cori reassured her. "I'll be fine."

"That's it," Applewhite said. "We've got to head out."

Cori forced herself not to resist as the marshal led her to the waiting patrol car.

MOST OF THE WAY BACK to New Orleans, Cori dozed in the back seat. Applewhite had released her hands when she'd offered no resistance. There were a million questions to ask, but she knew there was no point in asking him. She'd wait until Joey got back.

As they made their way into the busy city, Cori watched the familiar landmarks pass and wondered where they would take her. City jail? If she was in custody, that seemed the obvious answer. The thought was scary, but she was determined not to show that she was afraid.

As they pulled into the building that housed the federal officers, she tried to compose herself. At least there would be word of Joey. And Kit. They would have found him by now.

"Let's go." Applewhite opened the door and helped her out. "Clayton Bascombe wants to see you."

She didn't bother to ask why. She knew. She'd violated the agreement she'd made and now she was in big trouble. Clayton Bascombe had been the marshal who'd worked with her when she'd first entered the WP program.

She followed Applewhite inside and took a seat in a waiting room. Another officer stood at the door. Making sure she didn't make a run for it, she supposed.

Her wait was short. The door opened, and she was ushered into the room she remembered from two years before. Clayton Bascombe was a balding man with a patient smile.

"You're not injured are you, Ms. Wells?"

For a split second, Cori had forgotten that he'd known her as Brently Gleason Wells. "I've adapted to Cori St. John," she told him, "and I'm not hurt. I'm just very tired."

"Ken has given me an update." Bascombe frowned. "The question now is what to do with you. You realize that you can be called to testify against your will. As a material witness, you don't have a choice."

"I know that."

"Ben DeCarlo's retrial is only weeks way. We can hold you in protective custody until that time."

"I'm aware of that." Cori felt Bascombe took no pleasure in wielding his authority over her. He was stating the facts, and she was already aware of her limited range of choice now.

"We can detain you in jail, which I am loathe to do."

She waited. She'd never been in the city lockup, but she'd heard about the crowded conditions, the violence.

"Or we can put you in a safe house. It's up to you. One requires your cooperation. The other..." He didn't finish.

"Right now, I'd like a bath or shower and some clean clothes."

"That can be arranged." He picked up a folder. "What is your attitude about testifying?"

"I came to New Orleans to find my husband. I suppose you've been told that Kit was alive, and that he found me."

Bascombe nodded. "We were led to believe that he was dead, Ms.... St. John. Needless to say, we would have notified you if we'd had the slightest inkling that Detective Wells was still alive." A puzzled look crossed his face. "I expect Mr. Tio will be able to clarify some of these issues when he comes in."

"Have you captured Kit?"

Bascombe tapped the file against his palm. "I hesitate to tell you, but I think you have a right to know. No, he was not taken. We have two men in custody. Kit Wells and another of the men escaped."

Cori didn't believe it for a moment. They'd lied to her before, knowingly or not. Information that was supposed to be secret—such as her identity and location in Houston—had somehow been leaked. She had no reason to trust the man who stood before her.

"I don't believe you," she said, rising. "There was no way for Kit to escape. If you didn't capture him, then he's dead. And you wouldn't tell me the truth if he were dead. The entire time I've been involved in this mess I've been lied to by someone. Don't take it personally, but I don't trust anyone. Now, if I could go to that house you were talking about."

Bascombe rose, too. "I assure you, Ms. St. John, Kit Wells was not killed by the marshals or any of the other law enforcement officials on the scene. Two men were taken into custody. Neither of them was Kit Wells."

Cori felt bone weary.

"We'll keep a twenty-four-hour guard on you. No one should be able to find the house. And the time before the trial will pass quickly. Someone from the prosecutor's office will be in touch with you in a couple of days."

"Of course."

"Ms. St. John." He came around the desk. "I know you feel betrayed. Please don't let that color the truth when you take the witness stand. Keep in mind that Ben DeCarlo is a very dangerous man. He committed an atrocious act. He deserves to be punished."

"And I was deliberately set up as a witness to that act." Cori couldn't help her anger. "You're damn right I feel betrayed. By everyone involved in this. What happens to me after the trial?"

"Another identity. Another location. You'll be placed back in the program, as long as you cooperate."

"Will you send Joey out to the house?"

"I think it would be best if Mr. Tio backed away from this case. You'll be assigned a new handler."

Panic was the first emotion she felt, and she fought it back. "I need to speak with Joey."

"That wouldn't be wise for him. His career is already at stake. He's too involved in this case. He's lost his professional judgment. He'll be moved to other cases. Very likely another assignment post. As hard as it may be to believe, I'm taking his best interests into consideration. And yours."

Chapter Fourteen

The car that waited for her was unmarked. The man driving it was someone she didn't know. He opened the front door and put her inside. "I'm to stop somewhere and get you some clothes. I'll need a list of your sizes and preferences."

"Okay." She didn't care if she wore a flour sack. She would never see Joey again. He, too, would disappear from her life as if some hideous black magic had spirited him away.

They turned out of the parking lot and into the line of motorists. Cori glanced out the window, not interested, not really seeing anything at all.

Except the man with the thin face who had stepped out of the shadows near the federal building.

"Hey!" She pointed at the man.

"What is it?" The driver's hand went automatically to the gun concealed beneath his jacket. He brought it out at the same time he braked. "What is it?" he repeated, searching the area where she'd pointed.

"It was Danny Dupray. What's he doing hanging around the marshals?" Cori's weariness fled and a sick feeling of dread replaced it. What was Dupray doing there? Selling information? Or buying it?

"I didn't see anyone." The marshal surveyed the area while cars behind him honked and revved their engines.

Cori glanced at him, suddenly alert and completely distrustful. It was possible he hadn't seen Dupray. And then again he might have. She settled back in the seat. "Never mind. It was just someone who reminded me of...someone from my past."

He stepped on the gas and headed away.

"There's a shop in the Riverwalk. Could we stop there and get some clothes? I know exactly what to get. I won't have to try anything on." She didn't give a hoot in hell about clothes. She had to figure out some way to get him to stop the car and let her out. Some place where he wouldn't be able to watch every move she made. Shopping was the only excuse she could muster.

"I'm to take you straight to the house." He didn't look at her. "Just write down what you want, the correct sizes, where you want it purchased, and I'll make sure you get it."

"I'd really rather get the things myself."

"I'm sorry."

She sighed. "It's okay." With her past behavior, it wasn't going to be easy to escape. What was Danny Dupray doing hanging out with the federal marshals? Certainly no one was going to give her any answers, and she couldn't afford to wait around and find out. She might be on a ride to her own execution.

The car slowed and stopped at a red light. Canal Street, one of the major arteries of the downtown area, was swarming with pedestrians, cars, buses. Cori felt her body tense. They weren't too far from the Quarter, and Cori knew that was her best bet. She'd lived there. She knew many of the alleys and small private patios behind houses. If she could only get out of the car, she might stand a chance of getting away. And then what? She'd have to find someplace safe to go. Someplace where no one could find her until she figured out how to get out of town.

Her car was in the Riverwalk parking lot, unless they'd towed it away. There was no guarantee they hadn't done that, but she had to hope it was there. She'd kept her small handbag with her, with credit cards she could no longer afford to use because they were so easily traceable, and her keys. She had less than a hundred dollars in cash. Her mind spun onward with the tiny details that her survival now depended upon.

"Damn." The driver tried to edge into another lane of traffic because the right lane was stalled as a carload of six women began to unload in front of a shoe store. Without hesitation, Cori grabbed the door, pushed it open and jumped out into the street.

"Hey!" He reached for her and caught her sweater.

Cori tugged. Hard. And she was free, running as fast as she could through the crowd of pedestrians that choked the corner and waited for the light to walk. She ran with speed she never knew she had, making her way toward the old part of town where the brick streets were familiar and her only hope of hiding lay.

"Stop her!" She heard the marshal behind her call out. His panic produced some worried glances, but no one reached out to stop her. Before the marshal could get out of the car and pursue her, she was free.

JOEY STOOD AT THE EDGE of the swamp looking into the distance. The two airboats that had been brought from the parish sheriff's office had combed the swamp. Deputies had swarmed the small spit of swampland, but it had been Aaron who found the gun with the silencer, dropped in the mud, empty. Kit Wells was alive, and somehow he'd managed to escape with the assistance of the man called Bailey.

Joey thought of Cori and wanted to break something. She *had* seen Kit. He had doubted her, which was understandable. Kit had haunted them both—to the point that Joey was almost ready to believe in voodoo. What was unforgivable was that he had doubted her because he'd felt betrayed. When he'd seen her, bedraggled, terrified, blindly going after a man who'd tried to kill her, his good sense had fled and his defenses had gone up. He'd protected his heart instead of Cori.

He waved to the men on the airboat. He'd combed every inch of land, and they'd searched every foot of the areas covered by water. At last they found the muddy tracks disappearing into the marsh grass. Kit Wells had once again pulled his disappearing act.

"Let's go." Aaron walked up to him, covered in mud and wet from the knees down. "Laurette is fine. They got the bullet out and Cliff is with her. They radioed from the hospital. They've got the two men you hog-tied in Lafayette." Aaron's tone darkened. "Maybe you should go question them. I mean really question them. Since their pal left them for bait, they may be willing to talk."

"Don't worry, I'll have a few words with them."

"Where the other one went, who knows." Aaron looked out over the swamp. "Maybe Mr. Gator finally got his breakfast."

"Two, Aaron. The other two." Kit Wells and the man named Bailey. Bailey had abandoned the other two hit men, but he'd picked up Kit. "Aaron, did you call my office before you let those men abduct you?"

"You said not to, Joey. I did it the way you said. I hung around the fishing camp and waited for them to find your fancy car. Then I said I knew the swamps, and when they pulled the gun on me I let them convince me to take them, just like you said."

"Someone had to have called the office and given directions or else these guys would never have found us. Someone who knew how to get here."

"It's a good thing, whoever did it. We'd still be sitting here wondering how to get back." Aaron took his friend's arm. "Don't be angry, but I'm pretty sure it was Laurette who called. She was worried about you. She thought you were going to lose your job."

Joey nodded. Aaron was right. It was Laurette, doing her best to cover his posterior. And Aaron was right about another thing, too. It was good that someone had called or they would still be stranded there, with Laurette's wound building up more and more infection.

"When we get to Lafayette, can I ask those two guys some questions?" Aaron was tired, but the idea of wringing some facts from the two captives was more enticing than sleep.

"Not officially."

"That's exactly my point. Officially, I'm afraid you can't ask them forcefully enough. I, on the other hand, as a regular citizen, can ask in a way that they'll know I want the whole truth and nothing but the truth."

Joey looked at Aaron's bulging arm muscles. "I can't condone acts of violence against prisoners."

"You don't have to condone anything. You just have to step out of the room. I want them to tell me who sent them."

Joey smiled. "That's exactly what I intend to find out. And about Kit and Bailey."

"That, too," Aaron agreed. They could see the cabin in the distance, and they increased their pace. "We need to restock the cabin and season some more wood. After Cori testifies, I think you should bring her back here. You know, just the two of you, for a few days."

"I'll leave the restocking to you. I may not be back for a while." Joey, in fact, had no idea if he'd have a job once he got back to New Orleans. He hadn't exactly been a model employee. They walked out on the dock, their footsteps giving a haunted echo on the rain-soaked wood. Deputies from two parishes were standing in a small group at the boat, waiting. "When they radioed the information about Laurette, did they say anything about Cori?"

"Naw." Aaron picked up the two bags that someone had packed. In it were Joey's things, as well as Cori's and what Laurette had brought for herself. "Those men may tell you something, but they won't talk to me."

The deputy who held the tie line pointed at Joey as they walked up. "Hey, Applewhite just radioed in. They want you in New Orleans as soon as you can get there." He held the boat steady as Joey and Aaron got on. "They said it was urgent."

"Urgent?" What could be urgent now? "I need to question those two guys you took into custody."

The deputy shrugged one shoulder. "It's your butt, Tio. Applewhite didn't sound really happy."

"He's never happy." Joey felt an unexplainable sense of dread. "Did he say what was wrong?"

"He said that female witness you had out here had escaped from custody." The deputy couldn't deny himself a dig at the federal agents. "She must be a regular Houdini. Seems you boys can't keep her in custody longer than an hour or two."

"Escaped?" The very word made Joey angry. "Escaped from what?"

"They took her into custody as a material witness. When they were transporting her to the safe house, she jumped out of the car."

"She's somewhere in New Orleans, without protection?"

"That's what the man said."

Joey signaled to the officer in the rear to start the motor. "Let's get out of here," he said.

"I'll see to Laurette," Aaron told him. "You go after Cori." His brow was furrowed. "Why would she run away, Joey? Those men who want to kill her are still out there."

"I don't know why Cori would do that. Not yet. But I'm going to find her and find out."

The powerful boat cruised through the narrow canals and finally into a broader waterway. When at last land was in sight, Joey stood, ready to jump on the dock and steady the boat for the others to get off. He turned to the deputy. "Make sure those two men are charged with attempted murder. Ask your sheriff to hold them without bail, if he can. Once bail is set they'll never be seen again. I'll be back to question them when I can."

"We'll do what we can." The deputy waved down at the boat. "And we'll send a bill for all of this. You federal cops have a lot bigger budget than us locals do."

Joey didn't bother to respond. He dug his keys out of his pocket and ran to his car. It was close to three hours to New Orleans. How fast could he make it? And would he be in time to save Cori?

CORI INSTINCTIVELY HEADED for the areas of the Quarter where the tourists flocked. She could blend in more easily there, maybe find someone she knew. But could she embroil another innocent person in what was a fight for her life? The idea of calling her sister seemed wonderfully appealing, but Lane was more than a thousand miles away, in New York City. There was nothing her big sister could do now to help her. Without Joey, Cori knew she was on her own.

Had she jumped the gun by running away from the marshals? She didn't have an answer to that, but the very idea that Danny Dupray was comfortable entering and exiting the federal building was something she couldn't risk. Since Joey was out of the picture, she could trust no one but herself.

Ducking into a discount store she purchased a few necessary times and then recounted her money. She had only fifty-eight dollars left. There were plenty of fleabag hotels she could get for less than forty dollars a night, but it was cash up front. That would leave eighteen. She couldn't survive much longer than a day. She had to get to her car, but not until dark. If it was still in the parking lot, chances were that the marshals were smart enough to have it staked out. She'd wait until the last moment before she risked that.

The clerk in the store was eyeing her suspiciously, and Cori realized she was standing at the door as if she were in a daze—or intending to make a clumsy try at shoplifting. She went outside onto the street and hesitated again.

She had no idea what to do. How could she hide when she wasn't even certain who was after her? She walked two blocks to a bakery and bought a bagel and a cup of coffee. She wasn't hungry, but she hadn't eaten, and she knew she would need the energy. The bakery had small tables, and she took a seat, watching the people pass outside the window.

The faces were bright with laughter and anticipation of the coming holiday. She had simply forgotten all about Christmas. The past forty-eight hours had put her in a time zone that was outside the normal experience of the thousands of people marching up and down the sidewalk, huge shopping bags in their hands, laughter lighting their faces.

The coffee tasted bitter, and she added several spoonfuls of sugar. Once she had loved the Christmas season, but now...the very thought anchored her heart with sadness. She swallowed the last of the bagel and stood up.

A pay telephone in a corner of the shop caught her eye. There was one person she could risk calling. Someone who'd been in a tight place before, who knew Danny Dupray and might be able to give her a line on him.

Cori hesitated. She wasn't certain she could trust Jolene not to talk to Joey, and this time she didn't want Joey involved. He'd risked his life, Laurette's life and Aaron's in his determination to carry out his duty. Whatever happened, she didn't want Joey put at risk again. But there was also the very real possibility that Joey might not even make it back to New Orleans. If he'd been transferred, he might be on a plane at this very minute. Clayton Bascombe had not been happy with his marshal.

Searching a quarter out of the bottom of her purse, she picked up the directory and found a small white-page listing for Chez Jolene. The quarter almost slipped from her grip as she inserted it. Forcing herself to be firm, she punched in the number.

The one thing she had not expected was an answering machine. Jolene's cheerful voice said she wasn't in but to leave a message at the beep. The call would be returned.

"Jolene, this is Cori. Please don't tell anyone I've called you. I'm in big trouble. I had to run away from the marshals. Danny Dupray was down at their headquarters, and it frightened me. I was afraid I was being set up. I don't have much money and I don't know what to do. I'll call back in an hour." She hung up, picked up her shopping bag and went back into the street.

She had an hour to kill, and she had to find a safe place to hide while the minutes ticked away.

She heard the tolling of the bell, marking the hour at three o'clock. She had two hours of daylight left. They would come after her in the darkness, and she had to be secure by then. If only it had been possible to bring the shotgun Laurette had taught her to use. The irony of that thought made her smile. She could see herself strolling along the Quarter, shopping bag in one hand, shotgun in the other.

A patrol car turned the corner and she darted into the doorway of a leather shop. It struck her that the perfect hiding place was not far away, and no one would ever think to look for her there. Elated at the idea, she waited until the patrol car was gone. Then she made a beeline for St. Louis Cathedral. She could stay there for an hour, in the peace and quiet. And goodness knew, if she'd ever needed an hour of prayer, this was the time.

THE URGE TO RUN the car up on the sidewalk was almost too great to resist, but Joey managed to keep himself, and the car, under rigid control. It was three-thirty. The day was waning, and he had to get to the office. How had they let Cori escape? Alone, in the city, she didn't stand a chance. And she didn't even know for certain that Kit was still on the loose. He pounded the steering wheel with the ball of his hand and silently urged the clogged traffic to move.

This was his fault. He'd had a moment of doubt about Cori and her actions, and he'd allowed her to be taken from him. Never, never should he have let her leave his side.

He could see now that the forces moving around Cori were bigger than he'd expected. Bigger than either of them knew. There had to be someone placed high in the U.S. Marshals or in the NOPD who worked hand in glove with the people who wanted to kill Cori.

There had been too many leaks, beginning with her address in Houston. That information had come from a file that no one should have had access to except himself. Only another law officer could have possibly obtained that information. But it could be someone from any branch of law enforcement—marshals, police officers, court officials. The WP program was extremely well protected, but like any other system there were glitches. This particular glitch could cost Cori her life.

He slammed the steering wheel again. If he had been thinking, he would have put all of this together much sooner. Maybe even soon enough to save Cori's life.

His list of potential suspects was an arm long. There were too many people who had access, too many people who might succumb to the temptation of a big hunk of cash. It was often said that law enforcement officers and criminals were divided by a thin line. He'd never personally bought into that theory, but Cori's life hung in the balance. At this point, he didn't trust anyone except Laurette and Aaron. It didn't escape his attention that they weren't cops—and Kit Wells had been.

He traced the Danny Dupray connection with Kit. The two had joined forces with Danny as Kit's stoolie. The bribe to use Cori as a witness had probably come through Danny. It made sense, because Kit would have noticed Cori's acute memory when he took the complaint call she'd lodged against Danny and his treatment of the women who worked at the Twinkle.

Kit had obviously made it a point to start wooing Cori, a fact that made Joey's hand clench the padded steering wheel with a white-knuckled grip. Kit had dated her and set her up perfectly. Whatever the payoff had been, it had been worth a year of his time to continue to court Cori, even going through with a marriage ceremony. Spending time with Cori wouldn't have been hard duty, but whoever was behind Kit had plenty of money. Plenty. And that ruled out middle-level players like Danny. He had to look higher than that. And he had to figure out the motive.

Kit had been paid for having the perfect witness to a murder. He had provided that witness and kept her pacified until the trial. He'd seen to it that she testified, and then he had abandoned her to the WP program where she would be safe. So far that made perfect sense—to a criminal mind.

But Kit had returned and attempted to lure Cori back to New Orleans so she could be killed. That scenario had two purposes. One, Cori wouldn't be able to testify in Ben DeCarlo's retrial. Two, her death would serve the purpose of scaring off the remaining three witnesses. That was exactly what had happened to Emmet Wyatt. Joey knew for certain that Wyatt's death hadn't been a random act of violence, or the cross-purposes of some other deal Wyatt had involved himself in. He'd been brutally murdered to shut him up and to hold him up as an example to the remaining witnesses.

The problem was that the two uses of Cori were at cross-purposes—first to testify, now not to testify. And Kit was the common link. Had he switched sides? Had Ben DeCarlo gotten to him and paid him more than his original master? Those were the questions that had to be answered if Cori stood a chance of living.

At last he turned into the federal building. He didn't bother parking; he left the car in the first empty area and bounded inside.

Rushing through the maze of offices that marked all institutional complexes, he threw open the door of his office. Ken Applewhite looked up, startled, from Joey's desk. He closed the file he'd been reading. "We didn't expect you so soon."

"So I can tell." Joey closed the door and forced his fingers to unclench. He could feel them around Applewhite's throat. He lunged over the desk and grabbed the other marshal. "You'd better tell me what you're doing in here, or you're going to die a very painful death."

Applewhite's face paled, his freckles standing out in bold relief. "I was looking for your sister's home phone number. Her husband called and said it was urgent that he talk to you. He was upset and forgot to leave the number so I thought I'd pull it from your file. I was going to leave a message at her house in case you went there first."

"Right." Joey's white-hot rage made him want to do something that would cause the man he held great pain. "If anything happens to Cori, I'm going to make you regret the day you were born. I may go to prison, but I'll go a satisfied man that I've left pieces of you all over this city."

"Take your hands off me, Tio." Applewhite had regained his composure somewhat. "Call your brother-in-law."

Joey had no choice but to let him go. He slowly released him, but his gaze never wavered. "I mean it. I'll find out who's been leaking information out of here. If it's you, you'd better contact your priest. You won't have time for the final rites when I get hold of you."

"Making threats against a fellow officer is a crime." Applewhite straightened his tie.

"Murder is a crime. Selling information to thugs is a crime. There are lots of crimes going on here. If you're involved, you won't get a chance to hire a lawyer and get out of it."

"Chill out, Tio. You're in enough trouble here. Bascombe is ready to fire you, and after this display, that may be a good idea."

"Get out of my office while you still can." Joey picked up the file. It was his personnel jacket. Was Applewhite getting ready to sell information on Joey's family, or had he really been looking up Laurette's home phone number?

"You better cool it, Tio. That temper is going to get you in a big, bad mess." Applewhite opened the door and slammed it hard behind him.

Joey walked behind his desk and found a telephone message from Cliff at the Lafayette hospital. Fear for Laurette seized Joey, and he dialed. Cliff's voice, slow and steady, calmed Joey immediately.

"How's Laurette?" Joey asked, not even bothering to identify himself.

"She's better, Joey. She's worried about you. As soon as she came out from under the anesthesia she started nagging me to call you. She remembered something, or she dreamed something. Anyway, she's been on fire to have me tell you."

"What is it?"

"She said when she was in the emergency room waiting for them to take her into surgery, a police officer came in. He said he had to question her. She was woozy from the medicine they'd given her, and she knew it wasn't right. A real cop wouldn't have done such a thing."

Joey felt his apprehension begin to build again. "What did he want?"

"It was about Cori. He wanted to know where she was going."

"Did Laurette tell him?"

"She didn't know. Only to New Orleans."

"Was this man in uniform?"

"That was the strange part. He was. And she recognized the uniform as NOPD. When she came to, she was wondering why a New Orleans city cop would be in Lafayatte asking questions about a federal case."

"Was the guy tall and blond?"

"That's him," Cliff said. His voice grew more excited.

Joey leaned on his desk. Kit had returned, once again. And he'd brazenly walked into a hospital in uniform.

"Thanks, Cliff. And thank Laurette."

"How's Cori?" Cliff asked. "Laurette will be mad if I don't have an answer."

"Cori is fine." Joey lied through his teeth, but there was no point upsetting Laurette when she needed to concentrate on getting well. "Everything is fine here. You just take care of my sister."

"You got it."

Joey had no sooner put down the telephone when it rang again. He picked it up, expecting to hear Clayton Bascombe's voice ordering him into the office.

"Joey, it's Jolene." She sounded tentative, unsure. "I just got the strangest telephone message from Cori. She begged me not to tell anyone, but she sounds desperate. She's going to call me back at four."

Joey checked his watch. He had less than twenty minutes to get to Jolene's before the call. He'd have to make it.

"I'm on the way. Keep her on the line, Jolene. Keep her talking until I can get there. I have to tell her something." He hung up the phone and started out of his office only to run smack into the full figure of Clayton Bascombe.

"Tio, I want to see you in my office."

Joey didn't hesitate. "Not now." He held up both hands in a plea as he hurried out of the office in a backward trot. "There's no time for you to fire me. It can wait until tomorrow." He turned and ran.

He pushed the Supra to the maximum on every open stretch of road, brutally cutting in and out of traffic. Behind him horns blared and people made ugly gestures. He didn't slow.

He pulled into the quiet neighborhood that was sheltered by the huge old oaks, and he felt his anxiety begin to level out. He had made it. It was 3:58. Two minutes to spare. He left the car door open and ran to Jolene's house. The front door was unlocked, waiting for him.

"Jolene!" He called her name. "Jolene!"

Empty air answered him. Chills touched his lower back, creeping up his spine. He stepped into the living room and was surprised to find the French doors open wide, the sheer curtains billowing on the chill December air. On the stereo there was the sound of Christmas music, horns softly playing "Joy to the World."

"Jolene?" Joey continued through the house.

In the kitchen he saw the telephone. It dangled ominously from the cord, bobbing lightly.

Joey froze. Someone had managed to beat him to Jolene's. The telephone slowly stopped bobbing, and he knew that only moments before, Jolene, or someone, had held it in her hand.

Hoping against hope, he picked it up. There was only a dial tone.

"Damn!" He held the phone against his forehead and squeezed his eyes shut. "Damn, damn, damn."

He felt completely defeated. Totally lost. Until he remembered the answering machine. Jolene might possibly have waited for the machine to click on before she picked up the phone.

Running into her bedroom he saw the red light blinking, a beacon of hope to a drowning sailor. He punched the rewind button. Cori's voice came to him, clearly afraid but strong, determined.

"Meet me in the Aquarium at five. They'll be about to close, and that'll be a good time. We can mix with the people leaving."

"What do you need?" Jolene asked.

"Just a place to stay tonight. Some money. And maybe you could help me get my car. If I can get my car, I can get out of town. I can hide out until the trial."

"You're going to testify?" Jolene's voice quavered. "Maybe you should reconsider...."

Joey clenched his fists. Jolene was in danger, and she was trying to warn Cori.

"No, I believe the only thing I can do now is testify. If they want to kill me this badly, then I have to tell what I saw."

"Think about it, Cori. Maybe you didn't see what you thought you did."

"Are you okay, Jolene?" There was a rushed intake of breath. "Is something wrong?"

Jolene's voice caught. "No, of course not. I'm on my way to the aquarium. By the white alligator tank."

"I'll be waiting."

The line went dead.

Chapter Fifteen

Cori didn't hang up the telephone but retrieved another quarter from her purse. Jolene's tone had been off. She couldn't put her finger on it exactly, but there had been something there. The warmth that she had associated with the redhead had been absent.

Flipping through the white pages she found the listing she wanted. She punched in the number and waited for the receptionist.

"Farris Quinn, please," she said.

The phone rang once before it was picked up by a man with a harried voice. "Quinn, what can I do for you?"

"Mr. Quinn, this is Brently Gleason."

"The witness from the DeCarlo trial?" He made no pretense of not knowing instantly who she was.

"Yes, that's me."

"Where are you?"

"I'm in New Orleans, and I'm in serious trouble. I thought maybe you'd like to talk to me about it."

"When and where?"

"The Aquarium. Now. And bring a camera. I have to tell you, though, someone is trying to kill me. You may be stepping into danger if you meet me."

"I may be stepping into a Pulitzer. I'm on my way. Look, I'm no photographer, how about if I get a real one to come along?"

"No!" Cori was afraid it would turn into a production. She couldn't afford to have an entourage dragging after her. "Just you."

"You got it."

Cori replaced the phone and looked out across the street at the large, solid building that housed the aquatic display so popular with city residents and tourists. It had been a long time since she'd visited, but it was the perfect place for the meeting she had in mind. Anonymous, yet filled with spectators.

Quinn couldn't protect her, but it was her only shot at getting the truth out to the public. There was something terribly dirty going on with the whole Ben DeCarlo mess. She was no longer certain who were the good or the bad guys. Maybe the reporter could figure it out.

Checking her watch, she looked out the window of the small grocery-café across the street from the Aquarium. She'd give Quinn ten minutes, and then she'd go over and wait. The newspaper wasn't far away, and he sounded like a man intent on making his time count. If anything did happen, at least there would be a witness. Someone to tell the truth. It was exactly the sort of bet-hedging she didn't like, but she'd be damned if she was going to go down as a coward or let Joey take a rap for being a bad marshal. Telling the truth—one more time—was the least she could do for him.

Before she relinquished the phone book, she looked up the number of the U.S. Marshal's office. Not that she intended to dial it. It was a sentimental thing, a juvenile thing to do. She memorized the number, anyway, a sort of talisman, a last connection to the man she had come to love. She closed her eyes and saw him, handsome and so caring. A sigh escaped her. For Joey. For the future.

At the counter she paid for the soft drink she'd ordered and stepped into the fading sunlight.

A shop down the street played a continuing series of jaunty Christmas songs. "Up on the Housetop" was the current selection, and a young boy tap-danced to the number, using his feet to sound out the click, click, click. Cori passed by him without a shred of feeling. She was completely numb.

There was no admittance line to the Aquarium. The day was late, and the ticket seller tried to convince her to come another day when she would have time to see all the exhibits and to get her money's worth.

"I want to see the alligators. I'm going home tomorrow," Cori told her, pressing the point.

"It's your money you're wasting. We'll be closing in half an hour, and there's no way you can see everything." The woman pushed the ticket through the slot.

Cori entered, caught instantly by the light filtering through water in the big tanks where flashy-colored fish swam around. It had the feel of being underwater, a sinister sensation, yet also curiously pleasant.

She followed the most obvious path between the huge tanks, the strange creatures of the sea swimming up to the glass to stare at her. She felt a heartbeat of pity. She knew how it felt to be a prisoner in a controlled environment.

Even with the protective glass wall, she shifted back from the shark tank. The gray bodies sliced through the water, headed straight at the glass, their mouths open and teeth displayed. At the last second they would veer away. Cori hurried past, trying to shake the feeling of dread. Her goal was the display that contained a collection of rare albino alligators. It was fitting, she thought. The alligator had become the latest motif in her life, a creature that looked like a floating log until it lashed with its tail and opened its mouth. Until her trip to the swamp, she'd never given alligators much thought. City dwellers didn't spend a lot of hours worrying about reptiles crawling out of the wilds and snapping off a leg.

She found the tank and touched her fingers to the glass. The alligators were hideous. Their white skins made them victims as well as deadly aggressors.

"Less than half the baby alligators survive the first weeks of life. They're often eaten by birds." An Aquarium employee came up to stand beside her. "These albino alligators are even more vulnerable. They have none of the protective coloring they need."

Cori had to get the young girl out of the way in case anything went wrong. She turned to her. "I can read, you know," she snapped.

Confused by the ugly attack, the girl backed away. "Sorry," she said as she went to find someone nicer to talk with.

"Are you always that nasty-tempered, or are you just having a bad day?" Farris Quinn held out his picture ID and stepped toward her. He carried a notebook in one hand and camera in the other.

"I'm having a bad day, and I don't want to see an innocent young girl blown to pieces because she was trying to be helpful. I'm somewhat adverse to involving innocent people. I have some hesitations about talking to you, as well."

"Tell me your story, and I'll tell you what I've discovered. I don't have any proof, but I do have some very interesting theories."

Cori gave him the highlights of the past forty-eight hours. She kept her voice flat, her words factual. When she finished, he gave a low whistle.

"Sounds like the best story I've done in ten years. Any idea who's actually trying to kill you, other than your husband, who was supposed to be dead?"

She shook her head. "Do you?"

"Ben DeCarlo is the obvious choice." He scratched his cheek with his pen. "Maybe too obvious."

"I've worried and worried this. I can't make head nor tail of it," Cori confessed.

"When this story hits the streets tomorrow morning, you'd better be in a safe place. No one is going to be on your side. Especially no one in the U.S. Marshals. There has to be someone in that office who's leaking information. How else did your husband, for want of a better descriptive term, find you in Houston?"

"That's exactly what I wonder."

"I think with this information we can launch a full-scale investigation of the WP program here in New Orleans. Emmet Wyatt's death was terrible, but I couldn't find a single bit of evidence to support the fact that he had been lured back here and murdered. You've given me what I needed. You may have saved a lot of lives in the future."

"I want it clearly understood that Joey Tio was not involved in any underhanded business. He risked his life to save me. His sister is lying wounded in a hospital because she was protecting me. Whatever is going on, I want his name cleared, in print."

"If he's the guy in the white hat you say he is, then I'll do a special sidebar piece on him to make sure he's not dirtied by the guilty parties."

Cori nodded. This was what she wanted from Quinn. "Thanks."

"Thank you. You know, it's funny, but I suspected the NOPD. I mean, there are so many of them, and the press on

them lately hasn't been great." He made a wry face. "·
never would have suspected the marshals."

"I put my life in their hands."

"So where is Tio now?"

"They've sent him somewhere else. He's going to be
reassigned. Given new duties."

"You need a place to stay?" Quinn reached in and pulled
out his billfold. "The newspaper doesn't pay for stories, but
I could personally see my way clear to helping you out with
some cash for a decent hotel room."

Cori needed the money, but she didn't feel right taking it
from a man she didn't know. "Just print the truth. At this
point, I don't have anything to lose by telling it."

Quinn checked his watch. It was nearly five. He'd barely
have time to write the story and make his deadline. "You
sure you're going to be okay here alone?"

Cori wasn't sure that Jolene would show. But Quinn was
not the protection she needed. "Thanks for coming."

She stood to shake his hand when the wall behind her exploded in cement chips.

"Oh, my God!" Farris grabbed her arm and tugged her
down.

A loud voice echoed through the huge room. "Stay down,
Brently."

Cori glanced up at the second level of the exhibit. The
voice had come from there, and it was a voice she clearly
remembered. Kit's voice. Her eyes searched the walkways
until she saw a slight movement. Before she could determine who or what it was, a gunshot echoed and a wall on the
second level exploded. There were two gunmen—one
shooting at her, and one shooting at the other one.

"Who the hell is shooting?" Farris Quinn clutched his
notebook and peered around the concrete barricade long

enough to try to focus the camera. A bullet that came too close for comfort drove him back into hiding beside Cori.

"There are two of them." She could make no sense of any of it. How had they found her so easily? And who was trying to protect her?

"Where's security?" Quinn asked. He could hear the sound of running feet and panicked voices calling for backup into walkie-talkies. There were also screams and crying. Security and tourists, if they had good sense, were headed straight for the exits.

Cori scanned the opposite side of the big room until she finally found what she was looking for, the barrel of a gun extending from behind a concrete pillar. The shooter. Or at least one of them.

And it wasn't Kit. His voice had come from the other side of the room. For a split second, she saw him, standing in the window of the cabin. Staring at her, capable of killing her, but walking away. Dragging her through the swamp to be executed. It didn't make sense. Holding her breath, she stared at the upper landing.

The gun barrel extended, followed by a hand. Cori's heart was about to explode. "Kit, watch out!" She called the words and then ducked, herself.

Instead of shooting the gunman stepped out from behind his cover. The gun was no longer pointed at Cori, but at Jolene's head. The man edged out so that Jolene was in clear view of Cori and Kit.

Cori recognized the city cop. "It's Jake Lewis!"

Lewis's grin was self-satisfied as he held a passive Jolene. "Wells, you're a dead man. And unless our irritating little witness wants to see her friend here spattered against the wall, I think she should stand up and come along with me. We only want to make certain she doesn't testify. If she cooperates, I'll release Red here and now. After DeCarlo is found innocent in the retrial, we'll release her."

Jolene struggled in his arms, finally biting his hand and freeing her mouth. "He'll kill me, anyway, Cori. Run! Don't listen to him."

The man jerked her viciously. "You'd better shut up, little Red, or I'll have to really hurt you." He nodded down at Cori. "Decide, Ms. Gleason. Or your buddy here is going to take a tumble." He pushed Jolene closer to the guard rail. The walkway he stood on was suspended over several of the larger aquatic exhibits and framed the background for the exotic bird aviary. It was a good thirty feet to the ground— to the unforgiving concrete floor.

"She's right, Brently, don't do it. He's going to kill the woman, anyway!" Kit's voice came out of the dark shadows.

Cori had estimated where he was, but she couldn't catch a glimpse of him. She only knew that he had no angle for a shot at Lewis. She hesitated. If she stood up, he'd shoot her on the spot, then probably push Jolene over the railing and make a dash for it. Kit might get him, but she and Jolene would likely be dead. She had to try to come up with an idea that would at least give Jolene her life. She had to think of something, and it had to be quick.

JOEY HERDED THE LAST of the tourists and employees out of the Aquarium. "Don't let anyone have a key," he ordered a frightened security guard, taking her set. "Not the city police, not anyone." He flipped his badge. "I'm a federal officer, and I'm in charge here. If you open this door to anyone but me you can go to prison for the rest of your life."

The woman nodded so rapidly he heard her teeth click.

He felt a split-second's regret for his abuse of power, but there was no other way. He had no legal authority to commandeer the building, but he also had no choice. He had to make sure the building was secure.

The terrible truth was that he trusted no one else. Not the NOPD, not the marshals. He didn't know the source of corruption, but he was taking no chances with Cori's life.

He locked the door behind him, knowing as he turned the key that he'd possibly sentenced himself to death, but the gunman inside would never get out and escape. In another ten minutes television cameras would be out there, and the weight of the media attention would force the law enforcement officials to arrest the shooter, or to kill him on the spot. Joey grimly accepted the fact that the latter was the more likely scenario. He was a loose end that someone couldn't afford. Just like Cori.

At the sound of Kit's voice, shouting at Cori to stay down, Joey started jogging, softly, in that direction. With each word, his confusion grew. Wells seemed to be trying to keep Cori from getting killed. And they had Jolene in there. He'd suspected she'd been taken, but the solid fact sent a spurt of adrenaline to his already wired body.

At the wide doorway, he slowed. He couldn't afford to make a sound. His only hope was surprise, and the possibility that he could find a position before they knew he was in the Aquarium.

"Gleason, I'm going to count to ten. If you don't stand up, I'm going to push your little friend over the rail. Is that clear enough for you?"

"Don't do it, Cori! He'll push her and shoot you. Stay down."

Joey made a mental note of where the voices had come from. He thought he could locate all of them, except Cori, who'd remained silent. At last he heard Cori speak, and he placed her directly in front of him.

"Get out of here, Quinn," Cori whispered urgently. "Crawl over there and go, before you're killed, too."

"I wouldn't miss this for the world." Quinn didn't sound too certain, but he wasn't giving in to his fear.

Joey listened to the exchange with the newspaper reporter. He certainly hadn't expected an eyewitness from the media, but it was a smart move on Cori's part.

"I'm counting, Gleason. One, two, three . . ."

Joey sped around the building. Cori couldn't have picked a better place to stage a showdown, from his point of view. He'd always enjoyed strolling through the exhibits, and he knew the pathways that led to the second floor of exhibits. The area she'd chosen was his favorite. Especially the reptiles.

"Six, seven . . ."

He was on the second floor level, not far from the gunman. He stopped at the entrance, holding back in the shadows as he brought his gun up. He could just see the shooter's shoulder. Not the perfect target, but at least it was the gun arm. It was a risky shot, what with the point of the shooter's gun right against Jolene's head. His bullet could produce a reflex action that would kill Jolene.

"Eight, nine . . ."

Down on the lower floor, Cori started to stand. "Don't hurt her. I'm here."

Joey stepped forward and fired. There was no time for second guessing.

The explosion of the gun filled the vast room. Cori felt Farris drag her back down beside him, tucking her under him as if the Aquarium were going to fall apart in an earthquake.

There was a loud yelp of pain, and then a cry of terror.

Cori and Farris both peeked out, and Cori opened her mouth to scream, but nothing came out. She watched in mute horror. Jake Lewis tottered on the walkway.

He grasped at his shoulder, then the railing, leaving a bloody print. As if he were performing a choreographed move, he toppled from the walkway and fell into one of the tanks.

"Incredible," Farris said as he lowered the camera. "I may have actually gotten that shot."

Before he could say more, the man in the tank rose to the surface screaming. He flailed in the water, his shrieks rising higher and higher.

"Oh, my God, it's the piranha tank!" Cori started forward until Farris pulled her back to safety.

"There's nothing you can do," he said, holding on to her. Cori struggled for release, but Farris held her tight. "I'm not going to let you kill yourself after that dramatic rescue. There could be other killers out there. Besides, I haven't gotten a really good photograph of you yet." He ignored her pummeling elbows and held on.

"Take it easy, Brently, the cavalry has arrived."

Kit's voice made Cori stop struggling. She turned to find him right behind her.

Kit looked at the newspaper man. "If you're a man who values his life, I suggest you take that film and your story and get back to the newspaper."

"Kit!" Cori realized instantly that he couldn't have shot Lewis. She turned back to the upper level to see a dark-haired man who bore a wonderful resemblance to Joey Tio rushing to try and pull the NOPD officer out of the fish tank.

Farris lifted his camera, pointing it at Kit. Kit lifted his gun, pointing it at the camera. "I wouldn't do that if I were you," he said softly.

Farris lowered the camera. "It's a great story," he said.

"Yeah, it is. But so far, there's not a shred of evidence that I'm really alive. I'd like to keep it that way." He motioned toward the exit. "I think you should leave, Mr. Quinn. You'll miss your deadline if you don't go now."

Cori put her hand on the reporter's arm. "Thank you. You risked your life to help me. Now go." As he left, Cori turned her full attention to Joey, who'd at last pulled Lewis out of the tank. Even across the big room she could see that he was dead. But Joey was very much alive, and headed her way. He'd come after her! He hadn't given up on her.

"Cori, are you okay?" he called.

"I'm fine, Joey, see about Jolene." She could see the redhead clinging to the wall, obviously in shock.

"Where's Wells?"

"Right here," Kit answered.

Joey started toward them, his gun drawn. He didn't want Kit Wells anywhere close to Cori.

"It's okay, Joey, see about Jolene." Cori's fear of Kit was gone. She turned to face him. "Why?" she finally asked. "Why?"

"It wasn't ever intended to work out this way, Brently."

"Cori," she corrected him. "Brently is gone. She was used up."

"I don't have a lot of time." He looked toward the exit. "They'll be here, and it doesn't matter if it's the cops or the robbers. I'm not on anybody's side now. I want to tell you the truth."

"What happened?" She had once thought the answer to this question was the most important one in her life. Now she knew she could live without it, as long as she had Joey.

"It was a simple deal . . . Cori. Jake Lewis arranged it. Everyone in the department knew about your memory. I'd been bragging about you and how smart you were. So Lewis said if I could have you at Augustine's to witness an event, there would be a lot of money in it for me. A lot of money."

"And it didn't bother you that I would witness a double murder?"

"It wasn't supposed to be that. It was supposed to be an *attempted* murder. Ben DeCarlo didn't want to run for office. His father was pushing him hard. Lewis told me it was just a big press event, like a publicity stunt. Ben had set it up so that he would appear to try to nail his father. He'd get into big trouble, big headlines, and any political aspirations his father had for him would be destroyed. That would force his father to get off his back and leave him alone to run his wine business."

"He killed his parents, Kit. What I saw wasn't a staged press event. It was a double homicide."

"It wasn't supposed to be that. I swear to you, I would never have done that to you. It seemed like an easy way for us to get some money, a nest egg for a home, something to get started on. I had already begun to fall in love with you. I never intended for any of this to happen. It was supposed to be easy money for a harmless publicity stunt."

"At the price of my identity, my family, everything I cared about. I had to give all of that up, Kit. However much they promised you, it wouldn't have been worth it."

"It was only supposed to be *attempted murder*. Don't you see? There wouldn't have been witness protection. Attempted murder isn't that big a crime! I was double-crossed. And then I had to figure out the best way to deal with it."

"Which was walking out on me. How noble."

His grip on her shoulders tightened. "You don't understand. They had their hooks into me, and I couldn't shake them loose. The only way to protect you was to let you go into the WP program. I had to say I didn't know anything about where they'd placed you. I did it to protect you, Cori.

Once Ben was convicted, once the trial was over, they wanted to kill you. They were afraid maybe I'd told you about the deal. The only way I knew to protect you was to disappear myself and then let the marshals look after you. It was working fine, too, until the retrial came up. Then I had to come back because I knew they'd kill you."

Cori jerked free of his hands. "You lured me back here! You set me up to be murdered!"

"That's not true."

"You put those candies in my studio, in my car. You made me determined to find you. I dare you to deny it!"

"I did use the chocolates." Kit's eyes were intense. "I was hoping to frighten you away. I told them I could convince you not to testify again. I said I could make you quit WP and go away. That's what I was trying to do. But you've changed, Cori. You're not the shy girl I . . . fell in love with. I thought I could scare you, and instead you came after me, which was the exact opposite of what I wanted."

Cori considered this. "It doesn't make a bit of sense. They wanted me set up as a witness, now they want to kill me before I can testify again. What's going on, Kit? That isn't logical."

Kit looked up at the sound of Joey's footsteps. He was coming with Jolene, his arm supporting her as she wiped tears from her face.

"Nothing about this is logical, Cori. Nothing. I'm telling you, forget the past. Forget you saw anything at all in Augustine's. Don't testify."

"I only wish it were that simple." She felt an overwhelming fury. "How can I forget a double homicide? A man who killed his own mother and father? You think I can walk away from that and let that man go free? I'm not like that, Kit. I have a duty to tell the truth."

"But only if you know the truth." His smile was sad. "Forget everything you saw, Cori. It's all smoke and mirrors."

"Are you saying Ben DeCarlo didn't kill his parents?"

"I'm saying you have the best visual memory of anyone I've ever met. You were the perfect eyewitness. In this case, though, you can't trust your eyes."

Joey stopped on the last line Kit said.

"Cori, are you okay?" he asked. He kept an arm on Jolene, who gave Cori a tearful smile.

"Kit is telling me I can't believe my own eyes."

"Can you?" Kit's smile was bitter. "You saw me get attacked by an alligator. You knew that I was dead. Yet here I am, standing right in front of you."

"How did you do that?" Cori asked.

"That time, I got lucky. I had a gun with a silencer."

"How did you get off the island?" Cori asked.

"Bailey. He worked free of the ropes and waved some poor old fisherman down and got a lift over to pick me up off the back side of that spit of land. We took the boat."

"And the fisherman?" Joey glared at him.

"He's okay. I wouldn't let Bailey kill him. I knocked him out, and when we got off the boat I cast him adrift. When he woke up, I'm sure he was lost, but he'll find his way home."

A loud pounding came at the door. They all listened to it. Kit looked around the Aquarium. "I have to get out of here. If they catch me, they'll kill me." He looked at Joey. "You know they will."

"Who's the leak in my department?" Joey asked.

Kit shook his head. "As far as I could figure, it was Jake. I was never on the inside. I was just some poor sucker who got pinched up in a plan that was a lot bigger than any one person knew."

"Is there someone in the marshals?" Joey pressed.

"I saw Danny Dupray over there today. That's why I ran away," Cori said. Her gaze shifted from Kit to Joey. There was such a difference between the two men. She could see it now, in the set of Joey's jaw, in the way he kept a protective arm around Jolene. He was tough, and he was honest. Kit was neither of those things. How had she ever believed she loved him?

Kit laughed. "Strangely enough, Danny is the only person in this town who's tried to help me. And you owe him your life, Cori. He's the one who let me know there was a hit out on you. If it hadn't been for Danny, I wouldn't have been able to kill Benny Hovensky, Jake Lewis's right-hand thug and gun-for-hire. He'd kill his own mother for two hundred dollars. The world won't miss him."

"That was you who shot him?" Cori didn't know if she believed him or not.

Kit nodded. He looked toward the door where the pounding was more pronounced. "I was doing my best to keep you from getting killed. When I snatched you on the island, I was going to take you out in the water and pretend to drown you. I thought I could stage it so they'd think you were dead, and then you could get away. The alligator complicated things a bit." Kit backed up several steps. He looked only at Joey now. "I have to leave."

Joey's hand twitched on the gun. It was his duty to arrest Kit.

"Joey," Cori said softly, "let him go."

He stared at Kit, who made no effort to raise the gun he still held in his hand. "I won't fight with you, Tio. I only want to disappear. I can go away, out to some of the islands or down into Central America. If I know that Cori is going to be okay, I don't have to hang around trying to protect her. You won't see me again, I promise."

Joey hesitated.

"Please, Joey, just let him go." Cori placed her hand on Joey's arm, the one that didn't hold the gun. "He's in as much trouble as I was. If they do take him in, they'll get to him and kill him. There'll be some accident in the prison, or a fight. You know that."

Joey looked down into Cori's pleading eyes. He was afraid of what he might see—a flicker of love for the man she'd married only two years before. What he saw was pity. Nothing but pity.

Joey lowered his gun. "I'm breaking the law by doing this."

"But you're serving a greater justice," Cori whispered.

Jolene took a small step forward. "He tried to save my life, Joey. He could have killed me and then the man, but he didn't. Let him go. Let him disappear into the past."

"The records still show Kit Wells to be a dead man," Cori said carefully. "Let him rest in peace."

Joey finally looked into Kit's eyes. "Go on," he said, tossing him the keys. "One of those will open the delivery door. Go now before they get in here."

Kit held the keys in a clenched fist. He started away, then turned back to Cori. "I did love you, as much as I was capable of loving anyone," he said. "None of that was a lie." He turned and started running down the corridor, his footsteps fading slowly as the sounds of the front doors crashing open came to them.

Joey put his arm around Cori and motioned Jolene over. "We don't have all the answers about Ben DeCarlo. Maybe we never will. What matters most is that we're alive." He kissed Cori's cheek as he whispered in her ear. "And we have each other."

Epilogue

Cori stood before Travis Shanahan and waited. His handsome face was perplexed as he considered all of the evidence that had been presented to him. It was a tough call. Finally the prosecutor spoke.

"The two men captured and being held in Lafayette have been charged with attempted murder. Bail hasn't been set, and we're doing everything we can to hold them until they answer some questions. I can promise you, Ms. St. John, that we'll investigate the problem you and Mr. Tio have unearthed. Corruption within our law enforcement branches cannot be tolerated."

"It seems to be confined to Jake Lewis, but we have to be sure," Joey pointed out.

"There are grave issues here, and the manipulation of Ms. St. John as an eyewitness is of great concern to me," Shanahan said. "I don't believe it changes Ben DeCarlo's guilt, but it does change matters for you, as a witness."

"Do you still want me to testify?" Cori asked. She felt Joey's arm slip around her waist, and she had never felt as safe and secure and ready to face the future, no matter what it was. "I'm not refusing. I'm just not certain any longer what the truth is in the Ben DeCarlo case."

"This entire mess with the ghost of your husband has put your testimony in jeopardy." Travis wanted Ben DeCarlo to remain behind bars, where he belonged. Brently Gleason-Cori St. John had been through a rough time, and he wasn't certain she was stable enough to withstand the counterattack of the high-priced lawyers Ben DeCarlo had surely hired. What would be worse than not having her testimony would be watching her crack up on the witness stand. When a prosecution lost the credibility of a key witness, it could spell doom, no matter how strong the rest of the testimony.

He still had three very strong witnesses, one tough little waitress and an angry ex-model among them.

He examined the woman in front of him, noting the earnestness of her expression. She would testify if she was called. What he had to decide was whether, in her current situation, she would help or hinder his case. He nodded, his decision made.

"You're dismissed, Ms. St. John." He couldn't help but notice the relief of the U.S. Marshal who stood by her side. "You're released into the custody of Mr. Tio." He gave them a half smile.

Cori turned into Joey's arms with a cry of delight. "I don't have to leave New Orleans. I can have my old life back," she said. For the first time in days she felt the threat of tears. Blinking them away, she kissed Joey's cheek. "Or the parts of my old life that I want. My sister. My nieces. My art and studio."

Joey steered her out of the D.A.'s office and into the busy corridor. Kissing her cheek, he whispered in her ear. "Got any room for some new stuff in that life of yours?" he asked as he hugged her so hard he lifted her off her feet. He put her down and escorted her out into the warm December day before she could answer.

"What kind of new stuff?" Cori could hardly breathe. More than anything she wanted Joey Tio in her life.

"First a question. Is the annulment filed?"

"Filed and in the process. My marriage was in name only."

Joey lifted her left hand, kissing each finger. "Well, that new stuff includes a ring." He brought the case out of his jacket pocket and handed it to her. "And a proposal. It wouldn't have mattered if you'd had to testify, Cori. I would have gone with you into the WP program. Who better than me to figure out the best place for us to start over?"

"And leave Laurette and Cliff and the rest of your friends and family? You would have done that for me?" She knew he would have, but she was doubly glad that he hadn't been forced to make that choice.

"Do you accept my proposal, or are you going to make me get down on my knees in this very public place?"

Cori held the ring box and tilted her head as if she were considering making him get down on his knees. Unable to keep up the pretense any longer, she opened the box with trembling fingers. The diamond solitaire caught the sunlight and cast it back in a million glittering fragments.

"Joey..." She held the box so he could remove the ring and slip it on her finger.

"Will you marry me, Cori St. John?"

"Yes, with all my heart." She put her arms around his neck and kissed him. "I love you, Joey."

Across the street an old woman collecting for the Salvation Army rang her bell and cheered them on. "Merry Christmas," she called out.

Cori looked up at Joey. "This will be a merry Christmas for me. For both of us."

"And from now on, all of your kisses are going to be the real thing, Cori. None of those chocolate stand-ins. Real, live kisses, just like this one."

HARLEQUIN®

I N T R I G U E®

WANTED

12 SEXY LAWMEN

They're rugged, they're strong and they're WANTED!
Whether sheriff, undercover cop or officer of the court,
these men are trained to keep the peace, to uphold the
law...but what happens when they meet the one woman
who gets to know the real man behind the badge?

Twelve LAWMEN are on the loose—and only
Harlequin Intrigue has them! Meet them one per
month, continuing with

Sam Moore
#401 MAN WITHOUT A BADGE
by Dani Sinclair
January 1997

LAWMAN:
*There's nothing sexier than
the strong arms of the law!*

Look us up on-line at: http://www.romance.net   LAWMAN7

In steamy New Orleans, three women witnessed the same crime, testified against the same man and were then swept into the Witness Protection Program. But now, there's new evidence. These three women are about to come out of hiding—and find both danger and desire....

eye WITNESS

Start your new year right with all the books in the exciting EYEWITNESS miniseries:

#399 A CHRISTMAS KISS
by Caroline Burnes (December)

#402 A NEW YEAR'S CONVICTION
by Cassie Miles (January)

#406 A VALENTINE HOSTAGE
by Dawn Stewardson (February)

Don't miss these three books—or miss out on all the passion and drama of the crime of the century!

HARLEQUIN ®

Scandals

A passionate story of romance, where bold, daring characters set out to defy their world of propriety and strict social codes.

"Scandals—a story that will make your heart race and your pulse pound. Spectacular!"
—Suzanne Forster

"Devon is daring, dangerous and altogether delicious."
—Amanda Quick

Don't miss this wonderful full-length novel from Regency favorite Georgina Devon.

Available in December, wherever Harlequin books are sold.

Look us up on-line at: http://www.romance.net

SCAN

1997
Reader's Engagement Book
A calendar of important dates
and anniversaries for readers to use!

Informative and entertaining—with notable
dates and trivia highlighted throughout the year.

Handy, convenient, pocketbook size to help you
keep track of your own personal important dates.

Added bonus—contains $5.00 worth of coupons
for upcoming Harlequin and Silhouette books.
This calendar more than pays for itself!

 Available beginning in November at
your favorite retail outlet.

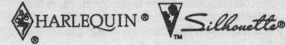

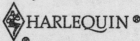

The collection of the year!
NEW YORK TIMES BESTSELLING AUTHORS

Linda Lael Miller
Wild About Harry

Janet Dailey
Sweet Promise

Elizabeth Lowell
Reckless Love

Penny Jordan
Love's Choices

and featuring
Nora Roberts
The Calhoun Women

This special trade-size edition features four of the wildly popular titles in the Calhoun miniseries together in one volume—a true collector's item!

Pick up these great authors and a chance to win a weekend for two in New York City at the Marriott Marquis Hotel on Broadway! We'll pay for your flight, your hotel—even a Broadway show!

Available in December at your favorite retail outlet.

NEW YORK

MARQUIS

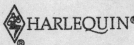

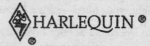